Texas Blues

Ashley Quinn

Copyright © 2016 by Ashley Quinn

All rights reserved. No part of this publication may be reproduced, distributed or transmitted in any form by any means, including photocopying, recording, or other electronic or mechanical methods, without the prior written permission of the author, except in the case of brief quotations embodied in reviews and certain other noncommercial uses permitted by copyright law.

To LP, you have so much kindness and compassion. There's so much chemistry between us, and that's important too, but ultimately your kind heart is why I love you. Being with you reminds me that there is still so much good in the world - And there is not enough gratitude I can give you for that. I am thankful for all of our days together.

To Texas, thank you for welcoming me with open arms. Thank you for the sunsets and the rivers and the vistas and the lakes and the cities and the desert and the country and the wide open road and the healing.

CHAPTER 1

One, two, three. Deep breath. One, two, three thirty-two year old London Foster counted silently in strict rhythm as her feet pounded against the crisp belt of the treadmill. Fatigue poured through every cell that made up all five feet, six inches of her body as she swallowed hard. She steeled herself and slowly turned the plastic dial to increase the machine's speed. Staring ahead, she hoped to ignore the persistent burning in her calves. London closed her eyes and reopened them as a thin trickle of sweat slid between her slick shoulder blades.

One, two, three. Deep breath. One, two, three she continued to count inwardly. Beads of sweat pooled at her hairline and snaked down her neck. She could feel her jet black hair was falling out of its short ponytail and matting itself to her face. She was also very aware that her thigh muscles were beginning to feel like jelly, but she refused to miss a beat. Stevie Nicks' unmistakable voice poured into her ears from tiny earbuds. She took another deep breath and continued running.

"Strange, she runs with the ones she can't keep up with
Ooh, it's so strange…He slows down, desperate to stop her
They meet in the middle
They both run from the one that haunts them…"

London stole a quick glance around the small gym as the beat continued. *This is my therapy* she thought smugly. *Why Dad would suggest I waste money on a counselor when I can work the pain out of me is beyond me.* The ground-floor workout facility of the 88-story skyscraper was one of the many perks of being one of the youngest and most talented Senior Copywriters at W.H. Young Advertising. The agency was the most prestigious in Chicago and, because it was housed on three levels of the looming building, London frequently enjoyed the corporate gym facilities on the main level.

At this hour, the gym is always empty she thought with a trace of satisfaction. *Just the way I like it. After all, who is still at work at 10 P.M. on a Wednesday? Besides me, of course.* She reached out and gently turned the dial to decrease the treadmill's speed. London slowed to a brisk walk and dabbed at her forehead with a small white towel. Through tinted windows, she watched as a spring breeze picked up outside and caused a few empty bottles to roll noisily down the wide sidewalk. A bright yellow taxi slammed on its brakes to avoid rear-ending a Mercedes that pulled in front of it. The driver punched his fist against the horn and threw his hands up in frustration.

London felt her stress give way to immeasurable fatigue as the last strains of violin, guitar and drums ended the song on her iPhone. She closed her eyes again and took a long swallow from her water bottle. *I'm too exhausted to think* she realized. *And that's the best part of working out. The pain is good. There's no room to feel anything else.*

Her mother's trademark grin flashed in her mind's eye. *She always had that smile, no matter how badly the sickness ravaged her body* London thought. A strange hollowness settled in her gut. *God, I miss her. Maybe I would have gotten through the shock of it all quicker if Kayley hadn't left me for Tara two months later.*

London quickly twisted the dial on the treadmill back to a 10. She ignored the cramped stitch in her right side and the memory of her selfish ex-girlfriend hauling boxes into her former best friend's S.U.V. *Tara didn't even have the guts to get out of her truck and talk to me* she remembered. *And she was supposed to be my closest friend. And Kayley? She never cared about anyone except herself.*

She took a deep breath as the tension grew in her legs. *I need to be too tired to feel anything else except this work out.*

It had been just over a year since her mother passed away and her former girlfriend had committed the ultimate betrayal with someone London had considered a close friend and confidant. She still couldn't believe how quickly the cancer, over eight months, had taken her strong, vibrant mother from newly retired to planning her own funeral.

A bright light out of the corner of her eye caught London's attention and she stifled a frustrated groan. She quickly tore out her earbuds and swiped at the screen of her phone.

"Hey, Holly," she panted.

"Damn girl, either you're *still* at the gym or you're getting some," Holly Brewer observed dryly. And London? I sure hope it's the latter. It's almost 10:15 at night."

London quickly slowed the treadmill. *She's a Chicago girl, through and through.* "Yeah, right," she retorted. "Getting some would imply that I'm actually interested in anyone. You know I like to work out after the day is over."

She could practically hear her forty-five year old boss and friend rolling her eyes. "Whatever you say," she replied. "You're going to want to hear what I'm about to tell you. In *confidence*, of course."

London's ears perked up as she ducked into the empty locker room. "Sure, what's up?"

"Word is that Daniel put in his two weeks' notice late this afternoon," Holly went on. "I don't know the details yet, but there's a rumor that Leo Burnett poached him and he's jumping ship to go to the bigger agency and our largest competitor."

London wrinkled her nose as she tried to picture Daniel's face. She didn't have much interaction with the Chief Marketing Officer. Holly, as the Director of National Accounts, had far more communication with upper management. "How's the C.E.O. taking that one?"

"Well, Mr. Hanson and the rest of the executive team want to fill his position as quickly as possible. Of course," Holly went on slowly.

"Of course," London agreed. She stretched as she opened her locker and relished the delicious feeling radiating through her legs.

"And he would prefer to hire from within…" Holly continued.

"Good opportunity for the right person to move up," London said as she stifled a yawn.

"Oh, for the love of God, I'm talking about *us*!" Holly finally spat. "I do nearly everything already that Daniel did. My eye is on that position and I have a good feeling that I'm a front-runner for it. That just leaves the question of who would fill *my* role."

London plopped onto the locker room's long wooden bench and anxiously waited for Holly to continue.

"London, I want to present you to the C.E.O. as the perfect candidate to slowly transition into my position if I were offered the C.M.O. role," she went on proudly. "I've mentored you myself for the last four years. You're the youngest and most talented Senior Copywriter that this company has. Your knack for advertising and your ability to write is something that can't be trained; people either have it or they don't. I know there's a lot of little things to learn in my position, but you're quick and I know you could pick it up with a transition period."

London stood and twisted a lock of sweaty hair around her index finger nervously. "Okay, you've got my attention," she replied after a short pause. "But I just don't know. I'm a writer. That's not only a strength, it's also my passion. Really, my only love. I've always steered clear of getting too involved in corporate things…"

"Look, I know I have a whole team to supervise," Holly started. "But you and I have always had a closer relationship. You deserve this upward mobility. I can't remember the last sick day or vacation you took. London, I *know* the C.E.O. is going to speak with a handful of us individually tomorrow to vet candidates for Daniel's position. He'll jump at the opportunity to replace him quickly and have someone ready to fill my role too. Your work speaks for itself. This could be really good for you."

London felt an unfamiliar spark of excitement inside her chest as the thought settled in. "I don't know, Holly. I just never envisioned myself as a corporate type."

"Tell you what, I'll speak to the Mr. Hanson during our one-on-one tomorrow and we can discuss it after," Holly replied. "Oh, and by the way, I got tickets to the After Dark gala at the Art Institute this Friday. It's an annual fundraising event hosted by the Board of Directors. Michael always gets tickets since he's a partner at the firm and they represent the Art Institute at a huge discount. Anyway, he's already booked for a speaking engagement at Northwestern's School of Law so that means you're accompanying me. Just so you know."

"I…What?" London asked as she ran a hand through her messy hair. She thought of Michael and Holly Brewer, movers, shakers and Power Couple of Chicago. *With Michael a partner at one of the biggest law firms in the city and Holly poised to move up the ladder at W.H. Young, they really do have it all. All of the important stuff, anyway. Money. Success. Influence. All of the things that I've learned matter most.*

"It's a lot of fun. You'll enjoy it," Holly said quickly. "There will be a cocktail party with hors d'oeuvres before. Plus live music, more food, more drinks and special exhibits during. Of course I can't forget the rubbing elbows part that I hate. But don't worry about any of that. Just put on your best little black dress and be my pretend lesbian date for the evening."

London laughed. "I don't wear dresses."

"Then your best mini-Power Lesbian suit!" Holly cracked. "Come on, London, when's the last time you've been outside of that apartment?"

London opened her mouth to reply.

"And being at work or at the gym doesn't count," Holly finished.

London closed her mouth and paused. "Fine, I'll go," she sighed. "But only because I know if I blow you off, you'll just show up at my door and drag me by my hair anyway."

"You got that right!" Holly crowed. "Good. You and I understand each other. That's why we've always connected so well. I'll e-mail you the details about the gala tomorrow. For the love of it all, please go home."

London grinned. "I'm on my way," she replied as she slung her gym bag over her shoulder. "Thanks for the head's up about the opportunity. I really appreciate it. You're one of the only people that's ever really had my back."

Holly was quiet for a moment. "I know neither you or I are good with the mushy feeling stuff, but you know I'm here for you, right? If you ever want to talk, you know. It's not good to keep things bottled inside you. Especially with what you've gone through in the last year."

London paused as she reached the glass doors of the gym. "I…I know," she stammered and then laughed it off. "I'm fine. I'm always fine."

Holly sighed. "Whatever you say, girl. I can't imagine how it felt to lose your mom so quickly after she got sick. And I know you don't have the best relationship with your dad or your sister…"

"*Half*-sister," London corrected her.

"Right," Holly continued after a brief pause. "Just know that I *am* here for you. I feel a little like a Mother Hen, you know? I've taken you under my wing since your first day at W.H. Young."

London glanced at the large clock above the doors. "Damn, it's getting late. You're right. I need to get home already, even though I feel like I'm suffocating in that loft most of the time. I'll talk to you tomorrow."

"I'll see you then," Holly replied with a sigh. London felt triumphant that her friend had given up for now. "I'll bring us some big-ass Frappucinos to get through the day."

London smiled at her casual cursing and pushed open the doors of the gym as they said their good-byes. A certain heaviness settled over her at the thought of holing up in the nondescript, but extremely expensive, high-rise loft for another night. *All this money, that glamorous building* she thought ruefully. *And I still can't seem to fill the emptiness.*

London quickly sidestepped a laughing couple that had piled out of the backseat of a taxi. She felt a glare settle over her features as the man's free hand casually fell to the small of his girlfriend's back. London rolled her eyes and continued walking briskly.

I'm bitter she realized weakly. *When will it stop? I've been jaded my entire life. After all, Mom and I were never part of Dad's plan. He didn't plan to get her pregnant while they were in college. He planned to be Chairman of Foster Oil & Gas, the company his grandfather started. So he paid her millions over the years in financial support but never took an interest in me. The checks came, but the birthday cards never did. He's a businessman and it was a simple decision. He chose money over love. Money is tangible. Love is messy.*

London paused at an intersection and took a deep breath. "Love doesn't mean anything anymore," she whispered.

The sparkling skyscrapers of Chicago loomed protectively around her, their bright lights twinkling in the velvety evening sky. There was something comforting about being another anonymous soul in the third-largest city in the United States.

Some days I'm suffocating and other days I'm so glad just to blend…And not think London thought as she quickened her pace across the street.

At least I have a possible promotion to look forward to she comforted herself. *Even if I'm not really sure I want it. It would be stupid to turn it away, right? Maybe I am my father's daughter after all. Maybe that's what my life was meant for. Climbing the corporate ladder, earning the mega-bucks and making a name for myself in advertising. Maybe other people are meant for all that love and romance and family stuff, but that's not me. I'm one of those people meant for money. After all, I was born to the heir of a successful Texas oil and gas company…Even if he barely acknowledged my existence before Mom passed away. I'll be a mover and shaker all by myself.*

CHAPTER 2

Thirty-year old Natalie Silva took a deep breath and enjoyed the feeling of warm morning air filling her lungs. She lay in the bed of her pearl-white Ford F150, her pride and joy, and let her feet dangle over the top of the tailgate. She blinked at the wide, expansive sky above her and yawned.

Nothing like starting your day before dawn to keep this bakery up and running she thought proudly. *But it's worth it. At what other job could I spend my morning experimenting with new pastry ideas and then take a break in the back of my truck before the A.M. work crowd comes through?*

The last streaks of light pink and yellow faded into clear blue as the bright morning sun rose. The incredible sunrises and sunsets were one of Natalie's favorite things about living just outside of Fort Worth. Not only did the sky seem to stretch on forever, but the sun and stars seemed close enough to reach out and grab.

Texas sky isn't like any other sky in the world she thought with a grin. *They say everything is bigger in Texas, and the sky is definitely one of those things.* She could hear the oil rigs far in the distance, a familiar sight along the lengthy highways in and out of the Fort Worth area.

She pulled her phone from the pocket of her worn jeans. *6:15 A.M.* she thought as she struggled to sit upright. *About two minutes until what I think will be the best lemon bars this side of the metroplex are ready and roughly five until Aunt Celia gets here.* Between prepping for two catering events scheduled over the weekend and readying the menu items for the food truck, Natalie knew it would be a long day but she couldn't picture it any other way.

She hopped out of the bed of her truck just as the faint *ding* of the stove sounded through the bakery's open back door. Natalie quickly smoothed her apron, already streaked with powdered sugar and flour, and ran a hand through her long brown hair. Natural blonde highlights from exposure to the hot Texas sun had lightened it considerably from the nearly black hair she'd had as a child.

Natalie swung the back door of Mission Bakery closed behind her just as a small bell above the front door trilled to announce a visitor.

"*Tia* Celia, you're right on time," Natalie greeted her aunt with a grin. She carefully removed two long, steel trays from the oven. "Are you ready to try the best lemon bars in Texas?"

Celia Silva laughed as she closed the door behind her. "You work harder than anyone I know, *mija*," she remarked good-naturedly. "I know Jane and I are co-owners of the bakery, but I think I may as well retire. I'm nearly fifty-eight as it is, why not? I ought to call her up right now and tell her to sell the house and get rid of the car because we're going to buy a camper and move to an island somewhere!"

Natalie laughed as she gently sliced a wedge of the soft yellow pastry and handed it to her aunt. "Oh no, you don't, she replied. "If I didn't have you and *Tia* Jane here to help me run this bakery and that food truck outside, I think I'd lose my mind. Speaking of, where is she this morning?"

"Your mind?" Celia cracked as she bit into the lemon bar. "Beats me, *mija*."

Natalie rolled her big brown eyes and grinned. "No, *Tia* Jane," she continued. "Where is that wife of yours?"

"Teaching morning yoga at that new studio in Southlake," Celia replied. She paused and licked her thumb. "*Ay mi dios*, Natalie! These lemon bars are fantastic. How many did you make?"

Natalie turned to the stove with a smile. "About three dozen," she answered. "I changed the recipe slightly to get a bit more of that zesty lemon snap in them. I thought we could put some on the food truck today and see how the lunch crowd in downtown Dallas does with them."

"That's a great idea," Celia replied. "I'll take the truck for the lunch shift and Jane can meet me from the studio." She cleared her throat and then flipped through a binder on the counter. "So we have the Robinson engagement party on Friday evening and then the Martinez baby shower on Sunday afternoon. Do we have everything we need to prep for those orders?"

Natalie nodded as she mentally scanned the huge pantry that housed most of the bakery's dry goods. "Yes, Jane confirmed the orders with both parties yesterday while I inventoried the pantry. We're ready for them."

Celia shook her head and grinned. "Of course we are," she replied. "I'm so proud of you, Natalie. Your baking is by far the best in all of the metroplex. Maybe even all of Texas! Is there anything that my niece can't do?"

Natalie laughed and took a carton of eggs from the wide stainless steel refrigerator. "You're too nice to me," she replied. "Texas is a big state. And you *have* to say that because you're my *tia*."

"No, no, no," Celia held up a hand. "Texas is the *best* state. And I say it because it's true. Are you making your French breakfast muffins this morning?"

"Oh, now you're just being sweet because you see the cinnamon on the counter," Natalie replied with a smile. "And *yes*, I'm making the French breakfast muffins that you love so much. With an extra dash of nutmeg, just the way you like them."

"You know, your mom and dad both enjoyed cooking but they never had the talent that you do," Celia mused. "I don't know where you picked up these baking genes, but fixing up this old bakery five years ago was one of the best things we've done."

"Oh Celia, Mom and Dad worked hard. They struggled just like the rest of us. That's why I got to live with my cowboy boot-wearing fairy godmother *tia* and her wife when I was twelve and why Mom and Dad are enjoying a nice, quiet life in Montana these days," Natalie replied lightly.

Thank God for my aunts she finished silently. *Dad never recovered financially after he lost his job on that oil rig. Years and years of moving all over the country to find work wherever there was oil took its toll on them. They wanted me to live a normal life, without having to move every year or two, and I've had just that with Celia and Jane.*

"You've always been more of a daughter to me than a niece," Celia went on with a smile. "The Good Lord blessed me with a wonderful family, starting with you and Jane. Maybe more if you'd stop focusing so much on this bakery and find the right woman."

Natalie paused and opened a large drawer. She took out a set of metal measuring cups and eyed several plastic containers of sugar before deciding on an organic cane. "You get what you give, Celia," she finally replied. "You put good into this world and good will come back to you in all forms. I'll find the *right* woman when it's the *right* time."

Celia clucked her tongue and crossed her arms. "The longer you wait, the slimmer the pickings. Especially out in these parts. I'd just hate to see you wait forever."

Natalie dumped a cup of sugar into a large metal bowl. "I appreciate your wisdom," she replied. "But let's concentrate on today, okay? And making some of the most popular breakfast muffins this side of the Trinity River."

Celia raised her palms in a conciliatory gesture. "Okay, okay, I'll stop," she conceded. "Jane always tells me not to worry so much about you. She understands that you're your own woman. I just want to see my beautiful *sobrina* happy and settled with a good woman. Your mom and dad always kept it together, miraculously. Jane and I have one another. Now it's your turn to find someone special."

Natalie turned from the counter with a wide smile and planted a kiss on her aunt's cheek. "I do have someone special," she responded brightly. "In fact, I have *many* special someones. I have you, for starters. I have *Tia* Jane, who is absolutely right in assuring you not to worry so much about me. I have Mom and Dad who, even if they're retired away from it all in Montana now, still call every other day. Did I tell you they figured out how to download Skype to their laptop?"

Celia smiled and patted her hand. "Say *mija*, have you gotten your truck fixed? I noticed the other day that the oil was low…"

Natalie grinned as her aunt went on. *Once these muffins are ready, she'll stop talking…For a little bit* she thought happily. *I wouldn't trade her for any other family in the world. She was the one who took me in so I wouldn't have to move all over the country for Dad to keep working. She was the one who would watch old Hollywood classics with me on Friday nights when everyone else at school was going to the big football game or the dance. She taught me to be compassionate and grateful, no matter the circumstances. She was the one who helped me figure out how to take my life's passion and turn it into this viable little business so I'd never have be a slave to work like my parents.*

"...Natalie, did you hear me?" Celia's voice interrupted her thoughts. "I was saying it might be time to trade that truck in while you can still get something for it. Especially if you're having problems with the oil pan..."

Natalie took a deep, satisfactory breath and sprinkled nutmeg over the dry muffin mix. "Yes, I hear you *Tia*."

CHAPTER 3

The phone was loud and unwelcome as London slowly opened her eyes and glared into the darkness. "It's not even light out yet," she muttered as she felt haphazardly around her bedside table. "It should be illegal to call someone before their morning alarm goes off."

She pressed the phone to her ear. "Hello?"

"London calling!" A male voice boomed. She cringed as she immediately recognized her father's cheerful tone.

Crap she thought. *I was avoiding him.*

"I don't think the joke works as well if it's you calling me and not the other way around," London replied coolly. *Not to mention you say that every time we speak on the phone. Which has been more times since Mom passed away than in the last ten years, but that doesn't make being absent from most of my life okay.*

"I know, but it doesn't get old," Vincent Foster went on jovially. "Look, I realize it's early. I'm in Dubai for a couple of business meetings and I honestly forgot about the time difference." He paused. "I'm glad I caught you. I tried to call a few times in the last month and haven't heard back from you."

London rubbed a hand over her face sleepily. "Sorry," she replied lamely. "I've been working."

There was another short pause. "Well, I know you're a workaholic," Vince continued. "A chip off the old block, I suppose. The reason for my call was to find out if you'd given any more thought to what I'd suggested when we spoke around Christmas."

London felt very close to whining and tossed onto her side in frustration. She briefly remembered his appearance at her mother's wake. She hadn't seen or spoken to him in years, but had recognized him immediately. *Whatever reunion he was hoping for wasn't going to happen* she thought. *I was far too upset and doing too much grieving to even speak to him beyond thanking him for coming.*

She wrapped her comforter tighter around her. *Has it been since Christmas when I last spoke to him?* She wondered in mild surprise. *I suppose I've been avoiding his calls longer than I realized.*

"Sorry, what did we talk about?" London asked. She racked her brain trying to recall their brief holiday conversation. Vince had regularly reached out since her mother's funeral and London knew he wanted to rekindle the long-lost relationship.

She shook her head in the darkness of the small bedroom. *Too little, too late Dad.*

Vince cleared his throat. "About you visiting," he replied. "Taking some time off work and coming down to Texas for a few weeks. You know, spend some time with your old man, hang out with your little sister…"

"Half-sister," London sighed tiredly. "I'll have to check my, um, calendar and see what's on for, um, this summer…"

Vince took a deep breath. "London, I know I wasn't around much. I know I've made a lifetime's worth of mistakes in the way I was largely absent from your childhood. I've told you before and I'll tell you again that I'd really like to start making amends. Let's get to know each other *now*. You have a sister that you haven't seen since she was in elementary school and she'll be at the house this summer. I'll be traveling some, but it's a start…"

London interrupted him with a heavy, impatient sigh. *Everything is always on his time.*

"We can all ease into being a part of each other's lives," Vince continued. "I've always provided for you, even from afar. I made sure your mom could afford to send you to the best private schools in Chicago and that you two lived in the biggest two-flat in the nicest neighborhood. I'll continue to support you so you can take some time off and regroup. Stop worrying so much and spend some time in Fort Worth. I know that city has got to be killing you after losing your mother so quickly."

London felt her blood simmer to a slow boil as she listened to her father's slow Southern drawl. *He's right, you know* a tiny voice piped up inside her. *The city is killing you. You feel hollow, suffocated and depressed every day. You struggle to get out of bed and you spend hours at the gym so you don't have to think.*

"You don't know how I feel or what I think about anything I may be faced with," London replied sharply. *But the thing is, I don't* want *him to be right. He never knew me, and now he thinks he can step in to rekindle the father-daughter relationship that never was? Yeah, right.* "I told you I would consider it and I haven't looked over my calendar yet. The only consistent family member I've had throughout my life recently passed away, so yes, I may be throwing myself into my work to cope. But that doesn't mean I'm ready to hop a plane to Texas just because you and Tiffany feel sorry for me."

She listened to her father's sharp intake of breath on the other end of the line. "I understand, London," he responded gently after a moment. "I can't imagine how hurt you must be and I'm just sorry that I wasn't there enough to be someone that you trust enough to turn to in a time like this. I really am. If you'd like, I can back off for a while. The last thing I want to do is upset you further."

London closed her eyes and bit her lip. "I'm sorry too," she replied. The malice she felt had evaporated. "It's just early. Look, I'll take a look at my calendar this afternoon and give you a call soon. Maybe we can work out a long weekend visit over the summer or something."

"Okay, London," Vince murmured. "That sounds good."

As they hung up, London pulled her leather-bound weekly planner from the drawer of her bedside table. She turned a few pages and then paused. She tossed the planner back onto the table with a shake of her head. *Maybe some other time.*

London sank back into her blankets and squinted at her alarm clock. *Two minutes until I'm supposed to be up.* She pulled a pillow over her face and groaned loudly.

"This is *not* my week. Or my month. Or my *year*."

Natalie took a deep breath as she climbed into the driver's seat of her truck. The sun was sinking into the horizon and she was exhausted after another busy day at the bakery. She rested the back of her head against the headrest for a moment and cranked the radio dial. It was set to a classic rock station. She thought of her Aunt Jane taking her to a Fleetwood Mac concert when she was just thirteen. The memory made her grin. She had introduced her to that band and Natalie had been a fan ever since, preferring classic rock to whatever the Top 40 was that week.

She smiled again. *Much to the chagrin of my friends growing up. Whatever. It's good music.*

The familiar honk of a Dodge Ram 1500 pulled her from her thoughts as she glanced in the rearview mirror. Her best friend, Paula Ortiz, rolled down the window of her truck.

"Hey, you!" Paula called out. "I was just headed over to your place, but I thought you might still be here. I'm so glad I caught you."

Natalie could barely make out a tousled head in the backseat, the small figure sound asleep. She smiled at her longtime friend's eight-year old daughter. "I won't wake her," she replied. "What's up?"

Paula took a deep breath. "I know it's a lot to ask, but would you be able to watch Isabella on Sunday? Rudy won't be done with his contract assignment on the rig in Odessa for another seven weeks and I have to drive all the way to Denton for my cousin's *quinceanera*. My grandmother will have a meltdown if I don't go because it would be the third family event I've missed since Rudy's been away at work. And I'd rather *not* drag Isabella because, as we all know," Paula paused and shot a glance at her sleeping daughter. "As angelic as she looks now, she finds trouble easier than any little girl I've known. Always wandering off, asking inappropriate questions, exploring things…"

Natalie laughed and held up a hand to cut off her friend's venting. "I'm going to be here and dropping off a catering order, but she's more than welcome to hang out. You know that. You're like my sister, Paula, and I've helped you and Rudy with Isabella since she was born."

Paula let out a sigh of relief. "Thank you, thank you, thank you!" She exclaimed. "I'll call you this week and let you know what time. For now, I'd better get this one home before she wakes up and finds her second wind."

Natalie nodded and waved as Paula rolled up the window of her truck and drove off. A large cloud of brown dust kicked up in its wake. *We may not be blood-related, but Paula has been my closest friend since middle school* she thought. *Besides, she's always helped in the bakery around the holidays when we've needed an extra hand. Celia always says that family helps family no matter what. Paula is just as much my family as anyone else.*

Natalie backed her truck onto the road, rolling over a few small tumbleweeds that bounced across the heat-baked pavement. As she turned the radio dial back up, she grinned at the setting sun glowing as far as the eye could see across the horizon.

"Take every day as it comes," she reminded herself softly. "There is so much to love and be grateful for. Today, it's this gorgeous sun and sky that you can't get anywhere else in the world. There's no place like home and there's *definitely* nowhere like Texas."

CHAPTER 4

London stood impatiently at the side doors of the Art Institute and scanned the crowds of well-dressed party-goers for Holly. She glanced at the window next to her and was taken aback by her reflection. *I look angry* she thought in wonderment. *God, do I always look like that?*

She absent-mindedly smoothed her hair with one hand. The glossy jet black bob was slightly grown out and rested just above her defined shoulders. She glanced surreptitiously at her reflection again. Her wide, ice-blue eyes held a certain hardness in them, even with her long eyelashes coated in mascara. Her pale skin that had once glowed brightly now looked pasty and sallow.

I can't even stand my own reflection London thought with a sigh. She played with a thread on the sleeve of her black blazer and startled as someone grabbed her waist.

"You look *hot!*" Holly exclaimed as London turned in surprise. "Wow, all that time in the gym has really been doing excellent things to your physique."

London smiled despite herself and embraced her friend. She had chosen her outfit quickly and wore a white silk shirt beneath her blazer and skinny black pants paired with motorcycle boots.

"See, and you tease me for spending so much time there," she replied with a laugh. "Holly, you look stunning. I would be honored to be your pretend lesbian date tonight."

They giggled as London gallantly stuck out her elbow. Holly slid her arm through and fanned herself with a black lace fan. They slowly made their way through throngs of people and had their names checked off a list by a tuxedoed man standing at the entrance to the ballroom.

"Pictures!" Holly exclaimed with delight as they were met with a red carpet. London stood patiently as Holly posed along the red carpet and paused at a backdrop as a few photographers snapped away. Her form-hugging yellow dress looked phenomenal against her cocoa-colored skin and her eyes shone with a confidence that London had always admired.

Holly laughed as she stepped away and grabbed London's arm. "I'm a sucker for a red carpet," she admitted. "Even at forty-five years old, the princess fantasy never goes away. Besides, I should be able to show off this way-too-expensive dress because I have a feeling Michael will have a stroke when he sees our credit card statement next month."

London nodded and pretended to listen. *I wonder if it's too soon to ask about her meeting with the C.E.O.* She wondered anxiously. *She's been holed up in meetings for the last two days. I've barely seen her and it's driving me crazy. Maybe this promotion* would *be good for me. Anything to get out of this funk.*

"Let's get a drink," Holly interrupted London's thoughts and nodded to a bar set up in the far corner. "All hail the open bar. What are you having, girl?"

London shrugged. "Vodka soda, I guess."

"Good call," Holly replied with a short nod. "Vodka for us both tonight."

London bit her lip as they made their way to the bar and finally sighed. "Okay, I give," she relented. "It's driving me mad. How did your meeting with Mr. Hanson go? How do you think he felt about you taking over Daniel's role and me transitioning into yours?"

Holly gave her a sidelong glance as the bartender approached them. "Two vodka and soda waters, please," she ordered with a smile. She turned to London. "I was going to wait until the end of the evening to discuss it with you. I thought we could both use a work-free night out at the gala. But I should've known, because I know how you are and you're never going to relax until your questions are answered."

London nodded. "So what is it? Good news, bad news, no news?" She glanced at the bartender with a short smile as he handed her a frosty glass.

The ice cubes clinked against the sides as she took a slow sip. "Holly, you're killing me."

Holly took a deep breath and met London's eyes as she steeled her gaze. "I have *great* news, but I don't know if you'll believe it's great news at first."

London blinked. "What does that mean? The promotion is great news if I have it in the bag. I never envisioned myself as the corporate type, but focusing on work has so far been successful in keeping me distracted and busy."

Holly pursed her lips and guided London to an overstuffed white sofa across the ballroom. "And therein lies the problem," she murmured.

"What?" London asked, unsure if she'd heard her friend correctly.

Holly placed her drink onto a glass coffee table as they sank into the soft suede. "Mr. Hanson offered me the Chief Marketing Officer position," she started.

London sat up and grinned. "Oh my *God*, that's amazing!"

Holly held up a hand. "Not so fast, London," she continued. "When I mentioned your name as the person I wanted to steer into my role, it brought up a long conversation about you."

London's smile faltered. "What…What do you mean, a conversation about me?"

"He made some excellent points that I wholeheartedly agree with," Holly went on. "So please listen to me and have an open mind. Take everything into consideration and understand that it's coming from a place of good intentions. I promise you, London."

"Okay," she replied slowly, unsure if she was liking the direction of the conversation.

Holly took a sip of her drink. "He mentioned that the transition into my role will, undoubtedly, mean more responsibilities, long hours and a widely expanded workload. I know you're familiar with what I do, but dealing directly with our national accounts means dealing with a lot of different personalities on any given day. Also, you're going to go from zero work-related travel to nearly 50%."

London wrinkled her nose. "Holly, I understand that there will be more expected of me. I'm prepared for that."

"There's no doubt in anyone's mind that you have the talent, the drive and the work ethic," Holly replied. "But we're both concerned that it could be too much for you at this time and you'll end up crashing and burning. That's what happens when you go full force ahead and don't take the time to slow down," Holly raised her hand to quiet London's protests. "I care about you and I want to see you succeed. Mr. Hanson is well-liked throughout W.H. Young because he has genuine concern for his employees. I've seen people crash and burn before. You can think you're the most ready person on the planet, but the fact is that the world relies on balance. You can't have one extreme or the other for too long before something has to give. You're so talented. I *don't* want to see you break down."

London rested her chin in her hand. Her drink was tasting better and better as Holly spoke. "I don't understand," she said stubbornly. "I don't get what everyone is so worried about. So I don't like to talk about things or wear my feelings on my sleeve, so what. A lot of people are like that. My father was the *king* of that so it's especially not fair now that he keeps calling me, trying to force a relationship and asking me to visit…"

"Wait, *what*?" Holly asked incredulously. "I know he was at the funeral, but you never said much about it. I thought you couldn't stand him. I thought he was a callous, absentee asshole for your entire life. What does he say?"

London shrugged slowly. "Ever since my mom passed away," she answered truthfully. "He's been trying to wedge himself into my life. We had a couple of decent conversations, I guess, but he wants me to take some time off and stay at his place in Fort Worth. Like I have nothing better to do than up and get on a plane. I may be the illegitimate daughter of some big-time oil guy, but I'm not sitting around and wasting opportunities. Unlike my ex-stepmother, I *work* and have a career that I care about. I always wanted to make my own name for myself."

Holly took another deep breath. She rubbed her thumb against the condensation pooling around the bottom of her glass. "London, the only time you've ever taken off was three days when your mother passed. Most people would take at least a week, maybe even a few. And with what you went through right after? I can't imagine going through *one* of those situations, let alone both within a few months…"

"I prefer to focus on work so I don't run myself into a depression," London cut in. "Please don't tell me that you think my father is on to something."

Holly stirred her drink and nodded slowly. "I'm going to give you some unsolicited advice," she finally responded. "I think you should take the summer off. You have six weeks of paid vacation that you've never taken. Mr. Hanson *is* willing to give you further consideration, but you need to take time to regroup first. He wants to see the focus and fire that you came into the agency with. And we both want to be sure that you're ready, given everything that you've been through personally."

London's mouth dropped open. "Take the summer off?" She repeated. "Where would I even go? What would I do?" She spread her hands helplessly. "Holly, that won't help me at all. All that time by myself is akin to torture. I won't know what to do with myself…"

Holly put a hand on her hip. "Have I ever steered you wrong?" She asked. "In the length of time that we've known each other, have I ever given you bad advice?"

London's eyes dropped to the marble floor beneath their feet. "No…"

"Then I'm telling you," Holly cut in. "I am *promising* you that this will be the most beneficial thing you've done for yourself. I'm afraid that, right now, Mr. Hanson thinks it's too soon. Once you're in my role, it's going to be go, go, go. All the time. Go refresh your mind and soul and come back guns blazing. Rent a house on a remote beach somewhere. Climb a mountain in Africa, I don't know! Hole up in a dreary, romantic European apartment and write the next Great American Novel."

"Oh sure, I'll just get on the next plane to Denmark…" London retorted.

"Actually…" Holly's eyes lit up and London knew that her mind was spinning. She groaned and picked up her drink.

"See this?" London pointed to her glass. "It's empty. I'm going to get another one. And I'm *not* going to Russia to get the vodka."

"London, wait," Holly called. "Come outside with me. Quick cigarette. I want you to hear me out."

She set her jaw and stayed silent as Holly guided them outside. They plopped onto the wide concrete steps of the Art Institute as London looked morosely at the cars speeding past on Michigan Avenue.

Holly lit a cigarette and breathed out slowly. "This is the most emotion I've seen in your eyes in at least a year."

"You think I should run off to Texas and spend time with a half-sister that I've only met a handful of times and a father that never wanted to know me," London stated sullenly.

"He wants to know you now," Holly replied. "That should count for something. When people get older and they reach that weird space just past middle aged, they start to reflect on their life. They see things differently than they did in their twenties, their thirties. Has he apologized and admitted his mistakes?"

London briefly recalled their morning conversation and swallowed hard.

"Then you should give him a chance," Holly continued softly. "It's not fair to blame your half-sister for him being a part of her life when you don't know her. It's all she's known. You don't control him or the decisions he's made."

London smiled despite the fact that she wasn't comfortable with the idea of temporarily leaving the city that had once held so much intrigue and promise. "Oh, I know that," she muttered. "He's hard-headed as hell."

Holly threw her head back and laughed. "I wondered where you got it from!"

"You're a good saleswoman, I'll give you that," London replied. "I suppose I can always hang out and try to do some work from afar. Mr. Hanson can't possibly pass me up then."

Holly shook her head and wrapped her arm around London. "Sure," she responded. "Whatever you feel you need to do. I can give *you* that. People love you, London. You just have to learn how to trust the world enough to let us."

London rested her head on her friend's shoulder, inhaling the smoke that curled upwards from the cigarette that rested daintily between Holly's thin index and middle fingers. "I trust your judgment," she declared. "I'll call my father tomorrow. Everyone wins. I'll try to work on some low-priority assignments while I'm away so they can be ahead of schedule," she paused and rolled her eyes. "When I return, of course."

"Good," Holly replied after a moment. "What do you say we go back inside and enjoy the night? Did you *see* that dessert table? Good thing you burn enough calories every night at the gym for us both." Holly rubbed London's shoulder and stood. "Because *I* cannot turn down a chocolate fountain."

London laughed and brushed off her pants as she stood. She turned one last time, taking in the traffic, the lights, the bustle and the hulking glass and concrete buildings against the dusky evening sky. *Could I live outside of Chicago?* She wrinkled her nose. *This city is loud, boisterous and big. But it's my home. Would I survive in a place like Texas?*

"Girl, what are you waiting for?" Holly's voice made London turn back. "When I say chocolate fountain, that means *let's go!*"

London laughed again and jogged up the stairs. *Weird* she thought. *I feel lighter than I have in ages.*

CHAPTER 5

Later that evening, London sank onto her bed from unsteady feet. The night had been a lot to take in and, as typical with Holly, one drink had turned into a few more. She laid back against the cool pillows and closed her eyes. A slight buzz from the vodka still pulsed gently through her temples. The bedroom was dark, except for one bright trail of yellow light beaming from a street light half a block away.

What do I do? She wondered. *Could I leave everything and take a chance in Texas? What if it's horrible, what if my father and I argue every chance we get? What if Tiffany and I hate each other? What if, what if, what if.*

The questions swirled through her mind and she took a deep breath. She opened her eyes and, in the deafening silence of the dark apartment, she took in her surroundings for what felt like the first time. The furnishings were modern but simple: black furniture, a flat-screen television, basic amenities.

If we're being honest, a person wouldn't know if they were in a hotel room or my apartment London realized. She was surprised at the disappointment she felt. *There's no personality here.*

She wondered if she had subconsciously done that on purpose. During the course of her and Kayley's relationship, they had collected a few pieces of art and a handful of knick-knacks; things that had given the apartment life and a splash of character. London hadn't fought it when Kayley took those items as she moved out.

I wanted her to leave as quickly as possible and I wanted every trace of her gone from this apartment London recalled dejectedly. *Any lingering reminders would have hurt too much. Between my mom and then Kayley and Tara, I was already at my threshold of hurt for, I don't know, the next twenty years or so.*

"I don't like this apartment," she whispered into the dark. She blinked at the ceiling. "I don't even like myself."

With her mind slowed by vodka and exhaustion, London carefully reached onto her bedside table and grabbed her phone. She knew it was late and her father was most likely asleep, but it was suddenly very important to send the text message she had in mind.

Before I lose my nerve she finished silently. *Maybe it's the alcohol talking or maybe I'm so tired of disliking myself and everything around me, but I give in. I'm sick of feeling this way. I'm sick of the days running together and the months passing me by. A short trip to Texas to get this promotion can't possibly be worse than sticking around here and feeling more numb each day.*

She smiled as she finished typing out the message and tried to read it over. The words swam before her eyes and her thumb hovered uncertainly over the Send button. With a decisive breath, London hit Send and watched as a blue bubble holding the message popped onto her screen with one small, intimidating word below: Delivered.

Dad, give me a call when you get this. I know it's late, but I've done some thinking and wanted to take you up on your offer. I'm ready to visit. I have some time off coming up and thought we could plan something soon. Let's talk more when you call. Have a good night.

London felt a satisfactory smile play at her lips and she closed her eyes again. "This is what I need to do," she whispered to herself as she curled beneath the blankets. Her mouth was beginning to taste like stale alcohol and cotton, but a sense of accomplishment surged through her. "I'll take a few weeks in Texas, come back ready for that promotion and then everything will fall into place."

For the first time in as long as she could recall, it felt as if the Universe had finally begun aligning. With a steely, unfamiliar confidence that she couldn't quite put her finger on, she knew in her heart that this was the right decision.

"Nat, Nat, Nat!" Natalie turned with a start as Isabella sprang from the pantry with a giggle.

"Isabella, what's going on?" Natalie asked. She glanced over her friend's daughter and mentally recounted the neatly stacked boxes for this afternoon's baby shower. "Is everything okay?"

Isabella laughed. "I was trying to scare you! You didn't jump at all."

Natalie smiled and ruffled her dark brown hair. "You are full of energy since you're out of school for the summer, huh?" She observed dryly. "How about you help me load some boxes into the food truck so we can deliver them for the party?"

Isabella nodded eagerly and held out her arms, patiently waiting, as Natalie selected a light box of mini cupcakes for the younger girl. "Yup and no more school for, uh…" She paused and began following Natalie to the truck. "Two and a *half* months."

Natalie laughed as she wrenched open the truck's wide back door. She turned to relieve Isabella of the box. "And then what?" She teased. "You'll start second grade, right?"

Isabella frowned and put her hands on her hips. "Natalie, second grade was *last* year," she pouted. "You know what grade I'll be in."

"Oh, right," Natalie bit back another smile. "Yes, of course. You'll be in kindergarten."

She burst into laughter as Isabella scoffed and stomped a foot. "*Third* grade," she corrected her with a sniff. "You know I'm not a baby."

Natalie held her hands in a conciliatory gesture and nodded. "Okay, okay," she conceded with a wink. "You got me. I just can't believe you're going to be in third grade this fall. I still remember the day you were born."

Isabella nodded seriously. "Eight years ago," she replied. "Soon to be nine. That's almost a decade."

Natalie groaned as she led them back into the bakery for another load. "God, yeah it was," she responded. "Did your mom mention what time she was picking you up today? I was too busy double-checking the order for today's party to hear much of anything she said when you were dropped off."

Isabella smiled. "Mom said she'd try to leave Denton around two. And she also says you work too much for someone your age."

Natalie grinned and handed her another box of mini cupcakes. "Your mom worries just like my *tias*," she replied. "I get out of this bakery plenty."

Yeah, right a small voice piped up in Natalie's head. *Except for when you dated Cristina, you've never gotten out much.* Natalie hoisted a heavy box of eclairs into her arms and marched back into the heat. *The two years I spent with Cristina were one big whirlwind of late nights, all day naps, zero ambition, raging parties and too much alcohol.*

She thought back to her single serious relationship as she neatly organized the boxes in the back of the truck. *I was so young* she thought ruefully. *Sheltered country girl who fell madly in love with the first outsider she met.* Natalie turned and took another box from Isabella's waiting arms.

I was barely twenty. She was, what was it? Thirty-three or thirty-four? Drifted into town from Los Angeles with her band, which I thought was just too cool Natalie thought. *I thought everything she said and did was awesome. She loved to rage and we partied our way through the metroplex for almost two years.* She laughed to herself. *Everyone wanted to be around her. Except Celia and Jane, because they couldn't stand her. I had no ambition, no direction in life and all she did was lead me from party to party. We'd drink together all night and lay around all day. But then the parties slowed, she got bored and moved on to a different location and a new young, eager girl.*

"And, just like that, it was over," Natalie murmured. "Easy for her, devastating for me."

Isabella's small figure appeared in the window reflection behind her. Natalie turned with a smile. "Is that the last box?"

Isabella nodded as she handed the cream cheese brownies to her. "Can I ride with you to make the delivery instead of cleaning the store room? I've never been in the food truck before."

Natalie shook her head and laughed. "Geez, I really spoil you, don't I? All you have to do is ask and you know I'll probably say yes."

Isabella grinned. "I don't think that's a *bad* thing, Natalie."

She laughed louder. "You *would* say that, kid," she replied. "Fine. You're too smart for your own good and I could use your help unloading when we get there."

"Yay!" Isabella shouted as she pumped her fist in the air. She ran for the passenger's side door.

Natalie rolled her eyes good-naturedly and resolutely shut the back door of the truck, ex-girlfriend forgotten except for one small lesson she had taken with her through the years. "Rule number one," she murmured. "Don't fall for an out-of-towner."

With that, she pulled her keys from the pocket of her jeans and hurried into the truck. She had just slid onto the seat when Isabella turned to her. "Natalie, can I ask you something?"

Natalie shot a look across the truck. *Uh-oh. Usually when Isabella asks if she can ask something, I know I'm in for it.* "I don't know, can you?" She countered as she put the truck into gear.

Isabella smiled. "What kind of girls do you like?"

Natalie blinked. "It feels a little odd having this conversation with my eight-year old pseudo-niece."

Isabella rolled her eyes and rested her chin in her hand. "Mommy and Daddy told me you're gay, like, *way* long ago."

"And I appreciate them being so honest from the get-go with you, but it's still a hard question to answer," Natalie replied wryly.

Isabella sighed heavily. "It's not hard," she pressed. "I mean, do you like girls that are tall? Short? Fat? Skinny? Blonde hair? Brown hair?"

Natalie laughed and shook her head. "To me, you have to be beautiful on the inside first. That makes you beautiful on the outside. I mean…" she paused and tried to put her words into a perspective Isabella would understand. "A cute person isn't very cute anymore if they're mean or lie a lot, right?"

The younger girl appeared to think it over and then nodded. "You're right."

"So maybe someone who knows what's really important in life," Natalie went on as they drove beneath I-20. "And, of course, cute. Whether that's tall, short, skinny, curvaceous, blonde or brunette."

"What's really important?" Isabella echoed in confusion.

Yup Natalie silently decided. They slowed to a stop at an intersection nearing a residential area. *This kid is way too smart for her own good.* "Love. Family. Happiness. Not necessarily things like money or…"

Isabella shook her head quickly. "No," she interrupted. "Money is important. Mommy and Daddy sometimes argue about why we don't have more of it. And then Daddy goes away to work on the rigs. I bet they wouldn't fight and he wouldn't have to go away all the time if there was more of it."

Natalie sighed. *How do you explain things like adult life to an eight-year old? A ridiculously perceptive eight-year old, but one nonetheless.* "There's a lot that goes into making a relationship work," she replied carefully. She knew that Rudy and Paula, high school sweethearts, had their problems but she also knew how dedicated they were to each other. "It's a challenge sometimes, but if the people involved love each other and are equally committed, it can work."

"Even for forever?" Isabella asked.

Natalie nodded. *Do relationships last these days?* "Sometimes even for forever."

Isabella grinned. "I think there's someone for *everybody*," she whispered.

"How many of those Disney movies have you been watching, *niña*?" Natalie asked as she raised an eyebrow.

Isabella shrugged. "There's even someone for a mermaid," she went on.

"Oh, you've been watching The Little Mermaid," Natalie replied knowingly. She peered out of the windshield and glanced back down at the handwritten directions in her lap. The neighborhood was gated, but she could tell the homes inside were massive by the size of the Spanish-tiled roofs peeking between tall shade trees. "That was one of my favorites when I was a kid too."

Isabella giggled. "I like it because the prince's name is Eric," she paused and sighed dreamily. "There's a boy named Eric at my school and he was the cutest boy in the whole second grade. Maybe I'll grow up and marry him."

Natalie smiled. "Focus on being a kid for now, okay?" She replied gently. "You have your whole life to find your prince. Or princess."

Isabella laughed. "*Prince*, Natalie," she said. "I like my girl friends but I don't want to marry any of them. They don't make my tummy feel fuzzy like Eric did when he would run past me at recess. But *you're* going to marry a girl and then I can help you both at the bakery!"

"Let's not get *too* ahead of ourselves," Natalie interjected quickly. "Let's just get these treats delivered and take this summer one beautiful day at a time."

Isabella nodded as they inched slowly toward the community's entrance gate. "Natalie, can I tell you something?"

Natalie felt herself tense slightly. *Here we go again. I never know what's going to come out of this kid's mouth.*

Isabella grinned. "I know that you're Mommy's best friend, but you're my best friend too."

Natalie reached over and ruffled her hair. "Love you too, Isabella," she replied and hoped her voice didn't catch. "When we get to the house, you just stand in the back of the truck and hand me boxes. I'll run inside and get everything signed off, okay?"

Isabella bunched her fists and flexed her skinny arms in the passenger's seat. "Yeah, I'm Superwoman!"

Natalie glanced at the girl, her heart swelling with pride. *Dorothy had it right* she thought. *There's no place like home.*

CHAPTER 6

London stood beneath the shower and closed her eyes. She savored the warm spray as it rinsed the feeling of travel from her skin. *This bathroom reminds me of one of those fancy spas on the Gold Coast* she thought. Marble tile floors, a Jacuzzi soaking tub peering into the property's expansive backyard, a separate dressing area and a large square stall with an oversized shower head installed right in the center gave the room a relaxed, comforting atmosphere.

The shower itself had a small sitting area in one corner and a tall, heated towel rack opposite the wide glass door. *I could stay in here all day* she thought, the idea not sounding half-bad. The muscles in her back and shoulders began to loosen as water pattered gently against her.

What a whirlwind these last few days have been she thought as she stepped further under the chrome shower head. *When Dad insisted on buying my ticket, I didn't know he was going to purchase it for this very weekend. Good thing Holly had my time off request covered.*

The early morning flight had been uneventful, but London was still tired from the travel and cab ride to the address her father had given her. She remembered him mentioning that he would be in Dubai until later in the week, but that Tiffany would be arriving this morning as well. London's heart sank. *Anytime now.*

What did Dad say she had been doing? London struggled to remember as she rinsed conditioner from her hair. *Oh, yeah. Teaching English to children in Cambodia. That's no small flight. At least she'll be tired when she arrives and we won't have to exchange awkward pleasantries. What could we possibly have to say to each other? Our lives have been spent completely separate.* London thought of her father's voice, bursting with pride, as he spoke of Tiffany's appetite for adventure and generous heart. He had said that, prior to her six-month assignment in Cambodia, she had spent a few months in Kenya to help install water filtration systems in small villages on the outskirts of Nairobi.

Saint Tiffany London thought with a roll of her eyes. She wrapped a thick Egyptian cotton towel around her body as she carefully stepped from the shower. *She's twenty-two. Young and idealistic. Maybe even how I used to be.*

London shook the thought from her head as she opened the bathroom door. She braced herself for the rush of air conditioning against her warm, flushed skin. She had only taken a few steps into the hallway when she stopped short at the sound of a voice.

"Hello?" The woman's voice called uncertainly. "Um, anyone home?"

Tiffany? London wrinkled her nose and assumed her half-sister was wondering if she had arrived yet.

"Now or never," she muttered to herself as she strode over cherry hardwood flooring through the sunken living room. London gasped in surprise when she spotted a lone figure in the kitchen. Her arms were filled with pink and white boxes and she whirled around at the sound of footsteps.

Definitely not Tiffany. "Who are you and what are you doing here?" London asked sharply. She wrapped her arms around herself and was acutely aware that she was completely naked beneath her towel.

The woman stood motionless and her mouth dropped open. Her brown eyes were wide and London watched as a slight blush colored her golden-tan skin. "I, uh…"

London continued to watch as her eyes traveled helplessly down her body. She suddenly felt vulnerable.

Too vulnerable she thought. "I asked what you're doing here," she barked. Her voice was louder than she'd intended but she took a breath and continued. "How did you get in? I'm calling the police."

The woman's eyes snapped up and she quickly set the boxes onto the long granite breakfast bar. "No, no, I apologize," she spoke quickly. "I'm with

Mission Bakery and my name is Natalie Silva. I was directed to use the key under the mat if no one was home. I'm sorry. I knocked a few times. I'm delivering the order for today's baby shower."

London's eyes narrowed. "Yeah, right," she replied suspiciously. *I've been in Chicago too long to believe her.* "What baby shower? What are you talking about?"

Natalie glanced helplessly at an order form. "The order was placed over a week ago and confirmed just a few days before," she tried to explain. She ran a hand through her hair in confusion. "This is 8667 St. Catherine Way in Fort Worth, correct?"

"Yes, but there's a misunderstanding," London declared. She felt her voice rise again. *This is not how I wanted to start my time in Texas.* "Besides, do you always go waltzing into peoples' private homes? I can't believe anyone would tell you to use a key. I was in the shower and you absolutely *cannot* just intrude…"

Another voice piped up as the front door opened and closed with a resounding bang. "*Sweet*, Mission Bakery is right on time," Tiffany paused as she walked down the wide hallway and grinned. She dropped a worn, overstuffed duffel bag onto the marble tile. It echoed with a light thud off the sixteen-foot vaulted ceiling. "I saw the food truck in the driveway and raced in as fast as I could. Sorry for the confusion, chicas. These are mine."

Natalie glanced at the order form in confusion. "You're Lorena Martinez?"

Tiffany burst into laughter as the morning sun filtered through the skylight above and bounced off her platinum blonde hair. It was tied back in a loose bun and she wore what looked to London like a patterned, hand-sewn headband to keep the stray pieces from falling into her face. "No," she shook her head and laughed again. "I'm Tiffany Foster and I ordered the goodies for the baby shower. But my very best friend from high school, who also happens to be very pregnant, is Lorena Martinez. She'll be thrilled when I surprise the shower this afternoon with sweets from her favorite bakery."

Natalie swallowed hard and thrust the order form at Tiffany. "Please sign at the bottom," she said stiffly. London could tell that she was shaken. "The form notes that we were given a credit card to keep on file when the original order was placed, so we'll charge that for the full amount. Otherwise, you're all set. Enjoy."

Tiffany grinned as she quickly signed her name and handed the paper back to Natalie. "Thank you," she responded as she peeked at the boxes. She threw a sidelong glance at London, who realized that she was still dripping wet in the middle of the living room. "I apologize again for the confusion. I just took an overnight flight home from Cambodia through Seoul and there were a few delays. That's why I asked that you use the key. I didn't realize my *sister* here would be joining us this summer until very recently. I'm sure she's tired from her travels and didn't mean to raise her voice."

Now that London had a chance to survey the situation, she realized that her eyes kept seeking out Natalie's slender frame. She subtly checked her out as Tiffany spoke. Natalie was wearing faded blue jeans with tears over both knees and a gray v-neck t-shirt. As she turned, a bit of her t-shirt rode up and revealed a hint of smooth, tanned skin along her hip. *God, she's gorgeous* London thought and then swallowed hard. *Wait, where did that come from?*

She realized after a moment that Natalie was refusing to look anywhere near her. Her heart kicked up a notch as it dawned on her a split second later that she desperately wanted Natalie to look at her again. *Say something, anything* she thought as her mind raced. *Rectify the situation. Apologize for acting like a complete snob.* She opened her mouth, but nothing came out.

London watched silently as Natalie gathered her papers and nodded a curt good-bye at Tiffany. The sound of the door closing as she left made her blink. She met Tiffany's sky-blue eyes and sighed.

"Thanks for, uh, clearing that up," she stammered. "Anyway, I should get changed."

There was a short pause as London made her escape, but not before she could hear Tiffany's hurt tone as she gently shut the guest bedroom door behind her.

"Wow, London, it's nice to see you too."

Natalie strode angrily to the truck still humming in the driveway. She couldn't remember the last time she felt so irritated and took a deep, calming breath. Maybe it was because she had been caught checking out a breathtakingly attractive stranger in a bath towel. *Or maybe it's because the gorgeous stranger opened her mouth and turned out to be kind of a jerk.*

She could tell from the woman's sure tone, the quick, measured way in which she spoke and the confident way she carried herself that she was not from around here. *Besides, I would remember a woman like that* Natalie told herself. *And not just because of those piercing eyes. Or those soft lips. Or those long, ultra-toned legs on display…*

Natalie willed her memory to stop its slow replay of the moment as Isabella glanced at her curiously. She quickly dialed a number on her cell phone and waited impatiently for her aunt to answer.

"Morning, Natalie," Jane greeted her pleasantly. "How's it going?"

"Could be better, *Tia* Jane," Natalie replied honestly. She quickly backed the truck out of the long driveway. "Did you, by chance, put the wrong name on the order form for today's delivery?"

She listened as Jane paused and thought it over. "Mmm, no. I don't believe so. Is there a problem?"

"There was a white girl in the house that chewed me out from here to El Paso. Let me reiterate, a *very pissed off* white girl," Natalie strained to keep the annoyance from her voice. "*Not* a Lorena Martinez."

"Right, Lorena is the mother-to-be," Jane spoke in confusion. "The order is for her, but was placed by someone else. Tonya, Tiffany…"

"Tiffany," Natalie confirmed. "Tiffany Foster. But her name wasn't anywhere on the order form."

Jane chuckled. "I'm sorry, Natalie," she apologized. "I took the call at the end of the day and it had been mighty busy. I must have forgotten to note her information. Honest mistake. Tiffany was upset?"

Natalie sighed. "No, she was fine," she replied. "But I happened to walk in on her sister. Who *happens* to be knockout-beautiful and was wearing nothing but a towel. Needless to say, she was less than thrilled and I was humiliated."

Jane roared with laughter, much to Natalie's chagrin. "Oh, God," she gasped between laughs. "I think that's the funniest thing I've heard in weeks. Oh, you poor thing."

Natalie's face was stone as she pulled into the parking lot of the bakery. "I'm glad you find it so amusing."

"Oh, honey, I know you're embarrassed," Jane continued. "You've always been a sweetheart. But everything is fine, right? The customer is happy, there were no serious issues with delivery and we completed one of the largest orders we've done all year. Be positive, Natalie. Our bakery has built an excellent reputation for itself over the last few years."

Natalie hung up the phone and sighed. She stared out the windshield at the entrance to the bakery for a moment before Isabella's voice roused her. "What do we do now?"

Natalie bit her lip. "Well, the bakery is technically closed on Sundays," she replied slowly. "But sometimes I like to get a start on the menu items for tomorrow."

Isabella clapped her hands excitedly. "Cool, do I get to bake with you?"

Natalie glanced at Isabella and then back at the bakery with a smile. "I think today is a day for cake pops, *nina*."

CHAPTER 7

London snapped her laptop shut with a sigh. The sun was sinking into the horizon and the guest bedroom was slowly growing darker. She had holed up nearly all day and tried to keep herself busy with editing website content for one of W.H. Young's newest clients. It had worked most of the afternoon, but for the last hour and a half she had been staring blankly at the glowing screen.

In less than twenty-four hours, I've already managed to piss off two people she thought. *That has to be a new record.*

She turned her and Tiffany's relationship over in her mind. *Ten years apart* she mused. *But in reality, we've always been worlds apart.* Her father had married his ex-wife, Diane, when London was barely in first grade. She vaguely recalled the elaborate destination wedding in Costa Rica. What she *did* remember was overhearing a hushed argument between the couple outside of the bridal suite door.

"Oh sweetheart, I really wanted to London to feel a part of this wedding," Vince spoke dejectedly. "I haven't been in her life much, but she's still my daughter. It would be special to have her as our flower girl."

Diane scoffed and London could hear the familiar jangle of the thin rose-gold bracelets that she always wore. "Really, Vincent," she replied. "How would that look to all of our friends? To Dallas-Fort Worth society?" She paused. "To your investors? The rest of the Board of Directors at Foster Oil & Gas? To have your illegitimate daughter parading down the aisle, front and center in photos that you know will run in the society pages back home. I don't want the whispers and I don't want the gossip. She lives in Chicago, for Christ's sake. Nobody even knows who she is; she's an outsider."

"But she's my daughter," Vince reminded her gently.

"And this is *my wedding*," Diane retorted. "I'm sorry, but you'll have to tell her tomorrow morning that she won't be the flower girl on Saturday. It's for the best."

London remembered sitting in a white chair in a row about five back from the ceremony. She swallowed as realization hit that the memory hurt just as much at thirty-two years old as it did when she was six.

"Tiffany can't possibly be as bad as Diane," London muttered to herself as she switched off her computer. She bit back a smile as she thought about Tiffany's work history in second- and third-world countries. "I bet that just *kills* Diane." Her father and Diane had divorced about three years ago and London knew her ex-stepmother resided in Dallas. *Now that's one person I don't want to see.*

London listened to the front door open and close. *Tiffany is back from the baby shower* she realized. She startled as her phone jangled loudly with an incoming FaceTime call in the quiet of the still room. She grinned as Holly's name popped onto the screen and grabbed her phone to accept the video call.

"Hey, London!" Holly's voice echoed excitedly through the speaker. London could see that Holly was seated at her dining room table, a tall China cabinet looming behind her. "How's your first day in Texas?"

London tried to force her biggest smile but faltered. "It's, um, it's good," she hedged. "I've been busy editing the copy for Westchester Solutions' new website so I haven't been up to much yet…"

Holly sighed and directed a disapproving look into the camera. "London, I can tell you're lying," she replied. "And I appreciate you getting a head start on your work, but this is your time. You're technically on vacation from W.H. Young, so that means *relax*."

London bit her lip uncertainly. "Fine," she replied. "It's horrible. I'm rethinking this. I snapped at a woman who was delivering baked goods to the house. And to say that Tiffany and I have gotten off on the wrong foot would be the understatement of the century. I think this was a bad idea and I should go home."

Holly raised an eyebrow. "London, you haven't even been there for twenty-four hours. You're tired, you're in a totally new environment and your nerves are shot. I'm not saying snapping at strangers is excusable, but give yourself a break. You and your sister haven't seen each other in over a decade. Put yourself in her shoes. This whole thing is probably just as strange to her."

London sighed heavily. "Half-sister," she muttered. "I just…I don't even know how to relate to her! We're so different. We don't know each other."

Holly shrugged. "You just have to do it," she replied. "Put yourself out there and start trying. If there's any hope of you two connecting, she has to feel comfortable with you too."

"I know," London admitted. "I know that I need to try too."

"Anyway, did you download the Instagram app?" Holly asked. "It's the best way to share photos of your trip in real-time."

London rolled her eyes good-naturedly. "Yes, I did," she admitted. "I even shared my first picture. Well, at least I *think* I did. I tried to post a photo of the sky as the plane was landing. I captioned it 'I don't know what I'm doing, but my best friend made me download this app so here's a picture of some cool-looking clouds.'"

Holly snorted. "You did not!" She exclaimed. "I'm going to search for you and start following right now."

"I did," London replied with a mock-serious nod. "Hashtag forced onto social media. Hashtag hi Holly."

Holly snickered again and shook her head at the camera. "Clever. So how's the weather there?"

"Hot…" London started. She paused as a dark shadow moved in the far corner of the bedroom. It darted up to the space where the wall met ceiling. "…But what the hell is *that*?"

"What's what?" Holly asked in confusion.

"I…" London squinted in the darkness and then widened her eyes. The shadow moved a few centimeters across the wall. "Oh my *God*, it's a spider! Holly, there's a huge spider in the corner!"

She jumped from her seated position on the bed and wrapped her arms around herself. "I hate spiders," she went on as her panic rose. "They're creepy and big and sneaky…"

London could hear Holly's sigh from where she'd dropped her phone onto the mattress. "London, just kill it."

She refused to take her eyes off the shadow. "It's in an awkward spot," she replied defensively. "And it's *huge*. I can see it as clear as day from across the room."

"London…" Holly started.

She darted to the bed and grabbed her phone. "I'm sorry, I have to cut this short," she apologized, not tearing her eyes from the spider. "It's an emergency. I'll call soon."

As London ended the video call, she quickly reviewed her small list of options for dealing with the eight-legged intruder. *I could kill it, like Holly said* she thought with a shudder. *But the odds of me actually killing it and not just throwing a shoe and then running away screaming are slim to none.* She ran a hand through her messy hair in distress. *Tiffany* she realized. *She's the only one here. She's my only hope. Great. She'll probably tell me to go shove it.*

London watched as the spider crawled a few more centimeters across the wall. She couldn't take it anymore. "Tiffany!" She shouted. "Are you home? Come quick!"

She listened as uncertain footsteps climbed the stairs and then paused. "*Tiffany!*" She tried again. "Hurry!"

Finally, the bedroom door swung open and her sister stood in the frame with a frown. Soft light from the hallway pooled around her and poured into the bedroom.

"What's wrong?" She asked. London detected both notes of irritation and concern in her voice. "Is everything okay?"

London pointed at the corner nearest her sister. "That…" she started in a low voice. "…is not okay."

Tiffany's eyes followed her finger and she crossed her arms. "You're going to have to be more specific."

"The *spider!*" London exclaimed. "The giant spider! I'm terrified. Can you maybe…kill it?"

"You're kidding, right?" Tiffany asked flatly. She scrunched her nose. "Don't you have spiders in Chicago?"

"Not *that* size!" London protested. She balled up her fists in fear as her short fingernails dug into her palms.

"That little thing?" Tiffany went on. "Geez, London, if you think *that's* big then I don't know how you would handle Africa or Cambodia."

London gritted her teeth. "Please," she continued desperately. "I have a big fear of them."

Tiffany rolled her eyes but London could tell she was holding back a grin. *She's enjoying this way too much* she thought.

She watched carefully as Tiffany removed one of her canvas slip-on shoes and climbed onto a desk chair. London let out a squeak as Tiffany smashed the spider with a single pound. She hopped off the chair and picked the lifeless spider in her bare hand from where it had fallen onto the carpet.

"You're…You're going to flush that, right?" London asked worriedly.

Tiffany laughed and then winked at her. "No, I'm going to bury him in the backyard with a tiny tombstone that reads 'Rest in peace, spider. Sorry my sister is such a wimp.'"

London tried to keep a straight face, but her mouth twitched with the absurdity of it all. Maybe it was because she'd had a long, tiring day or because she was relieved the spider was dead, but she burst into laughter. Soon, Tiffany joined her and they were both in near hysterics at opposite ends of the bedroom.

As their raucous laughter subsided, a questioning silence settled over the room. *What now?* London wondered.

Tiffany smiled and nodded once at the dead spider still in her palm. "I'll dispose of him," she said. "Good night, London."

London opened her mouth to speak as Tiffany gently closed the bedroom door behind her. A few seconds later, she heard the unmistakable flush of a toilet. She took a deep breath and realized there was one thing she had forgotten to do.

Carefully, London cracked the bedroom door open and padded down the hallway. She paused outside the bathroom and peeked in the half-open door.

Tiffany's back was to her and London watched silently as she unscrewed an orange prescription bottle and picked out an oblong orange and white pill. Tiffany popped it into her mouth, tilted her head back and took a long sip of water.

"I, uh, I just wanted to say thank you," London started uncertainly.

Tiffany turned and blinked. "Oh!" She fumbled the bottle in her hand and placed it quickly on the counter. "I didn't know you were there. I thought you were planning to stay in the guest bedroom forever."

London shook her head. "Thank you for killing that spider," she went on. Her gaze fell on the prescription bottle and she struggled to make out the tiny print on its white label. "I appreciate it. I wouldn't have been able to sleep knowing it was in the room with me."

Tiffany grinned. "No big deal, London," she replied. "You can loosen up, you know. I'm sure Chicago is a lot different, but you'll fall in love with Texas. There's a certain hospitality, a charm here that you don't get many places." She shrugged. "It's home."

London nodded and glanced at the plastic bottle again. Tiffany followed her gaze and quickly shoved it into the pocket of her white linen pants. "Adderall," she replied after a moment. "It's what keeps *me* awake enough to fly overnight from Seoul and then co-host my best friend's baby shower, what gave me enough energy to teach English every day to 30 seven-year olds and what balances me out."

London raised an eyebrow. "I thought that was for people with A.D.H.D.," she responded carefully. "If it has that effect on you, then you probably don't have it. Is that prescribed to you?"

Tiffany rolled her eyes. "Of course," she went on. "The doctor made a mistake and gave me a higher dosage than I normally receive. But it's fine," she paused and waved a hand. "I'll let him know when I get my refill."

London nodded once, not entirely convinced. She didn't remember her father saying anything about Tiffany having any type of attention deficit disorder. *But who am I to say anything to her?* She thought. *One day in, and I'm suddenly going to play the concerned big sister role? Yeah, right.*

"Well, good night," London said, deciding to let it go. "Thank you again."

Tiffany looked at her for a long moment and bit her lip. "No problem," she replied. "I'm sorry about your mom," she paused and then continued. "I can't imagine the pain you must have felt. I sent a card and a bouquet of flowers, did you ever get them?"

London opened her mouth and then nodded. "Yes, thanks," she murmured. "They were beautiful. Really. I appreciated it very much."

Tiffany grinned again and turned back to the bathroom mirror. "I'm glad. Good night."

London took a few steps down the hall and then, on second thought, turned back to the bathroom. "Hey, Tiffany?"

"Yeah?" She raised her voice over the sound of the sink.

"Do you think I should apologize to Natalie?" London asked, feeling foolish for the question. "It's been eating at me all day for some reason. She seemed upset."

Tiffany pursed her lips. "Well, you did practically bite her head off just for doing her job."

London nodded and then turned again. "I guess that answers my question," she said with a deep breath. "You know, I wasn't always like this. Believe me, I know what you and everyone else thinks. I'm cold, I come off rude and arrogant, I'm jaded, I'm a bitch, I'm…" she paused to catch her breath. "I'm trying to get back to who I really am."

She refused to meet Tiffany's gaze. She didn't want to see pity or sympathy in her kind eyes. London froze when she felt Tiffany jerk her into an enveloping hug.

"It'll be okay, London," she reassured her softly. "I swear it. And you know what? *Fuck* what me or anyone else thinks. *Your* opinion about you is the one that matters."

London blew out her breath. "Mine isn't very positive either."

Tiffany shook her head slowly and smiled at her. "Try to relax while you're here," she offered. "Forget about Chicago, step back and get outside of your bubble. Experience things, enjoy the days and I promise you'll start to heal."

As London wandered back to the guest room, she marveled at Tiffany's open heart. *She didn't have to comfort me just now. She didn't have to kill that spider either. Why doesn't she hate me?*

It wasn't until London closed the door behind her that she realized she had resented Tiffany for much of her life. *It was simpler to assume she'd turn out just like a mini-Diane and it was easy to write her off* London thought as she unzipped her suitcase and took out her neatly folded pajamas. *But she's not like her mother at all. She feels almost like a sister. Well,* half-*sister. How does she have the ability to forgive so quickly?*

Guilt bubbled up in London's chest as she settled beneath the thick comforter. She had the sneaking realization that she had been just as dismissive of Tiffany throughout the years as their father had been of her.

A single thought flashed through her mind as sleep took over. *I need to remember how to forgive too.*

CHAPTER 8

"Wake up, come on!" Tiffany exclaimed. "I come bearing gifts. I made you some coffee."

London cracked one eyelid open and groaned as the younger girl bounced onto the guest bed with a smile. *She is way too chipper for Monday morning.*

"Dad called earlier to check in, but I told him you were still asleep," Tiffany went on matter-of-factly. She held out a glass travel cup filled with steaming dark brown liquid. "He suggested taking you to get a car at Enterprise this morning. That way, you can actually get out and explore if you wanted. His Tesla is in the garage, but I'm sure you'll want your own car…"

London struggled to sit up and begrudgingly accepted the coffee. She took a long sip before blinking. "Did you talk to your doctor about your prescription yet?"

Tiffany rolled her eyes. "Very funny," she replied. "I'm glad you have such a fantastic sense of humor in the mornings. Especially after I slaved over a hot…cappuccino machine to make this amazing coffee."

London took another long sip and exhaled. "I prefer to ease my way out of bed in the mornings," she said coolly. "Instead of someone bursting into the room and jumping on the bed."

"My internal clock is so screwed after hopping all those time zones," Tiffany admitted. "I have a lunch date in downtown Dallas with my mom. I *need* Adderall to deal with her. She was livid when I left U.N.T. and now she's hoping that I'll go back to school and finish my degree."

London nearly spat out her coffee. "You *dropped* out of college?"

Her sister sighed and played with a loose thread on the comforter. "I prefer to think of it as voluntarily taking a leave of absence, but yes. That's one way of saying it."

London wrinkled her nose. "And you were at the University of North Texas? I thought your mom was on the Board at…What school was it?"

"Texas Christian University," Tiffany answered automatically. "And no thank you. Besides the obvious fact that I wanted to attend a secular school, there was no way that I was accepting a free ride just because my mom is on the Board of Directors. I wanted to do it my *own* way, so I moved to Denton instead."

"And what happened?" London asked curiously. The coffee was hot and strong and she found she was enjoying listening to her half-sister's tales of rebellion. *Maybe we're more alike than I thought.*

Tiffany shrugged. "I was there for two years and didn't like it," she answered honestly. "It felt stifling. Like…" She sighed. "Have you ever felt that everything was spinning out of control and the walls were closing in on you?"

London blinked in surprise. *She just described the last year or so of my life.* "Yes," she replied carefully.

"So you can understand," Tiffany continued. "How can *anyone* possibly expect a twenty-year old to pick a career path for the rest of their life? There's a big world out there." She smiled. "So I left. I've spent the last year and a half on volunteer assignments all over the world. It's far more fulfilling than studying for finals and drinking with fraternity boys. All I've ever wanted to do is make a difference in this world. Dad has been more supportive, but I think he secretly hopes it'll lead me to a career path."

London raised an eyebrow. "Has it?"

Tiffany looked sheepish. "Not really," she admitted. "I just know I want to keep impacting the world, one water filtration system and educated child at a time. And don't even get me *started* on how I would never work for Foster Oil & Gas…"

London looked at her for a long moment as her voice faded. A smile crept across her lips. "Hell, I'd vote for you to be President."

Tiffany burst into laughter. "London Foster, are you actually making a joke?" She cracked. "I can't believe it. My tough, stoic older sister has found her sense of humor."

London rolled her eyes and pushed the comforter back. "So is the public transportation system here really that bad?"

Tiffany nodded. "Non-existent," she replied. "That's why the first order of business this morning is getting you into a car. Can you just imagine how much better it would be if the metroplex had a viable public transit system? And no, I'm not counting the D.A.R.T. The Dallas Area Rapid Transit is a joke. Instead, millions of people clog these highways every day and slowly kill our air quality and environment with the fumes…"

London stifled a laugh. *Okay, she couldn't be more different from Diane. Thank the Universe.* "I'll take your word for it," she replied. She took another sip of coffee. "Let's go to Enterprise."

An hour later, London gripped the passenger door handle of Tiffany's silver Prius as it zipped in and out of traffic on I-20. She breathed a sigh of relief as she swung the hybrid vehicle into a compact parking space in front of the car rental facility. They were near downtown Fort Worth at Meacham Airport and she glanced around cautiously. A few of the tall buildings that made up the eerie, hulking Fort Worth skyline were visible in the distance, but they were mainly surrounded by older brick industrial buildings.

London stepped out of the Prius and was immediately taken with the late morning heat. "This is different than the type of hot we get in Chicago," she remarked as she pulled her black Coach sunglasses over her eyes. "It's muggy and humid there in the summers. This is different. This is…"

"The seventh circle of hell?" Tiffany supplied with a grin. She held a hand over her eyes to shade them. "You know, it's only going to get hotter as spring turns to summer."

The dry heat was a warming contrast to the air-conditioned car. It surrounded and relaxed her. *This is like a sauna* she decided. *A complimentary sauna every time you walk outside.*

London took a few deep breaths and enjoyed the feeling of the warm, clean air filling her lungs. She held the door to Enterprise for Tiffany and absent-mindedly ran her fingers through her hair. She nearly jerked her hand back as she realized the strands were already hot to the touch.

The rental office was small and empty. A bored-looking college student tore his eyes from the computer and forced a smile. "Hi, welcome to Enterprise. How can I help you?"

"I need a car," London started. She glanced behind him at dated posters along the wall. They were faded and baked from the direct sunlight filtering through wide windows. "Whatever you have."

He nodded and punched a few keys on the beige keyboard. "Unfortunately, y'all picked a heck of a week to come to the metroplex," he replied. "The Mary Kay Convention started this week, so most of my economy cars are out for the next seven days."

Mary Kay Convention? London thought amusedly as she imagined pink Cadillacs and big-haired women. *Only in Texas.* She took a deep breath. *But maybe that attitude is exactly what makes people think you're a snob.* Her mind briefly flashed back to Natalie Silva.

London nodded. "That's okay," she replied. "Whatever you have."

"I have a few luxury vehicles left." He glanced up and scratched his scraggly goatee. "We have a brand-new Audi R8. It'll be more expensive than the economy cars, but the manager just brought it over from the dealership two weeks ago."

She waved a hand. "Sure, that's fine. I'll give you a credit card."

He began entering the order as London reached into her back pocket for her wallet. She glanced out the front door and saw that Tiffany had stepped back into the heat. She watched for another moment as she quickly popped something into her mouth, uncapped a bottle of water and took a long drink.

Something doesn't feel right about that London thought. *Adderall is time-released. She seems to be taking an awful lot.*

A few minutes later, London joined Tiffany outside as they waited for the car. She closed her eyes for a moment as the heat coated her skin. She imagined the bright sun as a holistic medicine that penetrated her pores and fed her soul with Vitamin D and warmth. Tiffany's burst of surprised laughter interrupted her reverie.

"You've *got* to be kidding me," Tiffany exclaimed. "An Audi R8, London? *Really?*"

London shrugged but didn't meet her eyes. "The Mary Kay Convention is this week. I took what they had left."

"Whatever you say," Tiffany replied teasingly. "It's official. You're a thirty-two year old yuppie."

London glanced at her out of the corner of her eye. "At least I'm not a twenty-two year old hippie."

There was a moment of silence and then they both burst into laughter at themselves. *We're so different* London thought. *But we're alike too. How is that possible?*

"I'm off to Dallas to meet my mom in Preston Hollow for lunch," Tiffany continued between giggles. "I wish it was because she wants to hear about my time in Cambodia, but realistically? All she wants to do is gossip, pretend like I care about Dallas society and guilt me about getting back into school. Trust me, a Diane Foster guilt trip is unlike anything this world has seen. You have plans?"

London considered this. "Right now? Find the nearest Starbucks."

Tiffany groaned as she got into her Prius. "Don't even get me started," she replied. "You're killing me, sister." She paused as she began backing the car out of its narrow space and then rolled down the window and stuck her head out. "If you must, Google Brewed," she called. "Much better java and you're supporting a local business instead."

London watched as Tiffany waved and then sped off into a quick right turn toward the highway. She laughed to herself and sank into the smooth, toffee-colored leather seats of the Audi. She hit a button on her phone and smiled as Siri's familiar robotic voice greeted her.

"Siri, take me to Brewed," London commanded. *This afternoon's agenda? Frappuccino, some magazines and a bite to eat. Maybe this relaxation thing isn't half bad.*

"Y'all have a great day now!" Natalie called cheerfully after two of her lunchtime regulars. With the bakery empty, she took a deep breath and rested her elbows on the long metal cooking counter. Her hands were dry and powdery and her vintage Beatles t-shirt was stained with an errant streak of dried chocolate. The spring temperatures were soaring and she had worked up a thin sweat servicing the early morning and lunchtime crowds. She had stuffed her long hair beneath a faded Dallas Cowboys baseball cap that she had borrowed from Celia. Her aunt was in the back, counting the register and balancing the bakery's checkbook. Natalie closed her eyes and enjoyed the rare moment of stillness.

The moment was far too short. The bell above the front door jangled and she blinked. "Welcome to…"

The words died on her lips. The angry woman in the towel, who was now fully clothed, stood before her and gave her a small smile. Natalie got the feeling it was something she didn't do often.

Thank God she's clothed, thank God she's clothed, thank God… She repeated in her head. *Even if I wouldn't mind seeing her in that towel again.* Her body and mind battled for a moment before she realized she needed to say something, anything.

"Welcome to Mission Bakery," she finished and then cleared her throat. "What can I get for you?"

The woman smiled, wider this time. *Why on Earth would she ever keep that smile hidden?* Natalie wondered. *Maybe Celia is right. It's been too long since I've been on a date. Or there's something wrong with my hormones. My libido is going crazy.*

"I'll, uh, try whatever you recommend," she replied softly. She coughed once into her fist and it dawned on Natalie that this mysterious outsider may actually be nervous. "I've heard great things about this place. I was headed to Brewed, but it's closed on Mondays. I'd love a coffee if you have any left. And two of whatever you say is your favorite pastry."

"Of course," Natalie responded with a nod. "I'll have that right up for you, ma'am."

"Oh, it's London," the woman replied and then paused. "London Foster."

Natalie smiled. "Sure thing, London," she replied. She enjoyed how the unique name rolled off her tongue. "Calling people 'sir' or 'ma'am' around these parts is just a courtesy. Southern habits die hard."

Natalie handed her a lidded styrofoam cup over the glass counter. The bakery was silent for a split-second as their fingertips brushed against the other's.

All those books and movies talk about a jolt of electricity Natalie thought. *An electric shock when there's an attraction. But I felt the warmest sensation, starting where my fingers touched hers. And it feels a lot more sensual than an electric shock.*

"Thank you," London murmured. She opened the lid and blew on her coffee. Natalie watched, transfixed, as a thin curl of steam escaped the liquid. London pursed her lips and exhaled softly on the drink again. "Have you lived here you whole life?"

"What?" Natalie asked quickly. She had been drawn to London and thoughts of touching her again, melting into the deep warmth she had experienced for a brief moment, had clouded her brain. "Sorry, uh, what did you ask?"

She rolled her eyes at herself. *Nice going, Natalie.*

London took a small sip of coffee. "I was curious if you'd lived around here your whole life. Or elsewhere in Texas?"

Natalie nodded. "I was born in a small town outside of San Antonio. Even smaller than this town, if you can imagine. My parents moved around a lot because my dad worked on the oil rigs. Sometimes business was booming and other times it was deathly slow. The oil and gas industries ebb and flow a lot, so people like us had to move to wherever there was work. By the time I was twelve, I'd lived in Uvalde, Odessa, San Angelo and Abilene."

"Wow, that's a lot of moving around for a kid," London replied. She took another sip of coffee and met her eyes.

Natalie swallowed and glanced down at the counter. "It was, but I moved in with my Aunt Celia and her wife Jane when I was twelve. They gave me a great home and a stable life here in Weatherford. We're right on the border of Fort Worth and I've been here ever since."

"It's beautiful here," London remarked. "I've only been here a couple of days so far, but I'm excited to explore. I've never been to Texas," she finished with a sheepish grin.

"And where are you from?" Natalie cocked her head and put her hands on her hips. She studied London for a moment. "Wait, don't tell me. You're big city, that much I can tell."

"How can you tell?" London shot back. The smile and teasing gleam in her eye made Natalie want to say anything to continue having London's full attention.

"It's the way you talk, for one," Natalie continued. "You speak fast. And you pronounce things differently, almost with an accent."

London's mouth dropped open. "I don't have an accent!" She replied and then paused. "Maybe you have an accent."

"Sorry, honey," Natalie went on as she felt the twinkle in her eye grow. "You're the one with the accent 'round these parts." She carefully placed two cream cheese brownies on a small paper plate. "By the way, *these* are my favorite pastries. I made them myself this morning."

Oh my God, I called her honey Natalie thought. Her inner voice was screeching at her to shut up and to end the conversation with a shred of dignity. *I am positively flirting. What is wrong with me?*

"They're on the house," she blurted as she saw London reach for her wallet.

London opened her mouth to protest but Natalie shook her head firmly. "No, no, I won't hear of it," she continued before London could speak. "We like to make our guests feel welcome, so eat up and enjoy."

London smiled again and pushed the plate back over the counter. "One of these brownies is for you," she replied. "I wanted to apologize for how I reacted yesterday morning. I was startled and a little overtired, but I shouldn't have spoken to you the way I did."

"It's fine," Natalie responded. "Really, it's forgotten. You didn't know I would be there and you had no idea your sister directed me to use the key if no one was home."

"Half-sister," London automatically corrected her.

Natalie wrinkled her nose. "I guess," she replied, unsure how to respond. She met London's eyes. "You know, you never did tell me where you were from."

London laughed. "You never guessed."

Natalie leaned an elbow on the counter and rested her chin in her palm as she pretended to size up the newcomer. "New York City."

London shook her head and smiled enigmatically. "Nope."

"Hmm," Natalie drummed her fingertips against the counter. "Then I'm going to guess…"

"Natalie, do we have all our ingredients on the food truck?" Celia asked as she strode from the back of the bakery. She stopped short. "I apologize, I didn't realize we had a customer. Hi there." She nodded once at London.

"Hi, I'm London Foster," she stuck her hand over the counter and introduced herself.

Shit Natalie thought. She glanced at the baskets of dry ingredients along the counter. *I was so wrapped up in London that I forgot to load the food truck.* "I'm sorry, *tia*," Natalie replied. "I was just getting to that."

"I can help," London jumped in quickly. Both Natalie and Celia turned and stared at her for a beat. Natalie's face heated up as she felt Celia glance at her and then back at London.

"You ever work on a food truck?" Celia asked.

London shrugged and her cheeks colored. "No," she replied slowly. "I just thought, you know, if you need the help. I'm used to keeping busy and, uh…I mean, I'm not really doing anything today."

"Well," Celia said after a pause. "It's fast-paced. But we could always use an extra pair of volunteer hands to help out. We're headed to Klyde Warren Park in Dallas. The Dallas Independent School District is promoting a social in the park tonight for teachers, so just about every food truck in the metroplex will be there. I'm sure we can put you to work."

London nodded quickly and Natalie knew she had no idea what her aunt was talking about. "You'll have a good time," she tried to reassure her. "I hope. If not, at least it'll be a good story to take back to…Where did you say you were from again?"

London grinned. "Chicago," she finally said. "I'm from Chicago."

Disappointment crept into Natalie's chest as she turned to grab a container of sugar. *It's a lifetime and a world away from here* she reminded herself. *Besides, you don't even know her. She may have an entire life there.*

Natalie glanced at her distorted reflection on the metal counter and closed her eyes slowly. *To top it off, you had a giant chocolate stain on your shirt and your sweaty hair under a baseball cap the entire time you were flirting with her. Smooth, Natalie, real smooth.*

CHAPTER 9

London had no idea what had come over her or why she had offered to help on a hot, cramped food truck in a crowded park. *You know why* she told herself sternly. *And it has everything to do with the gorgeous woman exactly three steps to your left.*

She stole a glance at Natalie, who was ringing someone up on the cash register. The small ordering window allowed for some airflow inside the food truck, but the warm oven made the truck even hotter than it was outside. Natalie's aunt Celia was baking several dozen chocolate cupcakes to replace the several dozen that were already sold.

She surveyed the park and wiped her forehead with the back of her hand. Klyde Warren Park was built above the interstate smack in the center of downtown Dallas. Skyscrapers not unlike the ones she had left behind in Chicago surrounded them. Families set up picnics in the large grass field while others sat in the shade near pop-up bookshelves or beneath trees. On one side of the park, a jazz band played on a stage at the foreground while kids ran around a play area at the other side.

London stood and began restocking an ice chest with bottles of water. She had already scraped her hair back into a ponytail and changed into a forest-green Mission Bakery t-shirt. She had done everything that Celia and Natalie asked of her and realized there was something much more freeing about working on a food truck instead of the sterile office she was used to.

Natalie turned to London and nodded, gesturing for her to join her at the register. She tore a slip of paper from the pad and passed it down the counter to Celia. Her aunt glanced at it and turned from a metal mixing bowl to prepare the order. London stood next to Natalie and watched her work in awe. Her hands moved rapidly as she jotted orders, all the while punching keys in the cash register, sliding cards through machines and making small talk with the customers.

She really has it down to a science London thought, impressed. *This woman knows what she's doing.*

"I love those strawberry cake pops that y'all make," a middle-aged woman said enthusiastically. "I don't suppose you have any of those on your truck?"

Natalie smiled apologetically. "Not today, ma'am," she replied. "But we do have those at the bakery. If you stop in sometime, I'll have a batch just for you."

"Oh, I will," the woman said with a nod. "I'll take a vanilla-raspberry cupcake and a bottle of water then."

"Sure thing," Natalie replied. Her right hand scribbled furiously over the pad. "Will this be cash or credit today?"

"I'll pay with cash," the woman responded as she fished in the front pocket of her shorts.

London watched as Natalie slid another order sheet down the metal counter with her right hand and hit two keys on the register with her left. She turned back to the customer and grinned. "That'll be four dollars and eighty-five cents today."

She took a wrinkled five-dollar bill from the woman and punched three keys on the cash register. The drawer sprang open with a light *bing* and Natalie pulled out a few coins. "Fifteen cents is your change," she finished. "If you walk down to the small window on your left, she has that cupcake and water ready for you."

London glanced over her shoulder and saw Celia place a bottle of water and a cupcake on a styrofoam plate on the sill. She looked back at Natalie, who wiped her hands together resolutely.

"And that…" she began as she gently closed the cash register door. "…is how it's done."

London shook her head. *Natalie sure is something else* she thought. *I could watch her all day. She has such a sweet, friendly way with people.* She wanted to know more, hear more and learn more. There was something about Natalie that had caught her off-guard, capturing her full attention, and she was thoroughly enjoying it.

"How are you going to remember that one woman out of all the customers if she comes back to the bakery for a cake pop?" London asked. She met Natalie's grin and couldn't help but smile back. *That beautiful smile is positively contagious* she thought. *As soon as I see it, I have to grin too.*

"I remember *all* of my customers," Natalie replied. "Especially angry ones wearing bath towels, but…"

"Oh, stop it!" London exclaimed as they both fell into giggles. She caught the curious glance that Celia threw at them. "I'll never live that down."

"It's not hard to remember the customers," Natalie went on. "We're a small business and people around here appreciate being remembered, even if it's just for something like their favorite dessert. I make a point to ensure that my customers feel at home." She shrugged. "Anyway, I just like them all. Even the angry ones in bath towels."

London felt a strange fluttering sensation in her stomach. *Butterflies* she realized. *That's a new feeling.* "Must be that Southern hospitality I've heard so much about."

"Don't let what you've heard about the South fool you," Celia chimed in. London was enchanted by her accent, something between Hispanic and Southern with an extra twang.

"All people know is the politics and a few narrow-minded extremists who claim to speak for the whole state…" She waved a hand. "But Texas is a *big* state and it's impossible to speak for everyone. Where else can you go from a city steeped with culture like San Antonio and feel as though you're in a different world from Dallas? Or go to artistic, progressive Austin and feel as though you can't possibly be in the same state as the urban bustle of Houston?"

"My *tia* Celia is Texas, born and raised," Natalie cut in. "She's very passionate about the South."

"*Si, mija,*" Celia continued. She turned her attention to London. "There's nowhere like Texas in the world. You're lucky because you have the best tour guide." She nodded at Natalie knowingly.

London felt her face redden. She peeked at Natalie, who was busy chatting up a new customer at the window. She busied herself with organizing order slips and receipts as the line at the truck grew longer.

Keep yourself busy she warned herself. *You're here to help. You're not going to be productive if you keep letting your mind wander to...* she paused and pictured the hint of sunlight that had danced along the golden-brown tan of her arm just moments before. A tiny diamond pierced through the cartilage of her right ear had sparkled in the waning late afternoon light. *...Letting your mind wander to her* she finished sternly.

A cell phone rang just as Celia shut the oven door on her cupcakes. She glanced at the phone and then at Natalie. "It's Jane," she spoke up. "Mind if I take a breather and get this?"

"Of course not," Natalie replied as she handed change to the last customer in line. "Tell *Tia* Jane I said hello."

The door shut loudly behind Celia. Natalie took a deep breath and leaned back from the ordering window. She twisted her hair around her right hand, lifting it off her neck and tilted her head back. "It's slowing down."

London watched her for a long moment and felt a strange affinity for her settle deep into her stomach. *Uh-oh* she thought. It felt different and deeper than anything she had immediately felt for any other woman. The feeling rapidly turned to *want* as she studied Natalie's face, her neck, her arms and the way she leaned back casually.

She watched as a slow smile spread over Natalie's face, her eyes still closed. "What?"

"What?" London echoed, raising her eyebrow.

"I can feel you staring," Natalie went on as the smile continued to play at her lips.

"Sorry," London replied. *No, I'm not.* She tore her gaze away and set a neat stack of receipts on the counter resolutely.

"Don't be," Natalie murmured. She slowly stood and blinked at the sun.

"So what made a girl like you come all the way from Chicago to Texas? I get the feeling there's a story there."

London sighed and glanced at her nails. After an afternoon on the food truck, her bright red polish was steadily chipping away but she realized she didn't mind. "You could say that."

"Let me guess," Natalie turned and met her gaze. "Don't tell me you came here for a boyfriend?"

London laughed. "You really aren't very good at this guessing game," she teased. "No boyfriend. And no girlfriend either, after she admitted she'd been having an affair with one of my closest friends. They eventually made it official and were good enough to at least wait two months until after my mom passed away."

I sound bitter London realized with alarm. *That's not how I want her to hear me.* She forced a smile and busied herself with organizing a cup of pens and markers.

She felt Natalie watching her for a long moment before continuing. "And your half-sister, she lives here?"

London nodded. "We're ten years apart. Same dad, different moms. My dad is…"

She felt her voice fade as she recalled Natalie's words. *People like us had to move wherever there was work.*

"My dad lives here," she finished hastily. "And Tiffany too. He's no longer married to her mom. Tiffany's been doing a bunch of work overseas, I guess. Volunteering with some different non-profits."

"You sound like you haven't spoken to her in a while," Natalie replied.

"I haven't," London admitted. "Her mom was never a big fan of me, being that my dad and mom had me while they were still in college. I was young when they got together and she never liked me very much. I preferred to keep my distance as I got older."

"So your stepmom kept you from your half-sister?" Natalie asked. "That's a terrible thing to do to siblings."

London bit her lip. "A lot of it was me too," she replied. "I didn't make time to have a relationship with her. The last time I saw her, she was barely in second grade. Now, poof," London snapped her fingers. "She's an adult, driving a Prius and stomping around Southeast Asia with the biggest heart I've ever seen."

"I don't understand," Natalie went on. "She's still your family. Sister, half-sister, it makes no difference. She's your blood. Family takes care of family, despite the differences. That's what I was always taught."

London smiled. "Maybe I'm beginning to realize that," she replied. "I threw myself into work for a long time and it was only after a good friend encouraged me to let down my walls a bit that I decided to give my dad another chance. And Tiffany, of course." She took a deep breath. "With everything that had happened, I was losing myself up there. I needed the break."

London didn't realize she hadn't even mentioned the promotion until after the fact. *Weird* she thought. *That actually slipped my mind for the last few hours.*

Natalie shot her a smile. "You should do that more."

"What?" London asked.

"Let down your walls a bit," she finished softly.

I want to know everything about this girl London thought. "Has anyone broken *your* heart lately?"

Natalie shook her head. "Not since my ex-girlfriend deserted me once she got bored here," she said with a roll of her eyes. "Typical story, right? She was a cool older girl in a band, she was from L.A. and I fell hopelessly in love with her. We started going down a bad path with a lot of drinking, partying and no real direction in life. After a couple of years, she got bored and moved on. I've dated here and there, but nothing serious. My focus has mainly been on the bakery and my family. My aunts, my best friend, her husband, their daughter…We're all a big family here."

London nodded as she listened. *I want to be part of that* she thought. *I want a family. For once, I want to not be an outsider.* "At least you have people you love," she replied. "It's important to have good people around you. I realized that the hard way."

She could feel Natalie studying her closely again. She looked as though she was about to speak when Celia stepped back into the truck. "Hell, it's hotter in here than it is out there!" She exclaimed. "Customers winding down?"

Natalie nodded. "The park looks emptier. London and I are going to take a quick walk before we head out."

Celia waved her hand in acknowledgement as she peered inside the oven to check her cupcakes.

London watched, feeling almost intoxicated with something she couldn't quite put her finger on, as Natalie grinned and extended her hand. "Come walk with me?"

She grabbed her hand and let Natalie pull her to her feet. They climbed out of the truck and Natalie shoved her hands in the pockets of her jeans.

"Where are we going?" London asked. She couldn't help but notice how Natalie's jeans hugged her smooth thighs as she fell into stride beside her.

"You said you've never been here before," Natalie replied. "I wanted you to see the park. Not just from the food truck. I want you to *experience* it. The sounds, the life, all this energy. The music over there and the sun above us. Is there anything like this in Chicago?"

London thought for a moment and shook her head. "No," she replied honestly.

Natalie sat gently on a wooden bench facing the stage. A child, no older than four, raced around her as his older brother chased him. London stepped around the bench and plopped down next to her. They watched the jazz band for a few moments as London let herself soak up the atmosphere of the park. It was sunny and urban, warm and full of life. Hungry people wandered around the food trucks lining the curb and children screeched from the play area.

The energy is palpable London thought. She glanced at Natalie from the corner of her eye and drank in the sight of her. Her dark eyes were focused on the band and she blinked slowly. It was only when she hugged her knees to her chest that London realized how closely she had sat next to her. Their thighs pressed together and she swallowed hard.

I'm comfortable with her London realized. *And now I can't think of anything else except her thigh against mine and how close she is.*

"You're so different," London blurted out and blushed. Natalie tilted her head slowly and London was instantly sorry she had interrupted her dreamy reverie. "I'm sorry. That came out wrong. I meant it in a…good way."

Natalie smiled. "You're different too."

London shook her head. "You're not like anyone I've ever met," she went on. "Maybe it sounds strange, but I can't explain it. Everything just seems so…easy with you."

Natalie was perfectly content to listen to London's soft, rich voice as afternoon turned to evening. The jazz band played a slower tune and the stillness of the park bench, with activity flurrying around them, made her not want to move.

I could stay in this place forever she thought dreamily. "I don't like to be complicated," she replied after a moment. "So I'm not. I know you've been through a lot and you're only beginning to regroup here, but maybe we could see each other again sometime."

London sighed. "I'd like that," she agreed. "You're welcome to come over this week when you're not busy with the bakery and…and when I know what to say."

Natalie stole a sideways glance at London. "All you'd have to do is call and I'd be there."

That was not supposed to come out of my mouth Natalie thought as she mentally kicked herself. *London clearly has her walls up. But I don't know how else to be. Am I supposed to pretend that I'm not growing more attracted to her by the minute?*

Her thoughts collided to a halt as she watched London tear her stare from the grass. She turned and met her eyes. *Oh my God, she's going to kiss me* she thought as her heart suddenly pounded double-time. There was so much sizzle in London's intense gaze but Natalie couldn't help but recognize one other strong emotion. *Fear.*

She took a deep breath and let the fantasy of running her hands through London's hair and pressing her lips to her mouth repeat on a loop in her mind for a moment. She rested her fingertips atop London's hand gently. *Not yet* she thought. *Don't rush it.*

"I want to see you again," Natalie finally said. She felt London squeeze her fingertips gently and watched as she grinned.

"You'd better," London teased, her voice barely above a murmur. Natalie continued to watch as London took in the sights around her. "Thank you," she continued.

"What for?" Natalie asked.

"For the afternoon and evening," London replied. "For letting a total stranger jump onto your food truck and help out. And for accepting my apology. You're so different and I like it. I'm being honest when I say that you're not like anyone I've ever met."

Natalie realized that their fingers were still casually intertwined. She felt the same tender, sensual warmth she'd felt when she had handed the coffee to London. "You said that already," she replied with a grin. "But I like hearing it. Maybe different is good."

"I think so," London agreed.

Natalie raised an eyebrow. "You *think* so?" She teased.

London laughed as her cheeks flushed. "I *know* so," she replied.

Natalie took a deep breath and inhaled London's sweet perfume. "We should head back to the truck," she finally said. "I'll help Celia clean up for the night and we'll get back to Fort Worth in the next hour or so."

London nodded as they stood slowly. "You'll sleep well tonight," she replied. "Granted, I'm not a seasoned baker like you but if you're half as tired as I am after working on the truck? You'll be out the second your head hits the pillow."

Natalie smiled as they approached the truck. She watched as London opened the door and climbed up the high step in front of her. Her eyes slid down the toned arms that had been revealed after London casually rolled up the sleeves of her t-shirt. Her gaze moved to her strong back and dropped to her tight thighs. Natalie wanted to wrap her arms around her waist, hug her from behind and run her lips over the back of her pale neck, covering it with gentle kisses.

She sighed heavily. *London is under my skin and that's that* she thought grimly. *One thing is for sure, and that is that I definitely will* not *sleep well tonight.*

CHAPTER 10

A few days later, London turned from the wide dining room window and plopped into a polished wooden chair. She could sense Tiffany watching her over the brim of her coffee mug.

"What gives?" Tiffany asked. "You've been nervous since you woke up. Is your hot date with the Mission Bakery girl today?"

London gave her a look. "Her name is Natalie. And it's *not* a date. We're just hanging out. You know, friends."

Tiffany raised an eyebrow. "Whatever you say," she replied. "Why don't you get some grits? They're, like, a Southern staple." She nodded to the sleek black oven in the kitchen. "I know, I know. You're not from the South, but they're still good. I missed them when I was overseas."

"I've never been much of a breakfast girl," London answered with a roll of her eyes. "A big coffee and a good workout, and I'm set for the morning."

Tiffany pursed her lips. "Well, whatever it may be with *Natalie*, you ought to keep working on that food truck. Put a little meat on those bones. Speaking of, you never explained to me *how* you ended up at Mission Bakery and working on a truck all evening. Don't get me wrong, but you don't seem like the type who's itching for the chance to spend 95-degree afternoons over a hot oven. I'm sure it had *nothing* to do with that hot baker."

"A little manual labor is good for the soul," London replied defensively. She took a bite of toast from the plate at the center of the table. "All I've seen *you* do since you've been here is sleep. I don't know how someone can possibly sleep as much as you can. I know I've been wrapped up in work the last few days, but at least I have a regular sleeping schedule."

It was Tiffany's turn to be defensive. "I've spent the last year in, like, five different time zones," she responded. "My body is still getting used to being here. I've been trying to cut the Adderall, but…" she sighed and patted her pocket protectively. "I need it."

Maybe I should ask Dad about that when he gets back London thought hesitantly. *It doesn't seem right. She's either wide awake and zipping all over the place or sleeping for fifteen hours at a time. Something tells me there's something wrong here.*

"What are your plans today?" London asked conversationally instead.

Tiffany scraped the last of her grits from her plate and shrugged as she swallowed. "Going out."

London studied her for a moment. Tiffany refused to meet her eyes. "Wait a second, do *you* have a date?" She asked incredulously.

"It's *not* a date!" Tiffany replied vehemently. "God, everybody wants it to be a date. You, my mother, my friends…I am an *independent* woman who marches to the beat of her *own* drum. I don't need any man to complete me."

London blinked. "So who's the guy?"

Tiffany sat back and blew out her breath. "I'm going to lunch with an old school friend," she replied. "We may have *briefly* dated in high school, but today is *not* a date. His name is Wayne Paulson III."

London wrinkled her nose. "Wait, Wayne Paulson III? As in…?"

Tiffany groaned. "Yes, Wayne Paulson, Jr.'s son. Dad's best golfing buddy and the most famous plastic surgeon in the metroplex." She hid her face in her hands morosely.

"I haven't even been here a full week and I've already seen four of his cheesy billboards," London replied. "That's not even coming from the fact that I work for an advertising agency. That's coming just from me being human."

Tiffany burst into laughter and shook her head. "That family is everything I can't stand about this area. Rich, entitled, snooty, *boring*. I know we grew up privileged too, but at least Dad always made sure we were gracious. I don't know how they can be such good friends, especially when Dad is humble and Mr. Paulson is such a jerk."

London crossed her arms. "It was actually my *mother* who taught me to be gracious when *I* was growing up," she interjected coolly.

Tiffany looked away. "Wayne is different from the rest of his family," she went on after a beat. "He's a kind person and a gentleman. Even though we only dated for a few months of our junior year, he's probably the best boyfriend I've had."

London sighed and sat back down. "If that's so, then remind me why can't we call this a date?"

Tiffany groaned again. "He's so…so…*Texas*," she replied. "He, like, holds doors open for me and refuses to let me pay for anything, even though we're *just* friends. He has three horses on his family's vacation ranch in Hill Country, but he's especially attached to the one he learned to ride when he was nine. He has this *stupid* Southern accent and just finished his Bachelor's at Southern Methodist. He wants to go to law school and have his own practice."

London shook her head in confusion. "Am I missing something? Are any of those things supposed to be bad?"

"I'll never sit around and be some Real Dallas Housewife," Tiffany went on. "I won't be like my mother. Wayne has probably never been to Africa unless it was on some luxury safari."

London hid a smile. "Maybe you don't have to be exactly the same for something to work out. If you like him and he's good to you, focus on that instead of all the why nots."

Briefly, her mind flashed to Natalie Silva. They had fallen into the habit of talking briefly each night before bed and it was becoming harder for London to ignore her attraction to the other woman. *I can't help but want to be around her.*

"It's just lunch," Tiffany replied. "Maybe the Perot Museum afterwards. What time is Natalie coming over?"

London chewed the inside of her cheek and glanced at the time displayed on the microwave. "Soon."

Tiffany smirked. "You're nervous. Especially to hang out with, *you know,* a friend."

London stood and gathered her plate and glass. "You don't know…"

"Anyone with half a brain would see that you're nervous!" Tiffany said as she threw her head back and laughed. "You'll be fine. Natalie seems very cool. She's really pretty *and* nice. If you're that anxious, I'm sure I could scrounge up some Xanax somewhere…"

London glanced at her sister and realized she was completely serious. "I'll manage, thanks," she replied slowly.

Tiffany shrugged and slung her mini-backpack over her shoulder. "If you say so," she went on. "Personally, I don't know how anyone can manage *without* any happy pills. I'll catch you later."

London was momentarily dumbfounded as she listened to the front door shut behind Tiffany. *Okay, then* she thought. *Maybe this is bigger than I thought. What do I do about that?*

She was distracted as her phone dinged with an incoming text message. She glanced at the screen and a bolt of excitement raced down her spine as she skimmed over Natalie's words.

Be there in 20. Can't wait to see you.

As soon as the doorbell rang, London sprang from the couch and shakily ran a hand through her hair. *Okay, maybe Tiffany was right* she realized. *I am nervous.*

She strode to the door and tried to smooth her shirt as an unfamiliar knot of nerves chewed her stomach. *I can't remember the last time I felt nerves like this* London thought. She spotted Natalie's head through panes of stained glass along the top of the double French doors. *Focus* she reminded herself. *Natalie is a friend. A new companion, who was kind enough to let me tag along on her food truck and introduce me to Texas. After I insulted her.*

London opened the door and was immediately taken with Natalie's wide, sunny smile. There was something genuine in the way she looked at her and London realized she liked it a lot. *It's almost like she can see past the layers and the bullshit* she thought admirably. *It's like she can see* me.

"It's good to see you," London greeted her warmly. She held out her arms and expected Natalie to hand her the light sweater she carried. Instead, she stepped into her arms and hugged her.

"Good to see you too," Natalie replied. Her voice was inches from her ear and London closed her eyes. *She's a friend* she repeated to herself silently. *A friend.*

"So what are you up for today, London?" Natalie asked. "Stay close or explore more of Texas?"

Focus London thought. She was struck with memories of how badly she had wanted to kiss Natalie on the park bench and how it had seemed, for one tantalizingly short moment, that they might.

"I wasn't sure," she replied. They walked into the living room and London plopped onto the couch, tucking her legs to one side. "We could hang out by the pool. Or go for a walk if it's not too hot for you."

"Too hot for *me*?" Natalie laughed. "I think I'm immune to this heat by now. You're the one I'm worried about." She paused and her eyes lit up. "We could take a walk by that duck pond in the neighborhood. It looked like there were some big shade trees around there."

"There's a pond here?" London asked.

"Just to the left when you enter through the gates," Natalie replied. "You haven't seen it?"

London blushed and shook her head. "I guess my mind has been all over the place since I've been here."

Natalie smiled and gently rested her hand on her forearm. "That's okay," she responded. "I get the feeling you've been a little preoccupied."

London shot her a shy half-smile. "I get that feeling that you're right," she replied wryly. "I'm sorry, would you like something to drink? I don't know where my manners are."

Natalie shook her head. "No, thank you. That's what we'll do today then," she went on. "Take some time to smell the roses. Hang out and enjoy the little things. Relax by the duck pond and hope we don't get attacked by some fierce momma geese."

Natalie laughed and London found herself giggling along with her. *If I were in Chicago right now, I'd be sitting at the office* she thought. *Trying to tune out silly gossip, on my third coffee and editing more website content.* For some reason, the thought of sitting pond-side with Natalie seemed far preferable than the fast-paced, hard-nosed bustle of W.H. Young.

"Duck pond it is," London agreed. "Is that how you keep your sanity? Taking time out to enjoy the small stuff?"

Natalie shrugged as they walked through the front door and fell into step together. "I don't know if I'd want a job that had me constantly fighting to keep my sanity," she replied honestly. "If you have to spend so much of your life working, then you might as well make it something you enjoy. The bakery has never felt like work, though it definitely has been."

London glanced at her. "It keeps you pretty busy?"

Natalie laughed. "That's an understatement," she replied. "The bakery has been my *life* for years. We got the food truck about a year and a half ago and it has caused business to skyrocket. It's a great concept, being able to connect with people and bring your products to places outside the community."

"It sounds like you're very passionate about your business," London commented. "That can be hard to find."

Natalie shrugged. "It's our business," she said simply. "Mine, my *tia* Celia's and my *tia* Jane's. If it wasn't for them, Mission Bakery wouldn't exist. We've all dedicated ourselves to it and built the business together."

London felt Natalie studying her as they rounded a corner near the front of the community.

"And you?" She prodded. "Your career won't be hurt by this hiatus?"

London shook her head. "My best friend Holly also happens to be my immediate manager. She was the one who really pushed me to take this break and refocus."

That's strange London thought. *I really don't even want to mention the promotion. For all the times I could brag about my credentials or the success of W.H. Young, it's not something I care to talk about.* Somehow, she felt it was something Natalie wouldn't be particularly wowed by either.

"Sounds like a good friend," Natalie replied. "Good manager too."

"She's the only one that's really been there for me," London went on offhandedly. "I guess you could say Holly is sort of a big sister figure. We've always been close, but after my mom got sick and then the aftermath…" London paused and sighed.

I also don't care to talk about Kayley and Tara she thought. *They're part of my past. Not my present or future. I'd rather continue getting to know Natalie Silva than wasting the day complaining about how they wronged me.*

Natalie laid her hand on her arm. "It's okay."

London shook her head. "Sorry, I…" she took a deep breath and smiled. "I was just thinking how much more I'm enjoying getting to know you than lamenting about my past. Anyway, I think I would have gone crazy in that city if it wasn't for Holly's support."

"You're strong," Natalie replied as they walked past a wide cul-de-sac.

London shoved her hands into her pockets. "I think you're giving me too much credit," she admitted. *Just be real* she decided. *It is what it is.* "Trying to work my way through everything at once broke me."

Natalie stopped short. London took a few steps and then turned in question. "You're still here, aren't you?" She asked. London paused to ponder this as Natalie nodded. "You're strong."

They walked in companionable silence for a few moments as they approached a grassy hill. London studied Natalie out of the corner of her eye and let herself wonder for a moment what it would be like to hold her hand. *I could casually slip my fingers between hers* she thought as her gaze fell to her tanned arms.

London recalled Natalie's words and smiled to herself. *I wonder what it would be like to come home to a woman like her every evening.*

"Here it is!" Natalie's voice interrupted her thoughts. She pointed over the hill.

London tipped her sunglasses over her nose and raised an eyebrow. "Holy…" she shook her head and laughed. "I had *no* idea this was here."

The oval-shaped pond was filled with clear blue water and lined with square beige bricks. A wide sidewalk looped around the pond and a few benches were scattered in the grass beyond. Several ducks floated along the water and a few splashed at the east edge of near of drainage pipe.

"How about that one?" Natalie nodded at a mature tree with a thick trunk. It stood at the foot of the pond. Its long branches provided a square of shade about three feet wide.

"Perfect," London confirmed with a nod.

They settled onto the grass in the patch of shade. London rested against the trunk and stole a glance at Natalie from behind her sunglasses. She subtly shifted closer as a splash from the pond grabbed her attention. They laughed as two ducks quacked loudly. London pulled out her phone and quickly zoomed in with the camera. She snapped a photo just as one of the ducks spread its wings and let out another indignant noise.

"What do you think they're fighting over?" London asked in amusement. She quickly tapped a button to upload the photo to Instagram. Glancing at Natalie, she stilled as the other woman held her gaze.

After a long moment, Natalie reached with both hands and gently slid her sunglasses from her face. London blinked in the sudden sunlight.

"Don't hide your eyes," she spoke with a soft grin. "They're beautiful."

A breeze ruffled the back of London's shirt, causing a shiver to snake up her spine. *Or maybe it's the way Natalie is looking at me* she thought.

There was something about the feeling of Natalie near her, the thought of her closer to to her than anyone had been before, that both thrilled and terrified London. "Come here," she murmured. She stretched her legs so Natalie could sit between them.

London took a deep breath as Natalie's back relaxed into her front. They rested against the sturdy tree and watched the ducks for a few moments. *She smells like lavender and…just the faintest hint of sugar* she thought as she inhaled deeply. London gently wound her arms around Natalie's middle and relished the feeling of simply holding someone.

"Tell me something about you," Natalie spoke up. "Something no one else knows."

London took a deep breath and thought. She wasn't sure if it was the quiet of the duck pond or the strange feeling that holding Natalie was *right*, but she felt a guarded layer of herself begin to fall away. "I really hope that being here helps rekindle my relationship with my dad." She hadn't realized how true it was until she spoke. "My dad was absent from my life for so long. I grew up feeling like an impulsive college mistake, but one that he couldn't exactly cover up. I felt like an inconvenience. The unfortunate result of an idealistic but immature relationship by a couple of happy-go-lucky college kids."

Natalie twisted in her arms and squinted at her in the bright sunlight. "Do you realize you just called yourself a mistake, an inconvenience and an unfortunate result?"

London opened and then closed her mouth. "I mean, that's how I felt…"

"You're too good to think that way," Natalie replied honestly. "Don't say those things about yourself again."

London felt a surge of unexpected emotion and rested the tip of her nose and her lips against the back of Natalie's head for a moment. "Deal."

"You're scared that you and your dad won't know each other?" Natalie asked.

"Something like that," London continued. "I got used to being discarded by him and eventually wrote him off as a father. During the last year, he's been making a concerted effort to be part of my life. At first, it made me angry because I didn't understand it. Why now? Because my mother passed away and he has years of guilt stored? Because he and his second wife divorced and he's scared to be alone? Or maybe because he dedicated his life to Foster Oil & Gas and steered clear of any interpersonal relationships…"

"Maybe all of the above," Natalie replied. She sat up. "Wait, did you say Foster Oil & Gas? As in…"

London closed her eyes slowly. *Shit*. "Yes," she answered with a sigh. "As in, the company belongs to my father's family. He's the Chairman now, but has mentioned retirement more than a few times. It's his younger brother and his three kids that hold the main leadership posts nowadays."

"He wants to know you, London," Natalie replied after a moment. "Isn't that good?"

"Yes," she responded. "At first, I couldn't get past the whole *why now* aspect of it. I gave him hell. I wanted him to know I was raised without him and I'm well. My mother was a successful woman in her own right. She ran a special needs high school in Chicago and loved it. I needed him to know I was doing fine without him or the company."

"Understandable first reaction," Natalie agreed. "But once you got past that…"

"I realized I was curious too," London went on. "I want to know Tiffany. I want to understand him not just as a parent, but as a human being. Besides, he tends to keep people at arms' length. I know how difficult it must have been to open the lines of communication."

"He must have really wanted this, if he continued to contact you after you rebuffed him," Natalie chimed in.

"I got lost," London sighed. "*Really* lost. Then the Universe aligned in some strange way. My boss basically demanded that I take time off, my dad wouldn't give up on me and now I'm here."

Natalie smiled. "Do you believe the Universe works for a reason? That when you eventually look back that you'll understand why it happened the way it did?"

"I'd like to think so," London replied honestly. "Do you?"

"I *know* so," Natalie replied confidently. "Trust me on this."

"Okay," London murmured. She realized that she *did*, in fact, trust Natalie. "Your turn. Tell me something about you that no one else knows."

Natalie was quiet for a moment. "I haven't told anyone this," she started hesitantly. "But I want us to be open and honest with each other, especially since you were with me just now."

"I want to know everything that you're willing to share with me," London replied with a smile.

Natalie squeezed her fingers and took a deep breath. "I know it's probably not true, but I've always had a sliver of paranoia that the reason my parents gave me to Celia and Jane is because I'm gay."

London wrinkled her nose and wrapped her arms tighter around Natalie. "You were so young!" She exclaimed. "They couldn't have known. Even if they did, do you really think they'd leave you because of it?"

"I don't *think* so," Natalie said with a shrug. "I know times were hard for them and they felt guilty about moving around so much with me in tow.

They wanted me to have roots somewhere and be able to make friends at school."

"Of course," London replied. "Every parent wants to ensure that their child succeeds."

"I was twelve," Natalie went on. "It was an awkward age. I was figuring out what being gay meant and realizing why I always felt so different from other girls. I had been having a sleepover with one of my friends and my parents were due to pick me up. It was the first time I realized what attraction was and I had the sense that she felt the same way."

London had a feeling that she knew where this was going. "So you two acted on it?"

"We were kids," Natalie replied. "Her parents were very religious and, back then, so were mine. In small towns like that, churches and taverns are the only social spots and, well, you'll quickly get a reputation if you spend too much time at the latter. When I was young, we spent a lot of time at church. On this particular day, my friend and I were in the backyard and began kissing."

"Uh-oh…" London murmured.

"Yup," Natalie confirmed. "It was great because suddenly everything clicked and made sense. We had been kissing in the backyard for so long that we didn't realize my parents had arrived. Her parents took them to the backyard and, imagine their shock, found us making out instead of playing."

"Did they freak out?" London asked.

Natalie shook her head. "Mine never did," she replied. "They never said anything about it. The car ride home was quiet and I was too terrified to utter a word. The following week, they told me we had to move again. That was when they decided I'd have a better chance if I stayed with Celia and Jane."

"Oh, Natalie," London replied sympathetically. "I can only imagine." She knew the timeline was probably a coincidence, but she could also understand how an uncertain twelve-year old would mix messages. "If it was something they took issue with, you wouldn't be as close to them now, right?"

"I know," Natalie agreed. "Celia has been out since before I was born. Sometimes I wonder if I would have felt less comfortable with who I am if I hadn't been raised by them. I told Celia a year after I moved in with them that I was gay. She asked if I was sure and I said yes. They accepted it, but I think they still thought I was young. But I always knew what I liked. I never felt the need to try and convince myself differently."

"I admire that," London responded. "You're passionate about life and you follow your heart."

"Anything less and you're not really living," Natalie confirmed with a grin. "How else is there to be?"

London decided that she could sit under the tree all afternoon with Natalie in her arms and listen to her talk. "I think you're on to something," she agreed with a smile. "Are you thirsty? There's a big pitcher of lemonade at the house."

Natalie sat up and London immediately missed her soft skin. "Lemonade sounds great. Next time, I'll remember to bring scraps from the bakery so we can feed the ducks."

They stood, brushing off their clothes, and leisurely made their way back over the hill. London bit her lip and tried to hide the grin she felt straining across her face.

Next time she repeated silently. London felt downright giddy at the idea and took another breath as a second thought hit her. *I could fall for her.*

CHAPTER 11

Natalie took in the living room of the Foster estate incredulously as she followed London through the expansive home. Two crisp leather sectionals lined a corner while a 65-inch flat screen television hung across the wall. The dark hardwood flooring was cool beneath her feet and a thick Oriental rug spread beneath a long glass coffee table.

Everything about this place reeks of money she thought. *But there's a sense of comfort here too.* Natalie's eyes fell on the back of London's head and she smiled to herself. *Or maybe it's just her.*

Natalie followed London into the kitchen and studied her as she pulled two glasses from a tall, dark-stained cabinet. Gone was the stiff, serious businesswoman that she had first met. London looked relaxed and happy in the black yoga pants and gray striped tank top that she had been wearing all afternoon. Her hair was tied in a loose bun, but a few short strands fell around her face. *She's never looked more beautiful.*

Natalie glanced around the massive kitchen for a moment. *I can't believe we sat by the pond and talked for more than two hours* she thought. She briefly remembered their first run-in. *I never imagined talking to her would be so easy. After all, this is how the other half lives.*

She smiled at the careful, measured way that London handled the expensive glassware. She slowly stirred the lemonade in its pitcher with a long glass swizzle stick and then continued to fill their cups. *I like looking at her when she thinks I'm not* she realized as her heartbeat inexplicably quickened.

That's when I learn the most about her.

Natalie blushed, realizing she had been caught staring, as London turned and handed her a glass. She gently clinked them together and met her eyes.

"Cheers," London announced with a cheeky grin.

Natalie hoisted herself onto the granite island and let her legs dangle over the edge of the rounded countertop. "*Salud,*" she replied and then took a long sip of lemonade.

London took a step closer, facing Natalie, and lingered between her knees. After a moment, she reached behind her onto the island. Natalie felt her breath hitch the same way it did when she had sat close to London by the pond. Her nearness, and the way she casually leaned over her lap, caused Natalie's mouth to go dry. She quickly took another sip of lemonade.

I want her to kiss me so badly. The sheer desire she felt nearly knocked the wind out of Natalie. Her heart pounded as the moment seemed to stretch forever. *She's going to kiss me. She's going to…*

London straightened and held out a half-eaten box of doughnuts. She smiled brightly. "Powdered doughnut?" She asked. "I'm sure they're not nearly as good as anything Mission Bakery has on its menu. I apologize, we don't have much in the house right now."

Natalie closed her eyes slowly. *…She's going to give me a powdered doughnut.*

She reached in and plucked a small doughnut from the box. *Why won't she kiss me?* She thought as she tried to cover her disappointment. *We sat together so intimately by the pond and had great conversation. This magnetic energy, this attraction between us keeps growing. At least, it does for me. Maybe she doesn't feel the same way. Or maybe she's confused.* Disappointment washed through Natalie at the idea as she took a bite. *Or maybe she's* that *scared.*

"Is Netflix okay?" London asked. She nodded toward the living room. "We could see what movies are on."

I'd sit through a six-hour documentary on Persian cat grooming if it means you'll finally kiss me Natalie thought. She glanced up as she nibbled her doughnut and met London's gaze. It was then that she became all too aware of the fact that London hadn't moved from where she stood between her knees. Natalie wanted nothing more than to lock her legs around London's waist, nudge her closer and meet her soft lips. Instead, she remained still.

They watched each other, wary and unwavering, for a few quiet moments. After a beat, London reached up and ran her thumb over the corner of Natalie's bottom lip.

"You have something…" she started. Her voice was barely above a whisper. "Powder…" She glanced at her with an unspoken question in her piercing eyes before tentatively leaning forward. She slowly kissed the sugar from her lip.

Natalie sighed happily and closed her eyes against the warm feeling of London's lips against her own. She wrapped her arms around her and drew her closer. Their kiss deepened and Natalie was sure she was losing her mind as their tongues explored each other's mouths.

As the kiss slowed, a moment of hazy silence hung over them. Late afternoon sunlight filtered between the kitchen blinds and illuminated moving spots along the floor in the otherwise darkened room. London's hand tenderly cupped her face. She closed her eyes and pressed her forehead to Natalie's.

"Finally," Natalie whispered teasingly. She brushed her thumb along London's jaw as they both giggled.

"I wanted to kiss you," London admitted. "But I wanted it to be special."

"You're a romantic at heart, aren't you?" Natalie asked as the sweet realization dawned on her. She smiled and hugged London close to her. "Every kiss is special between us."

"You looked so cute with powdered sugar stuck to your lip," London went on with a wicked grin. "I almost didn't want to brush it away. But then I realized how much more I wanted to taste it."

A shiver raced up Natalie's spine. She was enamored with the seductive newcomer as she felt something deep and welcome, something she hadn't felt in years, open up inside her. She had an inkling that the explosive pangs she felt when they kissed held the possibility for something more profound than casual dating or a temporary crush.

Oh my God she thought as she leaned in and met London's lips once more. She smiled against her mouth and felt warm all over. *I could fall for her.*

Natalie blinked in the shadowy darkness of the Foster estate and realized she had no idea what time it was. Their exploratory kisses had led to innocent cuddles on the couch as they paid half-attention to some slasher movie from the '80's. She was beginning to enjoy the feelings that rose up through her stomach and chest as London relaxed against her.

"What should we watch next?" Her rich voice cut through Natalie's consciousness and brought her back to the present moment. She yawned as London stopped the credits of the movie and then lazily flipped through a few categories on Netflix.

"We could watch another cheesy horror movie," London went on with a laugh. She switched categories. "Or there's always an indie flick."

Natalie tried not to notice as London curled closer to her. She inhaled the light orchid scent of her shampoo and tried to focus. "What about a good old Food Network marathon? *Chopped* is my weakness."

London scrolled to the Reality Television category and selected Natalie's favorite show. "Would that be your ideal date?" She asked. "Going on a food and wine tour? Trying out all the top-tier hotspots around Fort Worth?"

"As fun as that sounds, I work around food so much already," Natalie admitted. "My ideal date is simple. I've always loved fireworks, ever since I was a little kid. Fourth of July is one of my favorite holidays. I used to get excited weeks in advance for the annual fireworks show. I don't know why. I mean, fireworks are fun and all, but nothing that a kid looks forward to like Christmas morning, right? But there's something special about them too. Cuddling up with the one you love, in the dark and under the stars, enjoying the celebration. It probably sounds silly, but…"

"No, it doesn't," London interrupted with a smile. "It sounds like a really good date. Romantic, even. Maybe I'm not the only romantic at heart…"

London's voice trailed off as Natalie pressed her lips to the top of her head and wrapped her arms around her tighter. "I guess we'll find out," she teased. "When do I get to see you again?"

"Anytime you want," London replied with a smile.

"Soon?" Natalie asked hopefully.

"My father's flight comes in tomorrow afternoon," London thought out loud as she scratched her knee. "So tomorrow is out, but this weekend I'm all yours."

"I'll take it," Natalie replied. She leaned in and kissed London's lips gently. "I didn't realize it's almost nine o'clock. I should get going. I have to open the bakery tomorrow and, believe me, the hungry people of Weatherford wait for no one."

London nodded as they stood and walked to the front door. "I understand," she said as she stretched. "Try to get some rest. Thanks for hanging out with me today."

She smiled and Natalie felt her chest tighten. "I had a really great time," she started and then paused. "I can't wait to see you again. I'll send you a text when I make it home, okay?"

Natalie started down the front path and turned once to blow a kiss back at the wide French doors. London waved and gently touched her fingertips to her lips in return.

Natalie managed to hold herself together long enough until she closed the door of her truck behind her. *Oh my Lord* she thought. *That woman is everything I want.* She placed her hands on the steering wheel and closed her eyes as she sunk further into the driver's seat. She wasn't sure how long she had been sitting in the winding driveway and replaying the day over in her mind when a silver Prius squealed into the narrow space next to her truck.

Tiffany she realized ruefully. *Guess I'd better head out before she fixes to tell London that I'm daydreaming away in their driveway like a nut.* Natalie pushed the gear into reverse and quickly glanced behind the truck. She eased her foot off the brake and then slammed it again as the driver's side door of the Prius jerked open wildly.

Natalie glanced out the window in mild annoyance and watched as Tiffany half-rolled and half-fell from the driver's seat. She sprawled onto her hands and knees in the tight space between their vehicles and disappeared from her sight. Natalie turned away and wrinkled her nose as the sounds of heaving floated up through the open windows of her truck.

She's completely drunk she realized as the heaving turned to unmistakable vomiting. *She doesn't even know I'm here. I could back away carefully and be out of these gates before she even realizes there was a truck in the driveway.*

Natalie bit her lip and sighed. "But I can't do that to someone, even if it's someone I don't know well," she muttered to herself as she unbuckled her seatbelt. She hopped out of her truck and gingerly stepped around the front. *Especially if that someone happens to be London's younger sister.*

Tiffany looked small, frail and young as she crouched against her car and shook uncontrollably. Natalie knelt quietly next to her and gently moved her shaking hands away from the mess on the asphalt.

"At least it's supposed to rain overnight," Natalie started gently. Tiffany's body quivered unconsciously and she sniffled. Natalie reached out and put a hand on her shoulder to steady her.

Tiffany jerked in surprise and glanced at her with glassy eyes. "Why do you say that?" She asked after a moment.

Natalie averted her gaze but nodded once at the puddle of vomit. "It'll wash away," she replied carefully. "Are you sick?"

She watched as Tiffany paused and then nodded slowly. "Must have the flu, I guess," she muttered. "I'm really sorry that you had to see this. I was having a good time with a friend of mine and…"

A once-over of London's sister confirmed to Natalie that she did not, in fact, have the flu. Her bright blue eyes were dull and glazed over while her mind seemed unfocused. She reeked of cigarette smoke, alcohol and vomit. *She's lying through her teeth* Natalie thought with a sigh.

"Tiffany, how much have you had to drink?" She asked gently. "And why did your friend let you drive home?"

She sighed heavily and stared at the asphalt. "I only had a few," she insisted. "I just, you know, don't drink often so sometimes, um, it hits me hard. I'm a…a lightweight, I guess," she stammered.

Natalie sensed something else was amiss but shrugged it off. She was about to stand and help Tiffany up when the younger woman's mini-backpack fell open and its contents clattered down the driveway. Natalie's mouth dropped open as several orange prescription bottles rolled in different directions and Tiffany struggled to grab them all.

Tiffany glanced at her suspiciously as she quickly shoved the bottles into her bag. "I have a lot of prescriptions," she spoke unnecessarily. "I've just had a rough day, okay?"

Natalie opened her mouth to speak as Tiffany's eyes suddenly lit up. "Oh shit, *Natalie*!" She exclaimed.

She was taken aback. *She just now realizes who I am?* She wondered silently. *She's slurring her speech. She can hardly get the words out.*

"Natalie, you *cannot* tell London about this," Tiffany continued desperately. "Please promise me! Don't tell London that you saw any of this!"

She hesitated. "I…I don't know if that's a good idea," she replied honestly. "I don't want to keep anything from her."

Tiffany gripped Natalie's hand and blinked rapidly. "*Please*, Natalie," she begged. "I don't want her to be disappointed in me. You don't understand. I've never had London in my life. *Ever*. We're finally spending time together and we're actually *bonding*. Well, kind of. But even still, I'm not ready for her to know all of this."

"Know all of what?" Natalie asked pointedly.

"That I take *pills*, okay?" Tiffany continued. "Is that what you wanted to hear? I just…I know they're bad, but some days are worse than others and those are the days I really need them. London isn't exactly the sister I've always envisioned, but it's too early to have her hate me."

"Tiffany, she's not going to hate you…" Natalie started. She gently pulled her hand away.

"She's *perfect*," Tiffany cut in. A single tear escaped the corner of her eye and rolled down her cheek. "She doesn't let anyone see her weak, at least. I just can't bear seeing her face when she hears about how truly messed up her little sister is. I drank a little too much and forgot exactly how much Adderall I'd taken. It could've happened to *anyone*." Tiffany threw a hand up in frustration.

Natalie opened her mouth to speak but closed it again as Tiffany continued tearfully. "I already ruined the most perfect date of my life today," she went on. "Wayne is like London, though. *Perfect*. I keep trying to find all these things wrong with him and I *still* had a great time."

"So how did it go from that to *this*?" Natalie asked as she gestured around them.

Tiffany sighed. "I got a text from my best friend Lorena," she explained. "My pregnant best friend who I ordered the baby shower sweets for, remember? She told me that I can't continue to be a part of her life until I get help for the drinking and the pills. I was supposed to be her baby's godmother, but she said it would be best if she asked her cousin instead. We've been the closest of friends since *high school*. I don't understand. Her life went one way and mine went another, I guess. She's married and starting a family. What am I? A pill-popping idiot who can't even finish college."

Tiffany stood and attempted to brush herself off. Natalie grabbed her and steadied her. "I was so upset when I got her text message," she admitted. "Wayne kept asking me what was wrong and why I had suddenly changed. But how do you explain all of that to someone who's *perfect*? He's never had an out of control day in his life. So I ditched him. I cut the date short, met up with some friends from U.N.T. for happy hour and we barhopped for a while…"

Natalie leaned over and picked up the last prescription bottle. "Who is Stephanie Curtis?" She asked as she glanced at the label.

Tiffany's arm shot out quickly as she grabbed the bottle and fumbled it back into her backpack. "One of my U.N.T. friends," she replied defensively.

Natalie raised an eyebrow. "Do I need to ask why you have a full bottle of her Adderall or should I just ask how much you spend each week to buy it off her?"

Tiffany's mouth dropped open. "You *can't* tell London, please…"

Natalie sighed. "You know, I understand," she started. "I really do. My aunt Jane used to do a similar thing. The only difference was that she would buy Vicodin from an elderly neighbor whose Social Security checks weren't enough to cover her living expenses. Granted, my aunt Jane had been through rehab and was sober by the time she met my aunt Celia but she's always been honest about her past. I suppose mostly as a warning to me, but I'm proud of her. Jane hasn't touched a drop of alcohol or a single prescription pill since she became sober, but she had to go through a *lot* of rock bottoms before she realized she needed to make a change."

"Adderall *helps* me," Tiffany replied insistently. "I'm the best version of me with it. I have an endless supply of energy and I truly believe I can change the world. But most of all? I'm so *happy* when I take it."

Natalie swallowed and felt her heart go out to the younger woman. "But Tiffany, hasn't anyone told you that the best version of you is…well, *you*? The real you that isn't enhanced by anything else?"

Tiffany shook her head slowly. "Would you believe it if I said no?" She paused. "Look, Natalie, I appreciate your concern. I get where you're coming from. I really do. But I promise I'm fine. Just please tell me that you won't say a word to London. We're just beginning to know each other." She leaned back against the Prius and closed her eyes. "I don't want her to be disappointed so soon, like everyone else in my life."

What do I do? Natalie wondered helplessly. *What can I do?* "Fine," she replied miserably. "I don't think keeping anything from London is the right thing to do. I'm not comfortable with this, so will you talk to her soon? Please?"

Tiffany shrugged. "I mean, I'll see what I can do…"

"You've got to talk to her. Or someone," Natalie prodded gently. Her face lit up as she remembered a thick paperback that Jane had tucked away in a corner on one of their bookshelves. *What is it called again? The Right to Make a Difference? No, it's The Wisdom to Know the Difference. That's it.*

"Can I bring over a book tomorrow?" Natalie asked. "It's one of my aunt Jane's favorites and she flips through it often, usually for a refresher or if she's struggling a bit. She's kept it on the shelf for years. It's called *The Wisdom to Know the Difference* and I promise it's not a science book or, like, a cheesy self-help book. Will you at least glance through it when you have some time?"

Tiffany smiled and squeezed Natalie's forearm. "Fine," she agreed. "If it means you won't say anything to London, then yes. I'll look at the book. Whatever you want."

Natalie nodded and felt pleased with herself that Tiffany had agreed.

"Good," she replied brightly. "Tell you what, I'll go into the bakery late tomorrow and stop by on my way. Promise you'll give it a chance? And then think about talking to London or someone else?"

Tiffany blinked and then smiled slowly. "I can see why my sister is so crazy about you," she replied. "You have a good heart. Don't let London fool you. She's tough because she has to be. She's been through a lot. But even *I* can tell that there's something special between you two."

She's intoxicated Natalie told herself as she tried to ignore the pounding in her chest. "You should head to bed," she replied carefully. "But for the record, I'm crazy about London too. I care about her and hope that she'll give me the chance to show her."

Tiffany took a few unbalanced steps toward the front door. *She looks like a baby deer learning how to walk for the first time* Natalie thought ruefully. She wasn't sure what to do, so she waited and watched as Tiffany picked her keys out of her bag.

"She will," Tiffany called over her shoulder. "Give you a chance, that is. She will."

Natalie leaned quietly against the grill of her truck as Tiffany dropped her key noisily on the front step and picked it up again. She didn't get back into her truck until she saw the front door close firmly behind her. Natalie sighed and chewed the inside of her cheek as she started the engine. A small pit of discomfort had lodged itself deep in her stomach at the thought of keeping a secret like this from London.

She bit her thumbnail as she pulled into the street and then she remembered the feeling of London's body against hers as they relaxed comfortably together on the sofa. She thought of her intense, trusting gaze and the taste of her welcoming mouth.

Natalie ran a hand through her hair. "What in the world am I doing?" She asked out loud. Her voice sounded strange and unwelcome in the humming stillness of the truck as it rumbled along the empty road. *Falling for an outsider, that's what. And if you're not careful, you're going to screw this up before it even has a chance.*

CHAPTER 12

The next morning, Natalie took a deep breath and stared at the familiar double French doors in front of her. The white-hot sun was blinding and a still morning heat permeated the air. She swallowed hard and stood on the wide front porch for another moment. She gripped the paperback in both hands and tried to work up the nerve to ring the doorbell.

This is what I get for making a promise against my better judgment she thought. *Now how am I going to get this book to Tiffany without London knowing?*

Guilt crept into Natalie's stomach at the idea of sneaking around right under London's nose. She glanced down at the book and then back at the doors before shaking her head slowly.

"I can't do this," she whispered to herself as she turned. "I'll give the book to London to pass along to her. If Tiffany gets upset with me, then so be it." *At least someone will be watching out for her and encouraging her to get help* she thought.

Natalie took two sure steps down the front walkway before hearing the door swing open.

"Natalie!" An excited voice called. "I thought I saw someone standing out here."

Shit. The single curse rang through her mind as she turned and forced a smile. "Hey, Tiffany," she replied uncomfortably. "I didn't know you'd be up so early."

Tiffany grinned. "I didn't sleep much. I'm making pancakes."

Natalie blinked. "You…You're making pancakes?"

Tiffany nodded and stepped aside. She gestured for Natalie to come in. "Of course," she replied easily. "My dad usually has a housekeeper that cooks meals for us, but he gave her four weeks off to visit her family in Greece. He's been traveling a lot anyway. I slept for a few hours and woke up feeling awful. So I doubled the Adderall just to get me through this morning and now I feel like a superstar. I feel great!"

Natalie followed Tiffany warily through the house and into the kitchen as she half-listened to her rapid chatter.

"…So you should definitely stay and eat," she finished. Natalie's mouth dropped open at the large stacks of pancakes towering on the granite countertops.

"Oh no, I can't," Natalie replied quickly. "That is a *lot* of pancakes, but, um, I'm actually running late to the bakery. I wanted to drop off the book before London wakes up."

"What book?" Tiffany asked. She poked at a sizzling pancake with her spatula and glanced at her quizzically.

Natalie was caught off-guard. *She really doesn't remember* she realized. "It's called *The Wisdom to Know the Difference* and I mentioned it to you last night. Remember? My aunt Jane swears by it and says it's helped her quite a bit. You promised to read it…"

Tiffany's face fell. "Oh," she replied flatly. "Yeah, that book." She sighed. "I'll give it a try, but I really don't think I have a problem. Look, I know last night looked bad. I was in a weak spot and you caught me. But I feel *great* now. I mean, check this out…" she paused and flipped the pancake with ease. "Would some desperate junkie be able to do that?" She grinned.

Natalie gently placed the book on the table as she realized the magnitude of Tiffany's issues. *Jane always said that most addicts are in denial* she silently recalled. *And easily defensive.*

"Flip through it by the pool or something," she replied. "Maybe you'll find it interesting."

"Sure, I will," Tiffany went on flippantly. She turned from the stove and shoved the book into her backpack. "It's too bad you have to leave. I may have misjudged how many pancakes London and I can eat between the two of us." She stepped back and surveyed the kitchen thoughtfully.

"Look, I really should go…" Natalie started quietly. She froze as the fine hairs on her arms stood. She felt London's presence before she even said a word.

"Hey, I didn't know you were coming over today," London spoke happily. The sleep was evident in her voice. Natalie closed her eyes slowly.

No she thought. She refused to turn around. *Don't look at her. I can't lie to her face. If I look at her, she'll know. She'll realize something is wrong and I can't keep this from her. I don't* want *to keep this from her.*

Natalie listened as London padded closer and stopped just behind her. She laid her hand lightly on the small of her back and suddenly all Natalie was aware of was how fast her heart was beating.

"She came over for my pancakes," Tiffany cut in confidently. She winked at Natalie. "I couldn't sleep, so I started experimenting with the Bisquick and whatever we had in the cabinets. I think I might really have a knack for the culinary arts, you know? Natalie, you'll have to let me know if you agree."

London stood next to Natalie and glanced at her. "You…came over for pancakes?" She raised an eyebrow.

Natalie felt herself flush under London's questioning gaze. She looked at anything but her. "Uh-huh," she squeaked nervously. *Dial it back, Natalie* she thought warningly. She took a deep breath. "Yup. Pancakes."

"Those ones are peanut butter and cheddar," Tiffany said as she pointed to a burnt stack in the corner. "And those are banana and creamed corn…"

London wrinkled her nose at the pancakes and Natalie finally met her eyes. They shared a slow, smoldering grin. London gently grabbed her hand. "Come with me to my room. I have a…a…question about my iPad."

"Wait, what does Natalie know about computers?" Natalie heard Tiffany's voice trail after them in confusion. "Don't you want breakfast?"

Natalie stopped short behind London as they reached a bedroom door. London quickly pulled her inside and resolutely shut it behind them. They dissolved into giggles as London took a step toward her.

"Are you okay?" London asked breathlessly. "I'm sorry if Tiffany was bugging you. I don't understand her. Sometimes she sleeps for days at a time and other times it's like she doesn't sleep at all," she paused and smiled. "But I'm really happy to see you."

Natalie looked back at her, torn. *I think I understand why Tiffany is so scared for London to find out* she thought. *She's incredible.* In that moment, she couldn't take it anymore. She had to be close to London, to feel her lips against her own and their bodies pressed together.

It'll be okay she decided. *Tiffany promised to read the book and then talk to her.*

Without another thought, Natalie leaned in quickly and kissed London. Her body reacted instantly to the other woman's gentle tongue as their kiss deepened. Stepping back, she bumped against the closet door and felt London grin through their kisses.

"I missed you," Natalie finally replied between breaths. *It's true* she realized with a start. *I did miss London last night. I missed her the second I walked out the door. I wanted to fall asleep next to her and wake up with her close to me.*

"I missed you too," London whispered as she toyed gently with Natalie's bottom lip between her teeth. "I'm sorry I dragged you away like that. But I..." she released her lip and worked kisses up her jawline. "Couldn't stop thinking about you all night..." Natalie nearly fell over as London's fingertips danced beneath the hem of her t-shirt and up her spine.

"...And then I woke up, came into the kitchen and it was like I conjured you up with thought or something," London went on as she nibbled at her neck. Natalie tilted her head back in response and stifled a moan. "Because here you are, you're gorgeous and I can't take my eyes...or lips...off of you."

Natalie's knees buckled as the heat continued to spike between them. London led her confidently to a suede chaise near a window overlooking the swimming pool and backyard. With one tug, she pulled the blinds shut and knelt over Natalie as she continued her exploration of her neck and shoulders.

I'm in heaven Natalie thought as she closed her eyes and gave in to the sensations. After a few moments, she blinked as the kisses paused.

"What time do you have to be at the bakery?" London whispered. A smile played at her lips as she watched her face carefully.

Natalie let out a small groan. "I usually get there around 5 A.M. But I told Celia and Jane I'd be there closer to 7:30 this morning."

London laughed. "It's 8:15."

Natalie quickly shot up but she snaked her arms around London's waist to keep her from falling off the chaise. "This weekend," she started with a smile. "I want to take you somewhere. I want to take you to my favorite place in all of Texas. Are you up for a small road trip?"

"With you?" London replied. "Of course I am. Where are we going?"

"My aunts have a country house in Haskell," Natalie replied as they stood. "Actually, it was the house that Celia and my dad grew up in. It stayed in the family after my grandfather passed away and Celia took it over. I spent a lot of time out there growing up. Nowadays, my aunts use it as a weekend getaway."

"So I get an entire uninterrupted weekend with you?" London asked with a grin. "Sounds amazing."

"It's a tiny West Texas town and there's hardly any cellular service," Natalie rushed. "I understand if you'd rather go to the city. It won't offend me if you tell me you'd rather spend the weekend sightseeing in Dallas. But this…" she shrugged and smiled shyly. "It's the *real* Texas and it's somewhere new for you. We're having a barbecue for my best friend's daughter's birthday on Saturday. You and I could stay through to Sunday. It'll give us a chance to spend more time and really get to know each other."

London looked at her for a moment and reached over to brush a lock of hair behind Natalie's ear. "I feel like I already know you," she murmured. "It's strange. As much as I thought I would never be saying this even a short time ago, there is nowhere I'd rather be this weekend than Haskell, Texas."

Natalie let out a breath she didn't realize she had been holding and admired London's form as she padded into the walk-in closet. "Give me two seconds to get dressed and I'll walk you out," she called over her shoulder. "I hope your aunts won't hate me too much for making you late."

Natalie leaned back against the chaise for a moment. "They'll get over it," she called back with a laugh. *Somehow, I'm breaking through all those carefully placed defenses that she's had since she arrived* Natalie thought proudly. *Gut feelings don't lie. And mine is telling me that maybe this was meant to be something…special.*

"London, I…" she started happily and then paused. *How do I articulate what I'm feeling for her?*

After a moment, London poked her head through the door of the walk-in closet and shot her a curious smile.

"Sorry, I didn't catch the last of what you said," she replied.

Natalie willed herself not to blush. "No, I just…I was saying that I'm looking forward to this weekend with you." She forced herself not to roll her eyes as she stammered. *Good save, Natalie* she thought sarcastically.

London wriggled into a faded Abercrombie & Fitch t-shirt and walked over to her. She smiled again and pecked her lips. "You know what? I'm finding that any time I spend with you is time I'm looking forward to."

Natalie stood, loathing to leave the darkened bedroom that smelled of London's perfume. She tried in vain to smooth her shirt. *Last thing I need is Celia looking me up and down and knowing exactly what I've been up to* she thought dryly. *But duty and family calls.*

A few hours after Natalie's surprise appearance, London wandered onto the back patio. The wide deck was paved with smooth tan bricks and housed beneath a black fence station. In one corner, a built-in fire pit took up most of the area closest to the backyard. Inviting wicker furniture was arranged around the fire pit in a lazy semi-circle. An oversized electric barbecue grill and grilling station was shrouded in a rare bit of shade at the opposite corner.

A row of padded outdoor chaises were scattered along a lengthier side of the kidney-shaped swimming pool. The water was clean and sparkling as the afternoon sun reflected from its ripples. Tiffany laid across the furthest chaise and tipped her sunglasses from her head over her nose.

London relaxed into the lounger nearest her and sighed happily. "This is nice," she murmured. "I bet you had some awesome pool parties here."

For a moment, London thought Tiffany might be asleep. She finally smiled in response. "What happens at the pool parties, stays at the pool parties." She flipped her sunglasses up for a moment and winked at her.

London nearly did a double take. *Her eyes are so red* she thought as she bit her lip. *She looks…bad. A shadow of the pancake-making energizer bunny from this morning.*

"Are you okay?" London finally asked. She casually tossed a cold bottle of water to her. "Drink up. You're going to shrivel up like a prune in this heat."

Tiffany smirked but uncapped the bottle of water and took a long swallow. "I wasn't feeling so great," she admitted. "I got queasy about an hour ago. Every time I moved, I felt dizzy. Laying by the pool is relaxing. The nausea is almost gone."

London took a deep breath as she recalled her recent memories of Tiffany taking pills. *Too many memories in the short time I've been here.* "Is there anything you want to talk to me about? Anything at all?" She ventured.

A strange look passed over Tiffany's face but she quickly shook her head. "No," she replied slowly. "Why are you asking me that?"

London shrugged. "You know I wouldn't judge you," she hedged. "I think I've finally realized that I'm not really in a place in my life to judge anyone else's. I don't know, I've been thinking about a lot of things differently lately. Maybe it's Natalie's effect on me. She's so unlike anyone I've met. She makes me see things in a new perspective."

Tiffany stared sullenly at the pool water as it lapped against the perimeter gently. "I don't have anything I need to talk about."

London looked at her for a long moment and sighed. *Maybe I'm blowing things out of proportion* she thought. *Am I that out of touch with the younger generation? Maybe Tiffany really does need that medication.* "At least tell me about your date yesterday," she tried for a change of subject. "This Wayne sounds like a pretty good person."

Tiffany grinned and slid down the chaise. "Oh my *God*, I think I blew it," she squealed as she pulled a pillow over her face.

"No way," London replied incredulously. *This is good* she reminded herself. *Girl talk. Isn't that what this is? Didn't Holly tell me to keep trying with her?* "Tell me everything."

"Okay, okay," Tiffany said excitedly. She grimaced as she hoisted herself back against the chaise but shook it off. "Only if you promise to tell me everything about *your* date with Natalie. She really cares about you, London."

London flushed. "You know, it's the weirdest feeling," she started. She glanced back at the water and momentarily fell silent as she watched a light breeze splash gently against a vent. *The complete and total relaxation, the fact that I'm dishing with my estranged half-sister like a couple of high schoolers or these strange feelings I'm developing for Natalie?* She wondered silently. *I guess they're all unfamiliar to me. Unfamiliar…but nice.* "I went all this time without feeling anything, because feeling hurt so much," she continued. "And now I can feel *everything*. One week into my four weeks in Texas and it's like she's cut me wide open. I feel so…so *alive* and happy. Weird, right?"

Tiffany shook her head but grinned. "Not weird, London. It's how regular people feel." She paused. "And P.S., you're falling for her."

London raked a hand through her hair and laughed but didn't deny it. "Wait, you promised you'd tell me about your date first," she exclaimed. "And you'd better do it now, before Dad gets home this evening."

No wonder Natalie is so big on family London thought as she listened to Tiffany recount their afternoon at the Perot Museum. She didn't offer any hints as to why she thought she blew the date, but London didn't press her. *This* is *nice* she decided. *For the longest time, I thought my mother was my only real family. But here I am by the pool, a million miles from anything I've known, listening to Tiffany talk about her date with an old high school flame. If I didn't know better, I'd say this almost feels like family too.*

CHAPTER 13

That evening, London listened apprehensively as her father's key twisted in the lock of the front door. Moments later, he shuffled into the foyer as he was weighed down by two wheeled suitcases behind him. London stood expectantly, but she wasn't sure what to do.

Running over and giving him a hug feels a little forced she thought. *Not to mention awkward. I can count the number of times we've hugged on one hand. But just standing here seems cold.*

Vincent Foster paused in the foyer and leaned his suitcases against the wall. He froze for a brief moment as he spotted London and then straightened and grinned broadly. He shifted for a moment from foot to foot and then held out his arms.

"There's a sight I never thought I'd see," he announced proudly.

As London gave him a quick hug in greeting, her thoughts were flying nearly a mile a minute. *He looks...different* she realized in shock. *There's something different about him.* Her father had always seemed so tall and statuesque when she was a little girl, with an untouchable air that fascinated her as a youngster and then frustrated her as she grew older.

His thick, dark hair, which he had always worn shaggy and long, had thinned considerably. He was skinnier than London remembered and he somehow seemed just a touch more frail too. Prominent wrinkles across his forehead and around the corners of his eyes deepened when he smiled. Small grayish spots were beginning to form across the backs of his hands and salt-

and-pepper patches colored the hair around his temples.

London took a deep breath as realization hit her. *He's getting older* she thought. She wasn't sure why the notion had never occurred to her before; after all, it was a natural part of life. *He was briefly at Mom's services* she recalled. *But I was so upset and there was so much going on that I don't know if I even spoke to him for more than a minute, let alone took a good look.*

"Good to see you too, Dad," she replied gently. "I'm glad I'm here."

"Me too, London," he agreed and then paused. "I'm just…I'm sorry it took us this long to get here."

London opened her mouth to speak but Vincent smiled kindly and patted her forearm. "Anyway," he cleared his throat and London immediately remembered that he was as bad with feelings as she was. "How are you liking Texas so far?"

"It's different," London hedged. "But I've been, um, exploring. Meeting people."

Vince glanced at her. "That's good," he responded. "I know you thought I was probably being overzealous by buying the plane ticket as soon as you asked about visiting, but I could hear in your voice how unhappy you were. Have you been settling in?"

London nodded, again at a loss for what to say. *Where to begin?* She thought ruefully.

"Hi, Dad," Tiffany's voice piped up as her light footsteps padded down the stairs. "How was your trip?"

Vince grinned and hugged Tiffany close. London watched their affectionate, familiar embrace, but didn't feel any of the resentment or bitterness that she had carried through the years. Holly's words rang in her mind. *This whole thing is probably just as strange to Tiffany* London admitted to herself. *How can I resent her for having a father when it's all she's ever known? Maybe part of growing up is letting old wounds go and letting things be.*

"Great," Vince replied. "But even better now that both of my daughters are here. Would you believe that Dubai is even hotter than Texas?"

Tiffany laughed. "*Everyone* knows that, Dad," she replied with a roll of her eyes. "Cambodia was hot too. Looks like the only one who enjoys the cold is London."

It was London's turn to roll her eyes as they made their way into the kitchen. "Well, I had to live up to my name somehow," she replied dryly. "Besides, Chicago has the best pizza in the world so it's an easy trade-off."

"Speaking of food, I hope neither of you made plans for tomorrow," Vince spoke as he opened the wide stainless steel refrigerator and pulled out a can of soda. "I thought we'd catch the Rangers game in the afternoon. London, Foster Oil & Gas shares a box at Globe Life Park with an energy subsidiary in the area. Surely being raised in Chicago you must love baseball."

London shrugged sheepishly. "I never got into the whole Chicago Cubs versus White Sox rivalry," she replied honestly. *We really don't know anything about each other, do we?* She thought as the familiar strains of apprehension chewed at her stomach. "I do have a soft spot for the Chicago Bears though," she offered.

Vince blinked. "The Chicago Bears? Oh London, we really have to talk football. We'll see if we can at least turn you into a Rangers fan yet." He smiled and took a seat at the kitchen table to next to her.

Tiffany crossed her arms suspiciously. "Dad, you're not going to be working at the game tomorrow, are you?"

Vince sighed. "The President, the Director of Operations and the Controller for Discover Explorations are in from Mississippi, so they'll be there…"

"I knew it!" Tiffany groaned. "I knew this would be a networking thing."

London watched the exchange in confusion. "What's Discover Explorations?"

"There's a lot to teach you about Foster Oil & Gas," Vince started with a nod. He took a sip of soda. "We're a small oil company. We've stayed purposely small and manageable through the years, which has given us more flexibility and less risk during the slower industry cycles. We run a pretty tight operation, if I do say so myself."

Tiffany rolled her eyes and headed back for the stairs. "Hey, Dad," she called with a laugh. "Your ego is showing. I've heard this five million times before, sorry London. I'm exhausted. Good night, y'all."

London met her father's eyes. *They're sort of shaped like mine* she observed silently. "So Discover is part of Foster Oil & Gas?"

Vince nodded. "Foster Holdings, LLC is technically where I'm Chairman. We do business primarily as Foster Oil & Gas and we have a few small sub-organizations that run under the umbrella of Foster Holdings. Discover Explorations is our off-shore drilling company, but they're really more of a unit. They work on mobile drilling units in the ocean and those generally progress into full production rigs when we've got oil. It's a much more complicated part of the business and I have a small, top-notch team that runs it. The executives are in from Mississippi, where they've been doing some drilling along the Gulf Coast for us."

London tried to follow along. "And your brother and his kids run most of the day-to-day operations?"

"That's true," Vince replied. "My older brother, your uncle David, is the President of Foster Oil & Gas. I was President for about fifteen years and then moved into the Chairman role. Over the last few years, I've been purposely entrusting David with more responsibility. He, in turn, has been giving his three children more responsibility. They've all come directly to Foster Oil & Gas out of college. Your oldest cousin, Kyle, is our V.P. of Operations. Then my niece Penelope heads up Human Resources. Finally, your youngest cousin, Ryan, is in the Communications department. Eventually we'd like to see him become our Chief Marketing Officer."

The unfamiliar names swam in London's head but one thing stuck out. "You must be planning to retire."

Vince smiled and London recognized a mixture of sadness and excitement in his eyes. "I am," he confirmed with a sigh. "It's bittersweet. I realize I gave up any semblance of a normal life when I agreed to take Foster's reigns from my grandfather. I sacrificed interests of my own and time with family. I don't want to say that my passion for the family business has wavered, but it's the right time for me. I'm looking forward to a new chapter."

London watched his face for a moment. *It's true* she thought. *He's so much older now and he's barely lived his life outside of Foster Oil & Gas.* "Life is short, Dad," she finally replied. "You should do what feels right."

Vince nodded and finished his soda. "I know you're a workaholic just like me," he responded. "Those long hours nonstop at the advertising agency, I understand. It's just the way our worlds work, I suppose."

As London said her good nights and excused herself to the guest room, she turned her father's words over in her mind. *Is that really the lifestyle I want?* She pondered as she changed into her pajamas. *I don't want to wake up one day at Dad's age, and realize how much I missed out on because I was too busy dedicating myself to W.H. Young.*

Natalie's face inexplicably flashed through London's memory. *Besides, I would never want to spend more time away from her than I absolutely had to.* The thought fired through her brain before she had a chance to stop it.

"What does Natalie have to do with anything?" She muttered to herself as she gently closed the closet door. Tiffany's teasing laughter from earlier in the afternoon echoed in her head. *And P.S., you're falling for her.*

At once, realization sunk in and London nearly lost her breath. She sat on the edge of the bed as things suddenly became clear. "Oh my God, I really *am* falling for her," she said out loud. Her voice bounced off the walls of the dark, empty room.

It was easy to dedicate myself to my career when I was so sure that love wasn't for me London thought. A million feelings raced through her at once and she wasn't sure if she wanted to laugh, cry or some combination of both. *And then here comes Natalie, entering my life when I least expected it* she recalled. *Well played, Universe. I feel like the rug has been pulled right from under me. One thing I know for sure is that I don't want to let her go.*

London flopped back onto the bed and stared in wide-eyed silence at the ceiling. Her mind flashed back to the sleek Chicago skyscraper that housed W.H. Young and the promotion that had been dangled in front of her. "I'm supposed to leave in two weeks, but all I want to do is get in the car, speed to Mission Bakery and kiss Natalie until I don't know where I am anymore," she murmured. "What am I going to do?"

Natalie sat on the porch of the modest home she shared with her aunts and traced her index finger around the rim of her juice glass pensively. She rocked gently in the white porch swing as she watched the early morning light rise over the horizon. The cloudless sky was washed in pastels as the temperature rose with the sun. She gazed at the open field across the quiet residential street and took a sip of her orange juice. A cloud of brown dust picked up in the light breeze and a small tumbleweed bounced along the road.

She shifted as she heard the front door creak open behind her. *Celia never understood why I didn't move closer to a big city when I got older* she thought. *Sometimes I wonder too. Surely I wouldn't have had to work so hard to make the bakery a success if I'd moved to Dallas, Houston or one of the big cities. But then Mission Bakery, as we know it, wouldn't exist and I wouldn't trade our bakery for anything.* She sighed. *I doubt London would want to live in a small town like this. It's already so different from what she knows.*

"You look deep in thought," Jane's kind voice spoke. She eased herself onto the porch swing with a sigh. "I've been out here for a minute now and I don't think you've blinked once. Is everything all right?"

Natalie glanced at her aunt and smiled. *Celia and Jane are a true study in opposites, aren't they?* She thought proudly. *Celia, with her dark hair, Hispanic roots, sturdy build and simple out look. Then there's Jane, the blonde-haired, blue-eyed aging flower child who grew up outside of Boston. They're the most perfect couple I know. Because of them, I always believed different was good, not bad, but London and I aren't just different. We're polar opposites.*

"I'm fine, thank you," Natalie replied quietly.

"We're all ready for Saturday in Haskell," Jane ventured. "Celia has all of her grill supplies ready and I bought an extra case of bottled water. I don't think there's anything left in that refrigerator from the last time we were out there. Is Isabella looking forward to her birthday party?"

Natalie nodded. "Yes, Paula stopped by the bakery yesterday to thank us again for having the barbecue," she replied. "She said Isabella has been a little down lately, with Rudy being gone so long for work. It's the least we can do for them, you know? Paula has been a good friend for so long and I relate to Isabella. Sometimes she reminds me of *me* when I was a kid. I always hated when Dad would leave for weeks at a time on a rig."

Jane smiled. "You have a kind heart," she responded. "It'll be fun to have everyone together this weekend. I can't remember the last time we were all in Haskell together. We've been so busy with the bakery. It's really taken it's own life over the last few years."

Could I leave Mission Bakery? Natalie wondered. *I've poured my heart, sweat and tears into it for years and it's been my first love for just as long. Could Celia and Jane handle it without me?* The questions seemed to compound on top of one another.

Natalie took a deep breath. "How did you know that Celia was the one?"

Jane smiled knowingly. "To be honest, I fell in love with Celia from the moment I met her. She was unlike anyone else I'd ever known before."

Natalie stilled, her glass halfway to her lips. *That's exactly what London said about me.*

"You Silvas," Jane went on with a grin. "You women have something about you. A way, I suppose. Celia and I couldn't be more different. She loves to barbecue all kinds of meat, won't miss a Cowboys game if her life depended on it and likes her life simple. I, on the other hand, have been all over the world, I've beaten addiction, I'm a vegetarian and I don't know the Cowboys from the Lakers." She took a deep breath. "But nothing compares to how I feel about her. It hasn't faded over our many years together. I look at her sometimes when she's grilling or washing her truck, you know, when she doesn't realize I'm watching. And I just know. We were meant to be."

Natalie nodded and took another slow sip of orange juice. The sun was higher than before and its rays reflected through the early morning sky. "I think I'm falling for London."

Jane patted her hand comfortingly. "Celia seemed to like her," she replied. "And you know your aunt Celia is a tough critic of anyone who spends time with you."

Natalie swallowed. "But she's just visiting," she blurted out. "She's not staying. Nobody comes from a big, grand city like Chicago and stays *here*. What if I'm just a fun distraction or someone to pass the time with? I'm scared that I'll be completely head over heels for her and then she'll leave."

"The heart is always a little quicker than the brain, isn't it?" Jane mused. She glanced at Natalie. "It takes the brain a while to catch up sometimes. By the time it registers what's happening, the heart has already made its decision."

"Nobody wants to fall in love just to be left," Natalie replied bitterly. "It happened once before and I learned my lesson the hard way. But there's something different about London. She was so broken when she got here. All I want to do is kiss her, hold her and promise that everything will be okay. But if she's just going to go back, like nothing…"

"Natalie, sweetheart," Jane interjected. "I know you're frustrated. I can see that you care deeply for her. Do you know that Celia told me London couldn't keep her eyes off you the entire time the three of you were on the food truck?"

Natalie felt a small glimmer of hope. "No…" she started.

"Well, she did," Jane continued. "What does your heart say about London's feelings?"

Natalie blinked as a rush of memories filled her mind. She thought of how London, bright and laughing, kissed her so passionately that she could feel it low in her stomach before it radiated out to every cell in her body. She remembered the deep content between them as they sat by the pond.

"She feels the same way," Natalie finally answered.

"Then it will work itself out, sweetheart," Jane responded. "London may have some tough decisions to make, but if she feels the same way then love will prevail. Be patient with her. It will be worth it. Every time I look at your aunt Celia, I remember just how worth it our own struggles have been."

"I hope I find a love like you two have," Natalie said with a smile. "Thank you for listening."

Jane stood and patted Natalie's shoulder. "You have all the love in the world, honey. If it's time for the next chapter in your life, then it's time. I'm going to head over and open the bakery. Come on by when you're ready."

Natalie stood and stretched. "I will."

"Don't worry about the uncertainties, Natalie," Jane went on as she paused in the front door. "You have the whole weekend ahead of you to enjoy with London. I, for one, am looking forward to meeting the mysterious woman that seems to have stolen my niece's heart."

CHAPTER 14

That afternoon, London surveyed the spacious air-conditioned box overlooking the batting cages at Globe Life Park and carefully took in her surroundings. An engraved marble nameplate outside of the box read "Foster Holdings, LLC" on the top line and "Hillside Energy", the company that shared the space with them, below it. She didn't feel the surge of pride she had expected upon seeing her surname etched as ownership of the opulent private box. She felt disconnected from it all and chewed the tiny stirring straw in her whiskey and Coke in thought.

I may be a Foster, but I didn't exactly grow up a Foster she thought. *I know nothing about the oil and gas industry and the little bit that Dad explained sounds like Greek or something.*

She glanced around the interior of the box. It was spacious, with a long granite countertop running the length of the left wall. A small sink, microwave and dry bar with tall stools were arranged around the countertop while a curved flat-screen television anchored in the far corner played the baseball game happening just below them.

A small step down led to a sunken social area, where leather couches and armchairs were scattered in two semi-circles around a square, marble-topped table. The dramatic floor-to-ceiling glass wall separated the social area from an outdoor patio by a narrow door. The patio held four miniature rows of seats that overlooked the baseball field and faced the large neon scoreboard directly across the expansive green.

A private restroom in the corner near the front door rounded out the box. London wasn't surprised that it had been occupied by Tiffany for nearly ten minutes. *First thing she did was make a beeline right to the bar* she thought as she continued to chew her straw. *I wonder if it's too soon to talk to Dad about that. That is, if I can catch him without his posse of oil executives for a moment.*

London eased herself onto one of the tall stools near the dry bar and sighed. Vince was sitting casually in one of the outdoor seats and spoke animatedly, erupting into laughter every few seconds, as he entertained his colleagues.

He looks just like I do when I'm talking to clients at work she thought ruefully. *If nothing else, I suppose the Fosters at least have the fake laughter memorized well.*

When they had arrived nearly an hour ago, Vince had politely introduced London and Tiffany to his colleagues. If they had been confused by the presence of a second daughter, they were gentlemen enough not to let it show. After the obligatory introductions were complete, the men had congregated outside with cold bottles of beer in hand. Tiffany had scattered to the bar, then to the long stadium hallway outside, and then back to the bar again.

London drained the last of her drink through her tiny straw as the amber liquid disappeared between square ice cubes. *How long do baseball games usually last?* She wondered dismally. She had the sneaking suspicion that they had quite some time left. *If this was Dad's idea of bonding time, he needs a serious lesson in separating business and personal.* She sighed again. *But why am I surprised? It's Vincent Foster.*

She perked up as she hard a flush from the small bathroom. She turned expectantly as the bathroom door opened and Tiffany leaned against the frame for a moment. A thin sheen of sweat shone over her face and neck. Her blonde hair was matted to her temples.

"Are you okay?" London asked, concerned. She knew Tiffany had downed two drinks in a record amount of time, but hadn't expected her to nearly lose her ability to stand upright.

Tiffany swallowed hard but nodded. She glanced up and met London's eyes. "I don't...I didn't feel so well, but I'm okay now."

London searched her sister's empty gaze. *She looks stoned* she thought in alarm. Her eyes were half-closed while the rest of her face was blank. London took a deep breath. She had had enough.

This stops now she thought in determination. *This is a problem. Tiffany needs help and I can't pretend like I don't notice or it's some normal personality quirk. She's going to end up hurting herself one of these days.*

"How much Adderall did you take?" London asked as she felt her voice rising. "Your pupils are the size of saucers!"

Tiffany glanced at the patio, but the glass door had been shut to keep the air conditioning inside the box. "Shh," she hissed. "I didn't take Adderall. It's the Xanax. I forgot that I needed some earlier."

"You did not," London replied flatly. She stole a glance at the patio and then glared at Tiffany. "Why? Why did you need it? You always say how much you *need* these pills and that you can't get by without them, but you've never said why. Because you know what? It's a lame, flimsy excuse. What you do to your body is *your* choice, but don't treat me like I'm stupid."

Calm down, London she warned herself silently. *It's not going to do either of us any good if we start yelling. Besides, Dad will never forgive us if we get into our own version of Family Feud right here at the game.*

Tiffany glared at her for a long moment. "Since when do you care what I do, London?" She retorted. "You couldn't care less about me through my entire life, and now you're going to judge me because I have issues? I don't have to take this. I'm going outside for some air."

Tiffany took a few slow steps toward the patio and then turned again. "I'm sorry we can't all be as perfect as you, London," she continued and then paused. "But you know what? I wouldn't want to be."

She turned again and London blinked. *Did I deserve that?* She wondered She thought of the years of resentment she had indirectly taken out on Tiffany by distancing herself and outright ignoring her younger sister. *Fine, maybe I did. But that doesn't make the pill-popping and drinking excusable. And there's no way she can go out there and mingle with Dad's colleagues right now.*

London hurried after her and gently grabbed her arm. "Tiffany," she started, her voice low and urgent. "I realize we have our issues and I realize

I'm just as much to blame for some of them. But I'm telling you as your…your…" she paused and faltered. "…Half-sister that there's no way you can go out there. Dad and the Discover guys are going to know you're intoxicated."

How can they not? She thought as she observed Tiffany's drawn, pale face. *She looks and sounds like she's been binging for three days straight.*

London was pleasantly surprised that Tiffany didn't argue it. She nodded after a moment. "I'm kind of dizzy," she admitted.

At that moment, the unmistakable ringtone of London's phone chirped loudly from the countertop. She knew from the ringtone she had set for her best friend that it was Holly on the other end of the call. London glanced back at her phone and then at Tiffany.

Crap she thought. *It's the middle of the day, so it has to be work-related. Do I take the call or get Tiffany situated?*

Her phone continued to ring and London bit her lip. *Work?* She thought again. *Or Tiffany?*

After a moment of internal struggle, London grabbed both of Tiffany's arms and pushed her forcefully into the nearest armchair. "Sit for a minute," she told her. "Relax. I have to take this call, okay? Please don't move."

Tiffany met her gaze and London stilled for a moment. She was caught off-guard by the complete trust in her sister's eyes. "Okay," she replied. She rested her head in her palm and closed her eyes. "You promise you'll be right back?"

Guilt wracked London's gut. "I promise," she confirmed. She wasn't quite sure why she felt so awful about turning her back on her sister and grabbing her phone, but the lingering feeling of guilt stayed with her as she hurried into the stadium hallway.

She needs me she thought. *I should be watching her right now.*

London quickly jabbed the redial button on her phone and tapped her fingers impatiently against her thigh as the call rang to Holly. The second big realization in so many days became clear as she glanced over her shoulder toward the door of the box.

My family means more she thought with a swallow. *What was it that Natalie* had said? *Family is family, and that's that?* Well, Tiffany is *my family. She's more important than work.*

London was about to hang up, turn her phone onto its silent mode and march back into the box when Holly answered breathlessly.

Damn London thought. "Hey, Holly," she forced the cheer into her tone. "How's it going? I just missed you."

"Oh thank God you're not saying 'y'all' yet!" Holly greeted her with a laugh. "How's the rest and relaxation?"

"It's a whole different world out here," London admitted. "I'm already feeling like a new…*er* person. I know we have a *lot* to catch up on, but I actually…"

"The reason for my call was that I wanted to talk to you about the promotion," Holly cut in. London fell silent. "Do you have a few minutes?"

London turned again and craned her neck toward the door of the box suite. She blew out her breath. "I guess."

"You don't sound enthused," Holly remarked. "Which is unfortunate, because I thought you'd be thrilled to know that Mr. Hanson had a private meeting with me over lunch. Your Instagram, London? It's gone viral in the office. Everybody, and I mean *everybody* from Accounting to Communications to I.T., is addicted to your adventure. Literally *everyone* at W.H. Young is following your account and waiting to know what happens next."

London blinked. That was not what she expected to hear. "Gone viral?"

"Yes," Holly confirmed with a chuckle. "Even the C.E.O. is following your Instagram account. You're practically a celebrity in the office now."

"Oh no…" London started as a wave of realization washed over her.

"Oh *yes*," Holly replied. "London, this is *great*. We love the photos you've been posting. In fact, Mr. Hanson told me in our lunch meeting that he now has no doubt in his mind that you're the right person to take over my role. He wants you back in the office as soon as your time off is up."

London sank against the wall and ran a hand through her hair. "Holly, I don't know…"

"In case you needed me to recite the *amazing* suite of benefits now available to you as the Director of National Accounts, you'll now have an office with a crystal-clear view of Lake Michigan, a $20,000 increase in salary and the admiration and support of every person at W.H. Young because we all feel like we're right there in Texas with you," Holly went on cheerfully.

"I don't know," London stressed again. "I didn't say I accepted it."

There was a long pause. "I don't understand," Holly finally replied. "This is what you wanted. What's going on?"

London sighed. *Where to begin?* She thought. "How did you know that Michael was the one?" She asked instead. "Was it, like, an instant thing or did you realize it slowly?"

Her friend was quiet for a beat. "You met someone," she started. "It's that brunette that you posted the Instagram of, isn't it? London, you sly dog! I can't believe it," she crowed. "Good for you, girl. I'm glad you're getting some action while you're in Texas. You deserve it."

"It's not just action, Holly," London tried to explain. "I really like this woman."

Holly took a deep breath. "Look, I get it," she went on. "It's been God knows how long since you've had a connection with someone. After the number that Kayley pulled on you, I don't blame you one bit for being closed off. But the fact is that this woman lives in Texas. You know as well as I do that long distance things never work out. The last thing I want is to see you being broken all over again, especially over something that wasn't attainable to begin with."

"Wow, Holly," London interrupted bitterly. Her annoyance was growing, but she wasn't sure why. "Thanks for that vote of confidence. I know what you're thinking, but she's not some rebound. I've had a year between Kayley moving out and coming to Texas."

"Well, what if you *are* falling for her?" Holly prodded. "What's going to happen? One of you will have to give and move to the other. You'll have to stay in Texas or she'll have to move to Chicago. And, London, I think you know what the obvious choice is. You have the promotion in the bag. Mr. Hanson confirmed it this afternoon. I know you wouldn't want to give up the single largest achievement in your career thus far to…to…what? Take a chance on some woman in Texas that you've known for a few weeks?"

London knew that Holly was making perfect sense. *On paper, she's right. It's the obvious choice* she reminded herself gently. Natalie's wide, contagious smile lit her mind's eye. *But I can't ignore my heart either.* "I can't push how I feel to the side," she replied. "I've done that long enough, and it's gotten me nowhere. I don't know that I've ever had such a strong, immediate connection with someone and that's worth something to me. I realize I have a lot of thinking to do…"

"London, the C.E.O. is not going to wait around for an answer while you explore this romance," Holly went on. "You know how he is. He's a fast-paced executive and he wants a plan in place right away. I can't give him a wishy-washy answer. Can I at least tell him you've verbally accepted? If you decline, you'll lose this opportunity."

London's heart pounded. *What if Holly is right?* She thought apprehensively. *What if things with Natalie crash and burn? Then I'm left with nothing all over again.* "I…I don't know what to say," she stammered.

"Say you accept, so I can tell Mr. Hanson that you've verbally agreed to the promotion," Holly replied impatiently. "And then enjoy your afternoon and the rest of your time in Texas, because it's going to be a whirlwind once you're back."

Speak now or lose the opportunity forever. "I accept," London said hastily. She felt a strange heaviness weigh down on her as Holly squealed in excitement.

"I knew you'd make the right decision!" She exclaimed. "All that dedication and commitment you've shown is going to pay off big time. London, this is going to be *dynamite* for your career! I'll let Mr. Hanson know as soon as we hang up."

London felt sick to her stomach. "Great," she replied, unable to keep the biting sarcasm from her tone. "Thanks a lot."

Holly plowed ahead, either undeterred or pretending like she didn't hear her, to London's aggravation. "One more thing before I let you go," she continued. "There's a client in Dallas that I'm overdue to see. I'm going to swing down for a day mid-next week. I was thinking a quick patio and margarita date, but I'd like you to be there when I visit the client. These responsibilities are going to eventually be in your hands now, so we might as well start training you right away."

"I'll e-mail you my dad's address," London replied. "I…I'll put the meeting on my calendar."

As they hung up, London closed her eyes and leaned back against the cool hallway wall for a second. "Shit," she whispered to herself. Her eyes flew open as she remembered her sister. "*Shit*," she repeated, louder.

CHAPTER 15

London threw open the door to the box suite and blinked. Tiffany had reclined back in her armchair and finished another drink with a long swallow. A quick glance through the glass wall revealed her father and his colleagues stepping closer to the door as they socialized. *They're going to come inside any minute* she realized as her heart sank.

She rushed to her sister. "Tiffany, I thought you were done drinking today," she hissed angrily.

Tiffany tried to roll herself to a seated position. "I had to…I needed to drink something," she slurred. "It's just, the Xanax, it makes my head, like…" she threw out her hands in an exploding motion. "Like, *whoa*."

"I can imagine," London replied dryly. "I hope you haven't been talking to Dad or any of his colleagues in this state."

Tiffany shook her head and hoisted herself upright. "No," she answered. "They've said a combined ten words to me all night. I knew when Dad mentioned that his colleagues would be here, I'd become invisible."

London couldn't help but assess how very visible Tiffany was as she stood and teetered against the chair. "You can't be here like this," London decided. She glanced outside again. "You're too intoxicated."

"In case you haven't noticed, we're stuck in a *box*," Tiffany replied. For some reason, this made her giggle. "There really isn't anywhere to go."

She's right London realized in defeat. As she looked around for a solution, one of her father's colleagues wandered inside from the patio and rubbed his hand over his belly.

"I'm glad the food arrived," He greeted them with a broad smile. He nodded at the trays of ballpark appetizers along the countertop. "Whoo-*eee*, I can't wait to get some of those tacos in my mouth!"

Tiffany snorted with uncontrollable laughter and London immediately pinched her wrist. "They do look delicious," she agreed with a forced smile. "Excuse me, we'll be right back."

London pushed Tiffany into the tiny bathroom and closed the door behind them. "What is the matter with you?" She whispered loudly. "In case you've forgotten, you're stuck in a box with Dad and a bunch of his executives until this game is over. You have to drink some water and pull it together."

Tiffany's head fell back as she giggled. "I'm stuck in a box and I'm not even a lesbian."

London rolled her eyes. "Are you happy?" She continued. "You got the obligatory lesbian joke out of the way. You have to get a grip."

Tiffany tried to speak but dissolved into a fit of nonsensical laughter.

London wasn't amused. "You can't go back out there."

A knock on the door quieted both of them. "Are you girls okay?" Vince called through the door. "The game is almost over. Rangers are up by two."

London glanced at Tiffany and noticed her smile had disappeared. Her pupils were still large and her face was turning a pale shade of green. "Are you okay?" She whispered.

Tiffany shook her head quickly. "No, I'm really nauseated."

"Girls?" Vince knocked on the door again. "Is everything all right?"

"Just hold it," London commanded. "I'll get you some water."

Tiffany shook her head again. "I don't think I can hold it. It's coming up, it's…"

London cracked the bathroom door with a smile. "Dad!"

He glanced quizzically at the slumped-over form behind her. "Tiffany?"

Her head shot up. "London…" she mumbled and then the vomit was everywhere on the shining ceramic tile of the bathroom floor.

London jumped out of the way and quickly shut the bathroom door in Vince's face. "She's not feeling well, Dad," she called.

"Food poisoning?" He asked through the door.

London stopped short. "Food poisoning?" She whispered to no one in particular. "*Really*, Dad?"

"You'll have to ask her when she's feeling better," London finally called back. She hated to lie.

I'm not covering for this she told herself silently. *Tiffany needs help.*

"Okay," Vince replied easily. "The game is almost over and we'll head straight home."

London listened to his retreating footsteps and cupped her hands over her mouth and nose. The bathroom reeked of sour vomit. Tiffany stared at the floor as a single tear snaked out the corner of her eye.

I shouldn't have taken Holly's call London thought guiltily. *I knew Tiffany wouldn't stay put and she'd go back to the bar. I can't leave her like this.*

"Come on," London finally said between her fingers. She nudged Tiffany's palm with her foot. "Let's get this cleaned up. Then I'm taking you to the car myself to sleep it off."

Tiffany blinked. "You'll sit with me in the car? While I try to sleep it off, I mean. Could you stay with me?"

London looked at her sister for a long moment. She nodded and swallowed hard. "Of course, Tiff. I'll stay with you."

Later that evening, after she had helped Tiffany into bed, London sat by the pool. She had rolled her jeans up to her knees and dipped her feet into the warm, still water. As it lapped gently at her calves, she ran a hand through her hair and pulled it into a messy ponytail.

Nearly midnight and it's still at least 85 degrees out here she thought. She lay on her back and stared up at the vast night sky twinkling through the pool fencing. Dozens of stars blinked back at her. Her mind wandered from the worry that chewed at her for her sister to her confusion about the promotion and finally settled on Natalie.

Her life is so different from mine she thought. *But that's one of the reasons I like her so much. Her heart is as big as her smile. Could I ask her to leave everything she's ever known?* She swallowed hard as she tried to picture Natalie living in Chicago, being part of the fast-paced bustle and blending with the loudness of the streets and the chaos of the city. She couldn't quite imagine it. *I could never take her away from Mission Bakery* she thought. *That place is her heart and soul. That leaves me with no choice. Do I stay? Could I give up my job at W.H. Young, the one consistent thing I've had over the years, and my life in Chicago for this?*

As she took a deep, relaxing breath and implored the stars for guidance, it didn't seem like the most outlandish idea. The hot stillness of the night air surrounded her like an invisible blanket and the water tickled softly against her bare legs. *This feels good* she thought lazily. *I could almost forget every…*

Just then, the patio door slid open and a figure strode to a nearby chaise. London sat up quickly, her reverie broken. Vince smiled and gave her a short wave.

"I didn't know you were still out here," he spoke. "You seem deep in thought."

London sighed. "Something like that."

"You've come to the right spot," he replied. "The pool deck is one of my favorite places to come when I need to decompress."

London glanced at her father. His eyes were on the water as he spoke and his mind seemed miles away. *Maybe now is a good time to say something about Tiffany* she thought. *But how do I bring that up? Say 'I've noticed in the short time I've been here that your daughter is a drug addict, how do you not see that?' What if Tiffany hates me for ratting her out and never forgives me?*

"Dad, how soon do you think you'll retire?" She blurted out. "You should be home more."

Vince smiled again. "That's the idea," he replied slowly. "It's going to happen sooner than later. In the next couple of years. Maybe less."

"I think, you know, that Tiffany needs someone," London went on. "It doesn't seem like she has many friends around here. Good ones, at least. And she doesn't seem very close to Diane."

Vince laughed humorlessly. "It's a miracle she even maintains a relationship with her at all."

London was momentarily silenced by her father's rare candor. She traced her fingertip along the blue tiled edge of the pool. "Was it a bad divorce?"

Vince scratched his nose as he appeared to ponder that. "Are there ever any good ones?" He countered and then sighed. "Diane wanted a lot of things in life. She wanted a comfortable lifestyle, a beautiful home, lots of spending money. She wanted to attend society events, charity galas and she loved the annual Margarita Ball. But one thing she *didn't* like was working at anything, even when it came to relationships. Ours had been deteriorating for a while, but I buried my head in the sand and ignored how unhappy we were. It was easy with the demands and travel required at the company."

"I throw myself into work when I'm unhappy too," London replied after a moment. "It just seems like Tiffany doesn't have anything. Or anyone."

"Her mother had all sorts of ideas for her when she was younger," Vince continued. "I think she thought Tiffany would be a mini version of herself. They'd go shopping, get their nails done, plan charity events, that sort of thing. But Tiffany is the opposite of her, really. She was always interested in different cultures, countries and learning about the world around her. Diane just never understood her. Instead of allowing her to develop into her own person, she gave up on Tiffany. I'm much closer to her than Diane is."

If you only knew. "I think she's lost," London replied. "She's crying out for help. You two may be closer, but you travel all the time."

"Has she mentioned these concerns to you?" Vince asked as he furrowed his brow.

London took a deep breath. "Well no, but her actions speak louder than words. She was happy overseas, but now she's back and she doesn't know what to do with herself or where to go in life."

"She's a free spirit, London," Vince replied gently. "Things like traditional schooling or business never interested her in the slightest. She's at a confusing age and I think she's feeling the pressure of having to decide on a career path. I'm trying to be patient with her and let her figure out what she really wants. After all, I never had that luxury. There was no question in my family that both my brother and I would take over Foster Holdings."

He really doesn't have a clue about Tiffany's problems London thought with a sigh. Suddenly, she couldn't bring herself to say anything more about the issues her sister faced. *Today was draining. I'm exhausted.*

"Do you ever wish you had done something else?" She asked, half-expecting her father to pretend he hadn't heard her question.

Instead, he shrugged and gazed at the water for a moment. "Doesn't much matter now," he answered honestly. "But I always wanted you and Tiffany to do whatever it is that your heart calls you to."

What if my heart is calling me to a person? London wondered. *A kind and beautiful person who owns a bakery and a food truck? What then?*

"I'm going away for the weekend," she said after a moment. "I'm spending the weekend in Haskell with someone I've been spending some time with here. She and her family were kind enough to invite me to join them for a barbecue and it…it means a lot to me. Just keep an eye on Tiffany, okay? Especially after I…" her voice trailed off lamely.

After I leave she finished silently. *Why is it so hard to say now?*

"She?" Vince raised his eyebrows and shot her a knowing glance. "All right, sweetheart. I hope you have a good time. I'm sure Tiffany will be fine."

London stood, shaking the water from her legs, and padded across the patio. She paused for a moment in the sliding glass door and stole another glance at her father. *I think that's the first time he's ever called me sweetheart.*

"Good night, Dad," she said. She waited as he met her eyes and then she smiled.

"Sleep well," he replied. "'Night, sweetheart."

CHAPTER 16

Exactly two days later, London rolled down the window of Natalie's Ford F150 as they flew over the back roads of Texas. She dangled her hand out the window, palm facing the wind, and took in the scenery around her. The long, single-lane farm highway stretched for miles ahead and there wasn't a cloud in the sky.

London stole a glance at Natalie from behind her sunglasses. Her left hand rested atop the steering wheel while her right hand held half an Oreo. She tried very hard to keep her thoughts P.G. as Natalie's tongue darted between her lips to lick some of the cream from the chocolate cookie. London shifted in her seat and took in the desolate ranch road.

I feel as though I can see for miles in every direction she thought incredulously. They had passed through a few small, dusty towns along the way. Tall white wind turbines, their distinct three blades casting long shadows over the ground, loomed further from the road.

"Oreo?" Natalie's voice cut through her thoughts.

London smiled at the open package Natalie offered to her, but she shook her head. "No, thank you," she replied.

"You're awfully quiet," Natalie commented as she set the package between them. "Is everything okay? I promise I'll try to make sure you have a good time this weekend."

London laughed. "That's not it at all," she quickly reassured her. She reached over the Oreos and squeezed Natalie's hand. "I've been looking forward to this time together. I'm just trying to take it all in."

Natalie wrinkled her nose and glanced out the driver's side window. "Take what in?" She asked. "There's nothing but ranches, farms and little towns that never progressed past 1950's."

London laughed again. "I didn't know places like this still exist," she replied. "The scenery looks like something out of an old Western movie. I've never been anywhere like this in my life."

Natalie smiled and rested her hand on London's thigh. The casual gesture made her swallow hard. She was sure the heat from Natalie's palm would sear a hole right through her jeans. *It's like she already sees me as hers* she thought. *I never wanted to be anybody's but my own. But now? Even though it's old-fashioned, I sort of...like the idea of belonging to somebody. Well, not just somebody. Natalie.*

"It's fun to see what you see," Natalie admitted. "To me, this is an old, boring farm road that I've driven hundreds of times before. But with you, it's something new and exciting."

Natalie took her hand from London's thigh and fiddled with the radio. The station had gone out a few miles back and left them with static. She twisted the dial until something finally came through the airwaves. "Sorry, it's country music," she went on sheepishly. "I don't mind it, but I'm sure you're not used to it. Unfortunately, I think this is just about all we're going to get out here."

"I don't mind," London replied confidently. "It's...fitting."

Natalie giggled. "I guess it is," she conceded. "I have some C.D.s somewhere in the back. Mostly classic rock, though. A lot of Fleetwood Mac, Rolling Stones..."

"You like Fleetwood Mac?" London asked incredulously. "They're one of my all-time favorite bands. My mom was a huge fan, she played their music all the time when I was growing up. I've always wanted to see them live."

Natalie's cheeks colored slightly. "They're one of my favorite bands too," she replied in slight surprise. "I know most people our age don't know them very well. Ever since Jane took me to a concert when I was thirteen, I've been in love with them. Granted, we were in the nosebleeds but it was still an amazing experience."

"I can imagine," London agreed excitedly. "They are easily one of the greatest rock bands of all time. Hands down."

"Definitely," Natalie started with a quick nod. She opened her mouth and then paused as London's eyes suddenly widened.

"Oh my *God*, that man is flying!" London interrupted in shock. She did a full 180-degree turn in the passenger's seat and winced as the belt cut into her ribcage. "Natalie, that guy is flying!"

Natalie eased her foot over the brake and looked at London as though she had grown a second head. "What?"

London pointed silently. "I…I don't know what else to call it," she went on excitedly. "He's just…*flying*."

Natalie leaned over the steering wheel and followed London's finger. She burst into laughter. "He's crop dusting," she replied through her giggles. "That's all."

"That looks so dangerous!" London exclaimed in awe. "He could fall at any minute. How can he just hang on a rope like that over that field? I'd be terrified I'd fall, or the wind would be too strong…"

Natalie's laughter was infectious and soon London was giggling too. "I'm *not* crazy," she insisted. She crossed her arms and tried to keep a straight face. "He's flying."

"He's spraying insecticide onto his crops to protect them from bugs and animals. Most people out here are born into farming. It's probably been a part of his family for generations," Natalie tried to explain.

"That," London continued as she paused and aimed her phone through the window. "Is the craziest thing I think I have ever seen." She bit the tip of her tongue in concentration as she carefully zoomed in on the farmer and snapped a photo. "And I'm from Chicago. I'd probably pee my pants if I was up there."

Natalie grinned. "So the tough and mysterious London Foster admits she's afraid of something," she teased. "Not a fan of heights?"

London shook her head. "Not at all," she confirmed. "And I am *not* tough and mysterious."

"Uh-huh," Natalie replied dryly. She slipped her fingers between

London's. "And that's okay. I know you've been through a lot and I know I've broken down a lot more of those walls than most. But I'm telling you right now that I'm going to break through them all," she paused and shot a shy smile at her. "As long as you don't keep anything from me. Deal?"

London leaned back against the headrest and watched Natalie for a long moment. *I have to tell her about the promotion* she realized as her stomach did a nervous flip. *But what if she stops seeing me? I don't want to let her go.*

"Okay," she murmured with a smile. She lifted Natalie's hand to her lips and kissed the soft skin between her thumb and index finger. "Do you always have this effect on people? Or am I just the lucky one?"

Natalie blushed. "I told you that day we were at the park," she replied. "Different is good."

London gazed out the window, their hands still intertwined. *I'm worlds away from W.H. Young, Chicago and everything I've ever known* she realized. *And Natalie is right.* This *feels right. Sitting next to her and holding her hand feels right in ways I don't fully understand.*

"Here's Haskell," Natalie announced proudly. She slowed her truck to a respectable 35 miles per hour as they entered the town limits and the farm road became First Street. A modest blue and white sign greeted them. Black plastic letters spelled out "Pray For Rain" just beneath the simple script announcing the town.

London looked around slowly. The small downtown area consisted of aged brick buildings with faded awnings reaching over a narrow, cracked sidewalk. Most of the downtown businesses were shuttered, with the exception of a pharmacy, a jewelry store and a tiny dive bar. They rolled slowly past a square brick building with an attached garage. A sign posted in front of it noted that it was the city hall. Old air conditioning units dangled precariously from each window of the building.

"Wow," London murmured as she craned her neck this way and that. "I've only ever read about places like this."

A small red and white sign with a large arrow advertised local church services and pointed down a wide side street. An image of a man kneeling before a cross, his hat in his hands and his saddled horse behind him, was below the words "Cowboy Church."

"Welcome to the Wild West," Natalie said with a teasing grin. She laughed as London took a quick photo of the church sign. "Is it as enthralling as you'd hoped?"

London nodded. "This is a whole new world, Silva," she replied with a smile. "Hey, what's a cowboy church?"

Natalie shrugged. "Not very different from a regular Christian church, just with a distinct Western…flair, if you will," she replied. Lots of these rural farm towns have them. They're huge in cowboy culture and there's a lot of that out here. Lots of singing country songs. Sometimes the services take place in a barn or rodeo arena, wherever they can find space. Baptisms are in wash bins or farm tanks. Think old-fashioned revival-type culture."

London felt her eyes widen. "I don't think I would fit in at a cowboy church."

Natalie laughed. "You and me both. What can I say? It's the Lone Star State."

London stared out the window as they turned down a residential street. The small ranch homes were scattered far apart along the flat landscape. She estimated it was about a half-mile from the last house before Natalie pulled into a long gravel driveway. Small rocks kicked against the undercarriage of her truck as the tires crunched up the driveway. She paused just before an aluminum carport. Two vehicles were already parked neatly in the shade.

London stepped out of the truck gingerly as she took in her surroundings. The yard was a flat square of fine brown dirt, with small patches of yellowed grass near the house. London could feel dry blades crunch beneath her tennis shoes as she stepped around the truck to help Natalie with their bags. Jagged lines split the dirt from where the baked Earth had opened up due to the omnipresent sun and stifling heat.

She glanced up as Natalie handed her a bag and met her warm smile. "Come on," she said as she nodded her head toward the door. "Everybody's inside and they can't wait to meet you."

London's nerves twisted in her stomach as she followed Natalie up the walkway. *I want her family to like me* she realized. *I want them to see that I can be good for her too.*

Natalie opened the front door and grimaced as it creaked loudly on rusted hinges. London stepped closer to her and felt Natalie gently squeeze her hand reassuringly.

A woman about their age, with thick brown curls tied back in a loose bun, greeted them in the tight foyer. She embraced Natalie enthusiastically.

"Hey!" She said excitedly. "I'm so glad you made it safely. Isabella is beside herself. This weekend is all she's been talking about."

Natalie grinned and glanced at London. "London, this is my best friend Paula Ortiz," she introduced. "Paula, this is London Foster."

London stuck her hand out politely, but Paula smiled and pulled her into a hug. "None of that handshake stuff here," she replied with a laugh. "We hug."

Natalie laughed. "I should've warned you," she went on. "They're huggers."

"Don't let her fool you," Paula spoke warmly to London. "Natalie is the biggest lover of us all."

London immediately felt her anxiety begin to melt away at her kindness. "It's nice to meet you."

"Nice to finally meet you too," Paula replied with a grin. "Natalie has told me a lot…"

"All *right*, Paula," Natalie cut in as a blush crept up her neck. "Where is everybody?"

"My little monster is outside in the backyard," Paula began. She paused and looked at London. "I love my daughter past the moon. But some days require more caffeine than others to keep up with her. This happens to be one of those days."

"She's not that bad," Natalie cut in with a wave of her hand. "She's a sweetheart."

"Must take after her mom," Paula replied as Natalie rolled her eyes. "Anyway, Celia has the grill fired up and she's getting ready to put the first round of meat on." She paused again. "Wait, London, you're not a vegetarian, are you?"

London shook her head quickly as Paula put a hand over her heart in relief.

"Oh, thank *God*!" She exclaimed. "We brought just enough bird food for Jane. She's got some discipline, that one. I don't know if you've ever been to a real Mexican barbecue before, but we're about to feast on some delicious *carne asada*, smoked tamales, brisket tacos, adobo pork chops…"

"All y'all brought all that food?" Natalie asked incredulously.

London bit back a smile. *She sounds so cute when she lets that Southern accent sneak through.*

"Yes, and *you* know how these things go," Paula countered. "We make food for twenty when there's only a handful of us. Even when Isabella takes three bites from everything on her plate and then says she's full."

"*Natalie!*" The elated voice of a child screeched from the yard. All three women turned as Isabella sprinted through the back door and down the hallway. She wrapped her arms around Natalie's waist. "You made it!"

Natalie laughed and bent to hug her. "Of course I did," she replied. "Did you really think I'd miss your birthday party?"

London observed the scene quietly. *These are some of the friendliest people I've met in a long time* she thought. *It's obvious they're a family.*

"No, I knew you'd be here," Isabella replied confidently.

"This is my friend, London," Natalie gestured to her. "Can you say hi?"

Isabella smiled at her. "Hi, London," she greeted her. "So are you and Natalie girlfriends?"

London's mouth dropped open and she quickly looked to Natalie, whose blush had returned with a vengeance. "I, uh…" she stammered.

Paula laughed and squeezed her daughter's shoulder lightly. "*Mija*, that's none of our business," she scolded her. "London is here as Natalie's guest and we're all going to have lots of fun today."

It was remarkable how much Isabella resembled a miniature version of Paula and London was about to say so, when a small dog yelped and raced through the open back door.

"What the…" Natalie started.

"Isabella's birthday present," Paula replied. "She's been asking for a dog for years. With Rudy on these long assignments, I wouldn't mind having a dog at the house either."

Isabella grinned and plopped onto the floor. The dog immediately hunkered down in her lap. She petted him gently and then looked up at Natalie. "This is Niko. Mommy and I picked him out yesterday."

"Wow, Isabella, that's awesome," Natalie replied. She knelt down and scratched Niko's floppy ears. "He's wonderful."

Paula smiled and then gestured to the kitchen. "She's barely let him out of her sight since we brought him home," she went on. "They're in love and I have to admit that it's pretty damn cute. Do either of you want a beer?"

Both Natalie and London politely shook their heads as they stepped around Isabella and Niko.

Paula rolled her eyes. "Fine," she continued. "But we're all doing a shot of Patron after Isabella goes to bed."

Natalie shook her head ruefully and glanced at London. "Yes, that's my best friend."

"Hey, *I'm* your best friend," Isabella piped up behind them. "Remember Natalie? You said."

Paula put a hand on her hip and pretended to be offended. "Is that so?" She asked. "You're replacing me with a younger, cuter version?"

Natalie laughed. "How about this? You're both my *family* and that's even better. And, speaking of, where are those aunts of mine? London, we'd better go track them down and say hello."

London grinned as a sense of comfort washed over her. *I've never felt so welcomed anywhere, so quickly* she marveled. *It's almost like this is what I've been missing for so long.* She quickly buried that last thought. *Whatever happens, I have a feeling this is going to be an unforgettable weekend.*

CHAPTER 17

"*Tia!*" Natalie called as she held London's hand loosely and guided them through the backyard. A cloud of smoke from the barbecue momentarily shrouded Celia, who stood tall behind the shining grill.

"My sweet *Natalia*," Celia greeted her with a smile and hug. "You got here just in time. I put the first set of pork chops on the grill just a minute ago."

Natalie gestured to London. "And you remember my friend, London."

"Ah yes, our hard-working food truck helper," Celia replied with a smile. She gave her a quick nod. "It's nice to see you again."

Natalie knew that her aunt had realized their relationship had progressed beyond the lines of friendship. *Not that I've tried to hide it* she thought with a small smile. *There's just something about her.* She didn't have much time to dwell on Celia's polite but distant greeting to London. She felt Jane's arms snake around her waist and give her a quick embrace from behind.

"Hi, honey," Jane said with a smile. "I was just getting the patio table set up. Why don't you two come sit with me in the shade and let Celia do the cooking for us tonight?"

"That's not much different from any other night," Celia cut in dryly. Natalie was happy to see the usual gleam that lit her aunt's eyes when Jane was nearby.

"Are you sure we can't help with anything?" London asked.

"No, no," Celia replied with a wave of her hand. "You girls sit and enjoy yourselves. Food will be up soon."

Jane fell into step with London as they made their way to the long, rectangular picnic table. A large umbrella shaded most of it from the brutal sun.

"It's lovely to meet you, London," Jane said. She paused as they reached the table and hugged her. "I'm so glad you could join us."

Natalie met London's eyes. "See?" She told her. "Huggers."

There was something in London's eyes when she looked at her that Natalie hadn't seen before. *There's this trusting openness in them now* she realized. *And it's making me want to kiss her right there on the patio.*

Natalie glanced at her other aunt, who was focused on the meat sizzling before her. "Is Celia all right?" She asked as they sat down.

Jane smiled kindly. "Oh Natalie, you know she thinks the world of you," she replied. "And you also know that she has a tendency to be, well…"

"Over-protective?" Natalie supplied.

Jane sighed. "I was going to say *caring*. She loves you very much." She turned to London and patted her knee reassuringly. "Celia just tends to be a little protective when it comes to her niece."

London smiled and sat up straighter. "She doesn't have anything to worry about," she replied. She glanced quickly at Natalie and then back at Jane. "I wouldn't do anything to hurt her."

Natalie felt those familiar butterflies flutter deep in her stomach as she reached over and held London's hand.

Jane smiled broadly. "I'm very glad to hear that, London," she said as she took a sip of sweet tea. The ice cubes clinked against the tall, skinny glass. "And what a unique name that is."

London shrugged. "To be honest, I'm not even sure how my parents came up with it. They split up before I was born. I'd like to think that maybe they just wanted me to be a little different."

Jane nodded thoughtfully. "Different is good."

Natalie watched as a look of surprise passed over London's face. "So I keep hearing," she replied wryly.

"I tell you, I wish I'd had a unique name growing up," Jane went on. "I can't tell you how many other girls named Jane went to my school. Sometimes there were a bunch of us in the same class! We had a Jane S., Jane O., a Jane C...In fact, I briefly changed my name to Sunflower around 1974."

London's eyes shot up. "Sunflower?"

Jane smiled mysteriously. "Yes, though it was short-lived," she replied as she stood. "But that's a story for another time. I'm going to bring out that pitcher of sweet tea. Do you girls need anything?"

"Two glasses would be perfect, thank you," Natalie spoke. She turned to London as Jane disappeared into the house. "You've got to try the sweet tea. My aunt Jane makes it herself and she lets it sit out in the sun for *six* hours…"

She paused when she realized that London was staring at her, a grin playing at her lips. "What?"

"Your family is *awesome*," she replied.

Natalie laughed. "I'm glad you think so," she said. "You fit right in."

"Really?" The dubious expression shadowing London's face told Natalie that she didn't quite believe her.

"*Yes*," Natalie assured her. She squeezed her hand. "We're all unique in our own way, London. It's our love and affection for each other that brings us together, despite our differences. That's *family*. We color each other's worlds and allow ourselves to see things from different perspectives because of it."

London grinned and held their hands in her lap. "Well, I *really* like your affection for me."

There was a lot that Natalie wanted to say, but she wasn't sure how to articulate it all into words that would make sense. Instead, she let herself watch how the sunlight sparkled in London's icy-blue eyes and danced across her face.

"You know what?" She said after a moment. "Your eyes look beautiful when the light hits them like that."

She watched as London bit her lip and appeared momentarily stunned. "Natalie Silva, I swear I could kiss you right here at this picnic table," she replied.

Jane set two glasses down in front of them and chuckled. "Now, now," she said lightly. "There will be plenty of time for kisses when the lights go down and y'all head to bed."

London reddened at being overhead, but Natalie didn't mind. She held her eyes for a moment longer and smiled. The sensual warmth that radiated between them made nighttime seem like lightyears away. *As much as I can't wait to be kissed good and hard, what I really want is to feel her sleeping next to me* Natalie thought.

Her mind was a million miles away as Isabella jogged into the yard with Niko energetically running beside her. Paula stomped outside from the kitchen and slid into a chair at the end of the table.

"Is everything okay?" Natalie asked. A quick glance at Isabella told her that she was too busy laughing and tossing a Frisbee to Niko to notice anything amiss.

Paula rubbed her forehead for a moment. "Rudy," she said flatly. "I just got off the phone with him. His boss let him know they need him for another two weeks once his initial contract is up."

Natalie looked at her friend sympathetically. "I'm sorry," she replied. "He's been gone a while, huh?"

Paula nodded and took a deep breath. "I feel like a single parent sometimes," she admitted. "It's hard. Isabella can be a handful sometimes and I'm the only one in charge of the house, our daughter, errands, cooking, cleaning. Plus I go to work part-time…"

"If there's anything I can do to help, you know I'm a phone call away," Natalie said gently.

Paula groaned but reached over and touched Natalie's forearm in gratitude. "I appreciate it more than you know, Nat," she replied. "But now we're *definitely* doing that shot of Patron later."

"Food is ready!" Celia shouted from the large grill. Thin clouds of gray smoke emanated from the hot cast-iron bars separating their dinner from the burning charcoal.

"Birthday girl," Paula called. "Let's put Niko back in the house while we eat, okay?"

Isabella nodded and trudged to the back door with the puppy at her heels.

Natalie turned to the table and smiled at Jane, who had fallen half-asleep and was snoozing in the shade. As she looked around at all of the people she loved, her gaze finally fell on London. With her faded jeans and navy blue tank top fitting her just right and her black hair down around her face, she looked far more like a laid-back Texas girl than a big-city business woman.

She's even more tan now than she was when I first met her Natalie thought as she cocked her head. *Not that she was ever really tan. I guess even London can't escape the Texas sun.*

London glanced at her and raised an eyebrow. "What?"

Natalie grinned sheepishly at being caught checking her out. She waited a moment for Paula and Jane to grab empty Styrofoam plates and head to the grill before stepping close to London. She didn't miss the tiny hairs that stood up on the other woman's arms. Her lips were mere millimeters from London's earlobe as she whispered quietly.

"You're gorgeous, you know that?"

London had never felt more full of food before in her life. Her first heaping plate of barbecued meat and grilled vegetables had filled her stomach, but Celia and Natalie had insisted she take seconds. After most of the food had disappeared, the group had migrated to the front of the home. London sat on a wooden porch swing in the shade and rested her hand lightly against her stomach. Flecks of white paint had chipped off the swing and two of its chains were brown with rust, but it was padded with a thick, comfortable cushion.

She watched with a smile as Natalie sat cross-legged on a patch of grass in the front yard and tossed a baseball to Niko. She threw her head back and laughed, her face tipped skyward toward the fading sun, as both the puppy and Isabella raced after the ball. Paula and Jane had shooed them out of the house to clean up the kitchen, ignoring their protests to help.

London swallowed as she heard the front door creak open and saw a shadow in her peripheral vision. Her suspicions were confirmed as Celia eased next to her onto the swing. She sighed satisfactorily as she relaxed back against the cushion.

"You full?" Celia asked. "We have homemade apple pie and vanilla ice cream for dessert, but I don't know if anyone is going to have any room left for sweets."

London smiled politely. "It sounds delicious, but I think my stomach is already sticking out two inches further than it did when I walked in the door earlier. Everything was so good."

The corners of Celia's eyes crinkled in amusement. "I bet you can't get good home-grilled Tex-Mex like this in Chicago."

London shook her head slowly. "No, you can't."

She knew the next question was coming even before the words were out of Celia's mouth. "How long are you planning to stay in Texas?"

There it is she thought. *What am I supposed to say? I never expected any of this. Or her.* Her gaze fell to Natalie again. The other woman leaned back on her elbows in the yard as Niko rested comfortably in her lap. Natalie and the puppy watched as Isabella demonstrated the cartwheels she was explaining she'd learned in P.E. class.

London opened her mouth to answer, but Celia continued. "You care about her a lot," she went on. London realized she had followed her eyes directly to Natalie. "I can see it all over your face. You are falling for her, no?"

She opened her mouth again and then nodded. She didn't take her eyes from Natalie. "Yes," she finally replied. "I am."

Clarity she thought. *Finally. It feels good to admit it out loud.*

"I know," Celia replied simply. "I know you are. And I know that Natalie feels the same. If I may, I'd like to tell you that there's something different about the two of you. Natalie doesn't fall for someone easily and she doesn't bring companions around often. Not that she's had many. You're special to each other and I don't know if either of you realize it just yet."

"It's beginning to sink in," London responded quietly.

"I won't tell you anything you probably haven't already thought about, London," Celia continued. "I won't waste your time with things that have already crossed your mind. What I *will* do is give you some insight to my niece. One of the reasons I'm so protective over her is because she's never lost that light that some people have inside them. You know what I mean? People go through things, tough times in life, and that light fades. They let themselves become angry or bitter and they're not the same. But Natalie? No matter what she's been through, she's never lost that bright shining light inside of her. She continues to smile, she keeps believing the very best in people and she doesn't let things destroy her."

I was that angry, bitter person London thought. *I let some of the worst things I've gone through in life change me when I should've been stronger instead.* She felt a smile pull at her lips as she stole another glance at Natalie. *But it's not too late.*

"You don't find many women like that," she agreed softly. "She's amazing."

Celia smiled and London felt a sudden sense of relaxation in the air between them.

"Her parents love her very much," Celia went on. "When they made the decision for Natalie to live with Jane and I, it was because they knew that she had potential and could do much better in a stable home. Not so much moving around and changing schools. She never had a chance to make many friends and she was a lonesome child. They knew it wasn't good for her. But, *Dios Mio*, she was always so smart. I thought eventually she'd begin acting out, getting angry and saying her parents had abandoned her, but she never did. She took everything in stride."

"I'm sure it was a difficult decision for them," London replied carefully. *I couldn't imagine being faced with a situation like that* she thought. *Having to sacrifice my child being raised by me to ensure she had the best life possible.* Her heart went out to Natalie as she thought of her at twelve years old, young and shy, saying good-bye to her parents.

"It tore their hearts apart," Celia confirmed sadly. "But she still talks to them on the phone or by Skype at least two or three times per week. My brother is retired now and they live in Montana. *Natalia* looks just like her momma."

London smiled. "I want us to be together," she replied suddenly. The words had jumped from her mouth before she had a chance to bite her tongue. *I never realized how true it is until just now* she realized.

"One thing that I can promise you about Natalie is that she will always have that light inside of her," Celia commented gently. "She will always uplift you if you're down or do everything in her power to make you smile if you're sad. My biggest fear is seeing that happiness disappear from her eyes and to see her get broken. She's a good girl. She's loyal to the ones she loves and she doesn't play games."

London glanced at Celia. For the first time, she genuinely noticed the worry that creased the delicate skin around her dark eyes. "I hope Natalie can see that I…" she started, but was interrupted by Isabella's ear-splitting scream.

CHAPTER 18

Both London and Celia shot up and scanned the yard. As if in slow motion, London spotted the sudden explosion of chaos. Niko had taken off wildly after a rabbit and was sprinting toward the street. A four-door pick-up truck was barreling down the narrow two-lane road in the distance.

"Niko!" Isabella screamed in terror. Without warning, she ran after him. Her brown hair streamed out behind her and her feet pounded against the Earth behind him as she tried to catch up.

"Oh my God!" Celia shouted at the same time that London bolted from the porch.

Natalie jogged behind them, but she was too far across the yard. She cupped her hands around her mouth. "Isabella, *stop!*"

"That's my puppy!" She yelled back. Her voice was high and frantic, but she didn't break her run. "I have to get him!"

"Get back here!" Natalie shouted as her jog turned into a full-blown chase across the property.

London caught up her quickly and easily sprinted around her. *Time for all those long nights in the gym to pay off for me* she thought grimly. She glanced down the road and could see the truck speeding closer. *They may have gotten a head start, but I know I'm faster.*

London guessed that the pick-up truck was flying down the road at about 60 miles per hour, judging by the swirling cloud of dirt in its wake. It showed no signs of slowing. With her eyes locked onto Niko and Isabella, she had one thought running on a single track in her mind. *Get them out of the way. Get them out of the way. Get them out of the way.*

She blinked and focused on the long brown hair flying in the breeze just ahead. *If I could just reach out...Get the back of her shirt...* She was so close that she could practically grab Isabella. Her lungs burned with the sudden sprint and her chest pounded with adrenaline.

London reached out with both arms. *Even if I push her down, as gently as I can...Anything is better than her running into that street* she thought. With a final burst, she propelled herself forward and fisted handfuls of Isabella's t-shirt. Their legs tangled up and they skidded over a wide swath of gravel shoulder that separated the road from the land.

She fell to the left, pulling Isabella with her, but managed to push her shoulder between the child's face and the hard, rocky gravel. They collapsed in a heap as the truck flew past with a deep bellow of its horn.

"Asshole!" London shouted into the wind. She was afraid to open her eyes.

Isabella lay still and crumpled on top of her for a long moment. London's chest heaved up and down as she panted for the air that had been whacked from her lungs with the fall. Her heartbeat was deafening in her ears. She tried to reach out with her left arm, but a throbbing sensation radiated from the shoulder they had landed on.

Please God, I know you haven't heard much from me lately she thought desperately. *But please, please let Isabella be all right.* She gingerly lifted her right arm and gently rubbed the young girl's bony spine. Several pairs of running footsteps reached them all at once.

Paula deftly lifted Isabella from the pile and clutched her to her chest. "What is wrong with you, *mija*? You could have died! Do you have any idea what would happen to me if you got hit by that truck? You are my world, I would die too! You can never go running into the street like that again, do you understand me? You are in *so* much trouble, young lady," she paused for a breath. "You are in so much trouble, but I love you so much. Do you understand that you can never do that again?"

Isabella blinked and appeared shell-shocked. She nodded silently and wrapped her skinny arms around her mother as the sobs finally came.

London was flooded with relief despite the pain. Two pairs of strong arms helped lift her to her feet and she tried in vain to brush herself off. She looked up and met Celia's eyes. Jane stood beside her and covered her mouth with shaking hands.

"I'm okay," London said quickly. "I swear." She rubbed her left shoulder. "I guess all those hours running on the treadmill were good for something." She grinned weakly.

"There aren't enough words to thank you," Paula said shakily as she held Isabella close to her. "All I can say is thank you, from the bottom of my heart, for grabbing my little girl. Who knows what could have happened. I just…" she paused and swallowed hard. "Just *thank you*."

London nodded, unsure what to say. She glanced up again and her eyes immediately locked onto Natalie's fiery gaze. She stood a few feet behind her aunts and her arms were crossed tightly over her chest. The intensity in her expression was like nothing London had ever seen. A silent tear rolled down her cheek.

Oh my God, she thinks I hurt Isabella London thought in horror. "Natalie, I…"

Before she could finish her sentence, Natalie launched herself into her arms. She buried her face in London's neck and wrapped her legs around her waist as she held herself tightly against her.

London caught her easily, despite the searing pain in her shoulder. She stroked her hair and held her close for a moment. "Hey, it's okay," she whispered. "Everyone is fine."

"I can't believe you caught up to her like that," Natalie's voice was muffled against her neck. "You were a split second away from being…" She sniffled. "I thought you and Isabella were…"

London rubbed her back gently. "But we're *not*," she reminded her quickly. "We're all okay."

Natalie took a small step back and held London's face in her hands. She studied her for a long moment. "And don't you ever think about doing anything like that again!" She went on as her voice grew louder. "You could have been *killed*! I was so scared that I was about to lose you and Isabella forever. Don't you ever go running off like that again and putting yourself in danger and nearly getting yourself killed and…and…I swear London Foster, you'd better kiss me right now or I'll…"

London grinned and wrapped her arms around her waist. She pressed her lips against Natalie's, swiftly silencing her. Natalie tightened her arms around London's middle and took a deep breath.

"I can't lose you," she whispered.

"You won't," London replied gently. *I never want to let her go.* "I promise."

An excited yip from across the road made them all turn in mutual astonishment. Niko stood a few feet from the road and shook his tail.

"No way," London said with a blink. "I thought that dog would have been halfway back to Fort Worth by now, with the way he was going after that rabbit. Never underestimate a puppy that's spotted a small critter."

"He didn't run away!" Isabella shrieked in glee. "Look Mommy, Niko is okay!"

"That damn dog better be thanking his lucky stars that we have a fenced backyard," Paula said. She took two steps toward the street. "See Bella, I'm looking both ways." She made a point of scanning the road each way for a long moment. It was deserted. "*Now* I will cross the street and get him."

Paula stomped across the street and plucked Niko from a patch of grass. She nuzzled him against her chest and checked him over. "From now on, when we're not at home, he needs to on a leash outside. Can you make sure of that, sweetheart?"

Isabella nodded quickly and jumped up and down in excitement as Paula crossed back over the empty road. She took the puppy from her mother and hugged him close to her. "Yes, Mommy," she promised. "He's already my best friend in the world. Everything happened so fast. One second he was running after the baseball and then the next second he saw that bunny."

Paula laid a hand on her shoulder and gently guided them back to the house. "He's so fast and I thought I was too, but I couldn't catch him," Isabella chattered away as she carefully carried Niko. "I don't ever want anything to happen to him. Maybe he should be on a leash in our yard too…"

Her voice faded as they got closer to the house and then disappeared in front door. Natalie wrapped an arm around London's waist.

"Come on, we need to get you cleaned up," she spoke softly. "This is enough excitement for one evening."

London half-listened as Jane told Natalie which linen closet had the fresh towels and toiletries. She felt Celia fall into step with her as they trudged toward the house.

"You did good, *mija*," Celia murmured. She patted her arm fondly. "I...We...can't thank you enough. You're going to be good for her."

London's head shot up in surprise as Celia continued ahead into the house. She grinned as Jane and Natalie, none the wiser, went from discussing bathroom towels to the water pressure in the second shower.

First Dad calls me sweetheart and now this she thought as her smile widened. *Celia called me mija.*

Natalie knelt on the cool bathroom tile and slowly swabbed a wet tissue over the thin, raised scratches that criss-crossed London's left shoulder, arm and ribcage. They were bright red and angry against her otherwise smooth, creamy skin. London sat gingerly on the edge of the bathtub in her bra and a pair of track shorts. Natalie didn't miss London's toes curling against the tile or the quick bite on her bottom lip as she tried to clean her scratches as gently as possible.

Luckily, all that gravel did was leave superficial cuts and bruises on both of them Natalie thought gratefully. They had taken turns showering, but she had demanded that London let her clean and bandage her cuts. She tried very hard not to stare at the soft cleavage resting snugly against London's black bra or the toned, strong stomach that betrayed the amount of time she spent in the gym.

Natalie paused and dipped the wadded tissue back into a large bottle of Neosporin. She caught London watching her warily and she smiled. She slid her fingers lightly up London's leg and paused just above her knee.

"Hey," she whispered. "I know it stings, but I don't want you to get an infection. Are you okay?"

London stared at a point on the wall just beyond Natalie's head. "I'm fine," she insisted. "Really. It's all surface wounds."

There she goes, trying to be tough again Natalie thought with a grin. She sat back on the balls of her feet and dabbed the tissue against the reddened, raw lines along her ribcage. A purplish-black bruise was beginning to bloom behind one of the deeper cuts. London winced as Natalie held the tissue over that area for a lingering moment.

"It's okay to let someone take care of you, you know," Natalie spoke casually. "You don't always have to be in charge."

London looked as though she was about to argue for a moment but then thought better of it. She leaned against the corner of the shower in defeat and sighed. "I know."

Natalie stood and held out her hand. "Come on," she replied. "Let's get comfortable."

She was surprised at how quickly London accepted her hand and lifted herself to her full height before her. They held each other's eyes and regarded one another for a moment. *We're the same height* Natalie realized. *Eye to eye. Face to face. Chest to chest. Body to…body.*

Natalie led London to the guest bed. It was smaller than the one at London's father's house and it was covered in a thick red and pink flowered quilt that her grandmother had knitted decades ago. The flooring throughout the home was brown clay tile and it was cold beneath Natalie's feet. She quickly wriggled under the quilt and situated herself against an oversized pillow.

London let out a satisfactory sigh as she relaxed against another pillow. She extended her right arm out to Natalie and smiled. "You feel so far away."

Natalie laughed. "I'm right here."

London shook her head. "Closer."

Natalie grinned as she settled herself against her warm body and felt London wrap her arm around her shoulders. She reached over and switched off the bedside lamp. They lay in silence for a few moments as Natalie memorized the sound of London's slow breathing and the way her chest would rise and fall in the shadows.

She took a deep breath and tried to ignore the lingering ache that had gradually developed between her thighs. *Lord help me if anyone else sleeping in this house tonight hears what I'm about to do* she thought. Natalie traced her fingertips along London's profile and down her neck. An excited thrill ran down her spine as London turned and met her lips in the dark.

The kiss started off innocently enough, but the feeling of London's tongue gently exploring her mouth and her body pressed against her own made it impossible to continue ignoring the desire that slowly burned its way from the inside out.

Natalie opened her mouth and deepened the kiss as London tightened her arms around her. A low moan escaped her throat as she pressed herself as close as she could and then found herself on top of London. The chemistry between them exploded and suddenly they were everywhere on each other's bodies.

The kisses never stopped as London's hands explored the small of Natalie's back and her fingertips inched their way further beneath the hem of her t-shirt. Natalie enjoyed the sweet sensations of the other woman discovering her body and wound her fingers in London's hair as she kissed along the shell of her ear.

A bedroom door further down the hallway opened and shut. They paused and stilled for a moment as someone padded into the kitchen and opened the refrigerator. They both giggled silently, holding their hands over their mouths, until the worn mattress shook under them.

Natalie met London's eyes in the dark. "So how many times have you actually let yourself get topped?" She whispered with a grin.

London shifted, but Natalie held her ground. "Just because you're on top of me doesn't necessarily mean…" she started.

"Yes, it does," Natalie cut in. She swooped down and kissed London defiantly. "I'm not done taking care of you yet."

London's mouth dropped open as the other bedroom door shut again. "You don't have to…"

Natalie kissed London again and realized the heat that simmered between them was quickly boiling over. In the silence of the old house, it was practically quiet enough to hear a pin drop.

"You better get used to being topped sometimes," Natalie teased. She sucked gently at the soft, sensitive area just behind London's ear. "I like *giving* as much as I like getting. Or giving *while* I'm getting." Natalie felt a small thrill as London met her lips with abandon and submitted herself to her.

Natalie gently guided London's hand over her underwear. She slipped her own hand into London's shorts and over the thin bikini briefs that were nearly soaked through.

"Do you feel what we do to each other?" Natalie whispered. She kissed further down London's neck and shivered as the other woman's fingers curled against her sensitive areas.

"Natalie..." London started.

She kissed the corner of her mouth. "Yes?"

"I...I want you," London said between breaths. She arched herself against Natalie's fingers, begging with her body for a closer touch. "I want you, Natalie."

"You have to be quiet," Natalie said with a smile. "Just focus on my body, your breath and my tongue against you."

London groaned softly, closing her eyes, and then clapped both hands over her mouth. Natalie instantly missed London's teasing fingers working slowly against her. She slid down her body, taking the quilt with her, and gently pushed London's bra straps over her shoulders. She kissed along the inside of her breast and slowly ran her tongue over her nipple. Natalie smiled against the soft ivory skin as she listened to London's breath hitch. She sucked her nipple into her mouth and let her tongue explore what London liked.

Natalie listened to London's quickened breath and the rustling of sheets in her balled up fists. *Slow and steady it is* she thought as London arched her back against her mouth. Satisfied that she was quickly discovering London's most intimate preferences, Natalie nibbled down the edges of her stomach and took extra care to brush feather-light kisses over the cuts and scratches on her left side.

Natalie slowly peeled London's shorts and underwear off together. She breathed deeply, feeling the urgency between her own legs increasing as she inhaled the scent of London's arousal. Natalie desperately wanted to take her time and tease London until her body exploded. She forced herself to take another deep breath.

She glanced up at London, her eyes closed and her nipples standing at hard peaks, and she momentarily lost her nerve. A thin, silvery slice of moonlight from between the threadbare curtains washed over London's face and shoulders. *She looks almost ethereal* Natalie thought, mesmerized. *She's gorgeous.*

"Hey, Moon Child," she murmured as she dropped a kiss onto London's inner thigh.

London's eyes opened halfway. A slow smile lit her face as she met Natalie's gaze. "What did you…"

I think I'm falling in love with you Natalie thought silently. Instead, she smiled back at her for a long, lingering moment. "You're beautiful."

Natalie eased herself between London's thighs as she gently explored her labia and teased the tip of her tongue in slow, lazy circles around her entrance. London let out a small, muffled cry between her fingers as her breathing grew heavier.

Natalie's tongue flicked over her as she slid her fingers over her hardened nipples. *Slow and steady* she reminded herself. Her tongue teased her most sensitive area, massaging and exploring, as London writhed against the bed. Her hands pressed against Natalie's shoulders and her short fingernails dug into her skin, but London dutifully remained quiet.

Suddenly everything that Natalie was kissing and licking was flooded with sweet wetness. She braced herself as London's hips lifted off the mattress and her body froze. She gripped Natalie's arms tightly and then her pitched inhales became slow, deep breaths.

Natalie gently eased herself next to London and reached over to curl a sweaty lock of black hair behind her ear. She laughed in surprise as London kissed her. She let her deepen the kiss and explore her mouth. After a moment, London pulled back and smiled at her.

"What?" Natalie whispered.

"I can taste myself on your mouth," London replied.

"You were really wet," Natalie murmured. She watched as London blinked sleepily.

"Your fault," London appeared to decide. Her voice grew thinner and Natalie knew she was fighting sleep. "You *made* me really wet."

Natalie shifted on the bed and pulled London under the quilt with her. She spooned London's bare back and wrapped her arm protectively around her middle. "We've always seemed to have that effect on each other," she whispered. "You know it and I know it."

Natalie felt London relax against her. She leaned over and kissed her earlobe. "Good night."

London stiffened for a second and tried to sit up. "Wait, I want to…"

"I know," Natalie murmured. She tried to ignore the throbbing between her legs. *I might kick myself for this later.* "And I know you're exhausted too. We have all weekend together."

Natalie felt herself fading into warmth as London relaxed again. Her own breathing slowed evenly and she was just about to fall into a deep, contented sleep when London's low, lethargic voice cut into her consciousness.

"I love you, *Natalia*."

CHAPTER 19

Natalie could feel her best friend's wary eyes on her as she chopped onions and spinach nervously against a bamboo cutting board. She took a deep breath, avoiding Paula's knowing stare, and dumped the contents of the cutting board into a pan. The vegetables sizzled in olive oil and Natalie poked at them with a spoon.

"Are you going to tell me what's up with you this morning or am I going to have to drag it out of you?" Paula finally asked. She eased herself onto a stool at the breakfast bar.

Natalie glanced furtively at the closed door of the guest bedroom. London was still sound asleep. She could hear stirrings coming from the master bedroom and she knew her aunts were getting ready for the day.

"London told me she loves me," Natalie finally murmured. She tried not to smile as Paula clapped her hands over her mouth.

"She did?" She asked with an incredulous grin. "Natalie, that's amazing! I'm telling you, I have a good feeling about this one. The way she looks at you…It's like you're the only person in the entire world. You're different towards her too. Like, you're extra caring and loving with her. Tell me everything. How did she say it?"

Natalie bit her lip and then peered down the hallway. "That's the thing…" she started hesitantly. "Wait, where's Isabella?"

Paula blinked. "In the backyard with Niko. Why?"

"She told me she loves me," Natalie started again. "But she was half-asleep.

Or maybe partially unconscious, I don't know. I don't even know if she remembers saying it. Maybe it was just one of those things that slipped out because she was relaxed…"

Paula narrowed her eyes. "Wait a second, did you two…?"

Natalie blushed. "We were both exhausted and fell asleep quickly, but…"

Paula burst into laughter as she peeled a banana. "I knew it," she replied. She held up a hand and shook her head. "Say no more. I know you too well. I knew there was a reason that you two took the bedroom at the far end of the house and Isabella and I slept in the room next to your aunts. You're a sly one, *mi amiga*."

Natalie's blush deepened. "It wasn't like that!" She protested and then quickly lowered her voice. "We didn't *plan* for it to happen. It just sort of…did. Anytime I'm around her, I feel like a magnet. Like I'm being pulled to her and we have to be close."

Paula rolled her eyes and bit off the top of the banana. "You're so gay."

"Anyway," Natalie chose to ignore her friend's ribbing. "I don't know if she said it in the afterglow of the moment or if she meant it. The scary thing is, I *want* her to really mean it."

"And you didn't say anything back?" Paula asked.

Natalie shook her head miserably as she took a carton of eggs from the refrigerator.

"Natalie!" Paula's eyes widened and her mouth dropped open. "I guess you'll find out soon enough. I thought I heard some movement coming from your room. If she's acting strange or distant, you'll know why."

"Thanks Paula, that makes me feel a lot better," Natalie replied with a roll of her eyes. She thrust the carton of eggs into her friend's arms. "Crap, I'll be back. I didn't want her to wake up in the room alone. Can you crack some eggs into the pan? I'm making a breakfast scramble."

Paula nodded and stood. "I can't believe you're putting me to work," she grumbled jokingly and then paused. She turned halfway and took a deep breath. "Natalie, can I tell you something? I can see that you're in love with her too. Anyone with half a brain can. You've always been a happy person, but honestly? I can't remember the last time I've seen you smile the way you do with her. Love doesn't have to be complicated. Just tell her."

Natalie felt her face heat up as she turned back and gently opened the bedroom door. She slid inside the room and silently closed the door behind her.

London blinked sleepily. "There you are."

Natalie knelt onto the bed and hugged her. She surprised even herself with how tightly she wrapped her arms around London. "I'm sorry," she replied. "I wanted to make everyone breakfast before they hit the road. You looked much too comfortable and adorable sleeping, so I couldn't wake you."

London grinned and covered her face with her hands. "How could I not be comfortable sleeping when you're next to me? Is everyone leaving early?"

Natalie fought the urge to crawl back under the quilt and relax the morning away with London. "Celia and Jane are heading back after breakfast and going straight to the bakery," she replied. "They prefer not to keep it closed longer for a day or so. Paula and Isabella are heading back too. I think Paula mentioned something about her parents and Rudy's parents visiting later with birthday cake and presents for Bella."

She doesn't seem to be upset Natalie thought. *Maybe she really doesn't remember saying that she loves me.* Her heart inexplicably sank at the thought.

"Are you hungry?" She asked as she stood. "I'm making an egg and vegetable scramble. Something healthy to offset all of yesterday's food."

London smiled and gently pulled Natalie back down to her. "First, kiss me," she murmured against the corner of her mouth. "One thing you should know about is that I do require good morning kisses."

Natalie laughed and met her waiting lips. London cupped her face in both hands and deepened the kiss. Almost instantly, the all-too-familiar stirring began somewhere deep in her chest at the same time as it did between her legs.

I need to stop kissing her before I lock this bedroom door shut and make love to London all morning she decided. The idea sounded deliciously enticing, if not for four of her closest friends and family members also awake inside the house.

"Noted," Natalie finally replied with a grin. "I happen to be a big fan of kisses myself."

London reached her arms overhead and stretched. Natalie tried not to notice the teasing way that her t-shirt rode slightly up her stomach and exposed the tiniest hint of bare skin just above her belly button.

Paula's right she realized. *I am in love with her. I can't even take my eyes off of her.*

London sat up and smiled as she brushed a lock of hair out of her eyes. "So what sort of trouble will be causing the town of Haskell, Texas today?"

Natalie laughed again. "You're in luck," she replied. "The Tri-County Fair is this weekend. Three of the surrounding counties come together and put on a festival each year. I think you'll get a kick out of it."

"I've never been to a county fair in my life," London admitted. "Do you think people will look at me strangely?"

"Doubt it," Natalie responded with a smile. She sniffed the air and felt her stomach rumble at the unmistakable scent of cooked onions. "But first? In any good Texas household, we eat. Let's go make sure Paula didn't burn breakfast to a crisp. She's never been one for cooking."

Natalie felt an overwhelming sense of content wash over her as they walked casually into the kitchen and joined the others. London's arm was loose around her waist and the smile she wore was open and sincere.

Something deep down tells me that London meant each sleepy word whispered into the dark.

London heard the county fair even before Natalie turned the truck down a dusty road between two brick buildings off of the main street. She leaned over in her seat and craned her neck to see where the loud music was coming from. Natalie pulled her truck beneath a wide yellow tent that took up nearly an entire city block. Rows of vehicles were neatly lined under the tent. Groups of people fanned themselves in the shade as they strolled toward a field just beyond.

"Is this it?" London asked. "Are we here?" *I have so many questions* she thought as she looked around. *Namely, why is every other vehicle under the tent a pick-up truck? Did I miss some sort of truck convention memo?* "Is that live music I hear or is there a D.J.?"

"We're here," Natalie confirmed with a smile. "Smells like they're already barbecuing the first batch of brisket," she commented as they wandered away from the truck. "As for the music, I'm sure it's the same local cover band that they hire every year. They're not bad, but I apologize in advance because you're not going to hear much other than Luke Bryan, Brad Paisley, Florida-Georgia Line, maybe some Lady Antebellum or Little Big Town…" she paused as she caught London's confused expression. "Um, country music."

London nodded. "Got it."

They walked closely together as they strolled through the fair. Rows of carnival games were set up along the right of the main thoroughfare while food and drink booths were arranged in squares down the left side of the grounds. Scarred wooden picnic tables, some with faded umbrellas, dotted the landscape behind the booths.

A semi-circle of carnival rides was set up at the middle of the far end, with a tall Ferris wheel its centerpiece. Kids chased each other from ride to ride and laughed loudly while the adults settled themselves at the picnic tables. The unforgiving sun beat down in waves of white-hot heat but didn't seem to deter the four-person band playing on a small, makeshift stage near the rides.

London paused to watch as a skinny thirtysomething man in a sleek black Stetson sang an upbeat country song.

"*Country girl, shake it for me, girl,*" he sang with a low twang. He glanced at his bassist and grinned as he bopped with the beat. "*Shake it for me, girl, shake it for me…*"

London glanced at Natalie out of the corner of her eye. She nodded in time with the music.

"Do you like country music?" London asked over the guitars.

"What?" Natalie asked loudly.

"Country music," London tried again as she pointed to the stage. "Do you enjoy it?"

Natalie blushed. "I liked it a lot more when I was a kid," she admitted. "I'm more into rock, mainly classic rock, these days. But I'll still turn up the radio for the occasional country song. And, besides, I still know how to line dance."

London's mouth dropped open at this new information. "Wait a second, you *line dance*?"

Natalie laughed. "When you're a kid growing up in certain parts of Texas, you can't *not* eventually learn to line dance. Don't get me wrong, I haven't done it in years but it's like riding a bike. You don't really forget."

"Show me," London replied, feeling a twinkle light her eyes. "Please."

Natalie's blush deepened. "Oh London, only you would think that's something special," she protested. "I haven't line danced in years and I don't even listen to country music very much."

"But you said it's like riding a bike," London pouted. "I don't think I've ever seen real line dancing, except maybe in the movies."

Natalie grinned and shifted to wrap her arms around London's waist from behind. She rested her chin on her shoulder. "So if I show you, what do *I* get?"

London felt her cheeks redden. "What do you *want*?" She replied teasingly.

"*Somebody's sweet little farmer's child, got it in her blood to get a little wild, ponytail and a pretty smile, roped me in from a country mile…*" The lead singer continued to croon in the background.

Ain't that the truth London thought ruefully.

"I'll think of something," Natalie replied with a quick wink. "Be right back."

London watched curiously as Natalie walked to the stage. The band had just finished the song and paused to mop the sweat from their foreheads. The lead singer spotted Natalie and leaned over the stage. He cupped his hand around his ear as she spoke to him for a moment. She turned once to point at London and then he nodded and shook her hand.

"Dare I ask what you told him?" London ventured as Natalie stood next to her and refused to meet her eyes.

"I asked if they could play something that we could do a simple A-B line dance with," Natalie replied. "I may have also mentioned that I'm trying to show off, Texas-style, for this beautiful woman accompanying me this weekend."

London burst out laughing. "You did not!"

Natalie grinned. "Actually, what I'd said was that it was your first time here and you're from Chicago, so I'm going to teach you how to line dance."

London held up a hand. "Hold on, I never said *I* was going to…" The rest of her words were drowned out by guitars and percussion as the next song started.

"It's easy, I promise," Natalie called over the fast-paced country music. She grabbed London's hands and squeezed them. "Just watch me for a minute."

London crossed her arms and watched dubiously as Natalie took a few steps closer to the makeshift stage. She paused and nodded slowly in concentration. London studied her as her lips moved silently and she mouthed the count to herself.

Natalie took the first few steps slowly and held London's eyes for a moment. Her pace quickened and fell in line with the music as her steps became sure and measured. London couldn't take her eyes away from her.

Never in my life did I think line dancing could be sexy she thought with a lopsided smile. The way that Natalie's hips flared with each quarter-turn and the way she swayed with the beat had rapidly changed her mind.

"*But when she says baby, oh don't matter what comes, ain't goin' nowhere, she runs her fingers through my hair and saves me…*" the chorus of the song cut into London's lascivious thoughts. "*Yeah, that look in her eyes got me comin' alive and driving me a good kind of crazy…When she says baby.*"

Guess he says it better than I could she thought as she realized the song wasn't half-bad. *It sure describes how I feel about Natalie, that's for sure.*

She openly gazed at the other woman. Her eyes were closed as she grew lost in the song and her dark hair was loose down her back. Her long, tanned legs didn't miss a single count. Natalie clapped her hands together once and took a few steps back and then to the left as her hips flared and swayed to the beat.

Beauty London decided. *This is beauty.* She briefly recalled how she had thought Kayley was a beautiful woman because, by any standard definition, she was. She took countless hours getting her hair and make-up just right and spent way too much money on skin products and designer clothing. In fact, London couldn't think of a single time that she had left the apartment without looking together and polished.

But this... she thought as she was entranced in Natalie. A few passerby had joined her and they formed a straight line as they danced in time with the music. *This is a different kind of beauty.* Natalie's brown eyes sparkled in the sun as she danced with abandon. She looked every bit the happy, free spirit.

London pulled out her phone and smiled as she watched Natalie through the short video that began recording. *This is raw beauty, genuine and real* she realized. *The kind that you can't buy with all the Lancome and Louis Vuitton in the world.*

Natalie smiled and motioned for her to join them. London quickly shook her head as she pocketed her phone.

"Come on," Natalie called, not missing a beat. "You can do it, London."

"I don't know how to dance to this," she called back. "Not like you. I'll look like a fool."

"Nonsense," Natalie replied. "If you mess up, just try again."

"Ah, come on," a middle-aged woman dancing next to Natalie chimed in. "We're all just having fun."

London shook her head firmly. "I don't..."

"Hey, you only live once, right?" The woman called. She swayed into a quarter-turn and then her back was to them.

London blinked as the stranger's words sank in. *Didn't Mom always tell me that she didn't want me to stop living because of her illness?* She recalled. *She didn't want me to stop discovering or loving.*

She took a few tentative steps to the line that had expanded to nearly ten laughing, smiling dancers. *But somehow, along the way, I ended up living like I was half-dead already. I thought it was easier to turn off my emotions and give myself no chance at feeling anything. But that's not living, is it?*

Natalie jogged down the line to her and grabbed her hand. She smiled breathlessly. "Come on, it's okay," she reassured her. "I'll show you."

London gingerly tried to follow Natalie's slow, exaggerated steps. *Pay attention* a small voice in her mind piped up. *She's showing you more than just line dancing.*

The dance came easier after a minute or so of copying Natalie's movements. London felt the butterflies stir in her stomach as Natalie rested her hands lightly on her hips to guide her through a turn. The line clapped once and then it was a quick one, two, three to the left and again to the right.

They slid into the last step as the song wound down and the music faded. London threw back her head and laughed as the dancers that had joined Natalie dispersed amongst the small crowd.

"That wasn't so bad, right?" Natalie asked. "Now you can say that you've not only seen *real* line dancing, but you've learned it too."

London felt high from the excitement and adrenaline of doing something she had never done before. *That. Was. Awesome. I can't believe I just did that. I, London Foster, learned how to line dance. In public. Sometimes you have to throw pretenses to the side and go for it. Besides, I have a feeling that I'll always have a soft spot for country music now* she decided in her rapid-fire thoughts.

She paused, still reeling from the last few minutes, and grabbed Natalie's hand. "Thank you."

Natalie searched her eyes and smiled. "For what?"

"Thank you for making me feel alive again," London finished simply. Natalie opened her mouth to reply, but London ducked her head shyly and instead pointed to the food tents.

"Are you hungry?" She pressed quickly. Natalie closed her mouth and blinked at the abrupt change in subject. "I think I've actually worked up an appetite for brisket."

As they walked casually across the field of fine brown dirt, London noticed an ominous black cloud far over the horizon. She wondered briefly if it was headed their way.

That doesn't look promising she thought dubiously. Her phone buzzed in her pocket and she quickly turned her attention to the incoming call. *Great. It's Holly.*

Her stomach did a nervous flip as she let the call go to voicemail. She knew exactly why her friend was calling and a text message less than thirty seconds later only confirmed it.

Hey girl! I know you're having a lot of fun in Texas with that mysterious brunette - Ha. I wanted to check in and find out if you'd had a chance to make your return arrangements to Chicago. I'd like to give the C.E.O. a target date for your return to W.H. Young. We're so excited to officially have you promoted!

London swallowed and re-read the text message two, three, four times until the tiny words blurred together. A wave of anxiety washed over her as she again wondered what exactly to do. An impending sense of dread crept low into her belly and worked its way up through her chest until a lump formed in her throat.

No matter what, something big is going to happen. Something is going to change. I've already *changed* she thought nervously.

She was so deep in thought that she didn't realize Natalie had stopped short outside of a white food tent. London walked directly into her back and then jumped to the side.

"Oh my God, I'm sorry!" She exclaimed. "Are you all right?"

Natalie turned and touched London's face affectionately. "Of course, don't worry about it," she replied and then peered at her closely. "Hey, are *you* okay? You look like you've seen a ghost."

London wasn't sure if it was a blessing or a curse that Natalie could read her so easily. "Yes, sorry," she replied. "My friend Holly texted me from Chicago. I was reading it when I walked into you."

"Is everything okay?" Natalie asked.

Tell her everything, London she thought. *Tell her about the promotion. Tell her how you don't want to leave. You're not ready to go back. Tell her how she's the best thing that's happened to you and you're ready to take a chance. Tell her that you want to build something together, because you have the one thing you've been missing for so long and that's faith. Faith that the two of you can be together. Tell her... Tell her that you meant what you said last night. That you love her.*

"I, uh..." London closed her eyes briefly. "Yeah, she was just checking in. Seeing how I'm doing."

She immediately wanted to kick herself as Natalie nodded in

acknowledgement. They stepped up to a card table beneath the tent, the moment was gone and then London lost her nerve.

"One barbecued brisket sandwich…" Natalie started and then paused. "You want one, right? Never mind, you *have* to get a sandwich too. It's easily the best brisket in Texas."

London allowed a small smile. "Well, if you say it's the best…"

Natalie nodded vigorously. "It is," she confirmed. She turned her attention back to the high school student taking their order. "Make that *two* barbecued brisket sandwiches. And two bottles of water, please."

As the kid punched in their order, Natalie turned to London excitedly. "You'll really like this sandwich," she went on and then winked. "I *love* this brisket. Almost as much as I *love* spending time with you."

London felt her heart swell with pride, but Holly's text lingered at the back of her mind uncertainly. She opened her mouth to respond, but a sliver of lightning split the sky above them in a bright burst of white. She jumped as a clap of thunder boomed strongly enough to shake the table before them.

"I thought it didn't rain much out here," London commented. They carried their sandwiches and stepped around the tent.

Natalie glanced pointedly at the south-facing sky. The horizon was nearly pitch-black and an unseasonably cool breeze blew across the grounds warningly. "It's Texas, not the *desert*," she replied with a laugh. "I guess we're still catching the tail end of storm season. So how fast can you eat?"

London raised an eyebrow and glanced again at the dark clouds swirling their way. "How long do I have?"

Natalie bit her lip. "Maybe ten minutes?" She guessed. "This is Tornado Alley, so storms can blow in fast and strengthen quickly. We'd be better off leaving before it gets too bad."

London watched the wave of low-hanging black clouds for another moment. She sat on the edge of a picnic bench and bit into her sandwich decisively. "Okay," she agreed. "Ten minutes it is. The calm before the storm."

CHAPTER 20

Natalie licked the last drops of tangy barbecue sauce from her fingertips. A gust of wind blew their empty water bottles across the picnic table. The thin plastic clattered noisily over the thick wood as London jumped up to gather them.

It seemed as though the impending storm had brought a strange electricity with it. It buzzed and crackled intangibly in the air as Natalie stole a glance at London.

Something is different she noted silently. *Something's shifted between us, and I can't put my finger on what. The energy between us has changed.* Natalie couldn't quite tell if the sudden, urgent shift in atmosphere was a good thing or bad. Her heartbeat increased as she caught London staring at her and then looking away quickly once she had been caught.

Natalie glanced up as the sun seemed to fully disappear behind the wave of fast-moving dark clouds. The band had just finished packing their instruments at the back of the stage and streams of festival-goers hurried for their vehicles.

"Maybe we should head back," London spoke, filling the strangely heavy silence between them. "It's going to pour any second."

Natalie nodded. "You're right," she agreed. They stood as another bolt of lightning lit the sky in warning. "Do you like storms, London?"

London shrugged. "I guess I've never really thought much about them."

The invisible electricity crackled around them as another gust of wind nearly knocked them over. "You know, I love storms," Natalie started. "One of my favorite things to do is sit on the porch with a glass of wine and watch the storms roll through." She stole another glance at London. "I know it sounds crazy. Even my aunts think it's crazy. There's something so mesmerizing and beautiful about them though. It's, like, this enchanting show that Mother Nature puts on you remind you who's really boss. You can feel it so deeply with *all* of your senses. The sight of the lightning, the sound of the thunder and the wind, the feel of the raindrops against your skin. Have you ever *really* felt the rain against your skin?"

London glanced cautiously at Natalie as they walked. "I have…" she started and then stopped short. "But I guess I haven't."

Natalie was well aware that she sounded crazy, but she was wrought with a tickling sense of urgency and the strange gut feeling that she had to somehow get through to London. *For some reason, as quickly as her guard went down, it shot right back up again* Natalie thought. *But there's this change in energy, in atmosphere. I know she feels it too.*

"It's cleansing," Natalie continued, softer this time. "These storms come in, they shake everything up and the rain pours down in buckets. By the time it's all over, everything is *new*. It feels like your little corner of the world has been rocked and then somehow, by the end of it, everything is calm. The sun returns and everything is cleansed and new again. It's…*amazing*," she finished.

She paused for a moment and watched as London opened her mouth to respond. Just then, the skies opened up and rain beat down in sheets of cool, fat drops. They splattered across the grounds, into the dirt and against their faces and clothing.

"Oh my God, it's *pouring*!" London exclaimed. She turned her face to the sky, closed her eyes for a moment and grinned. "What now?"

Natalie burst into laughter and grabbed her hand. "Now we run!"

They jogged, arm-in-arm, through the rest of the fairgrounds and burst into giggles as they swiftly dodged mud puddles and slick patches of browned grass.

It's coming down hard Natalie thought. She wiped the back of her hand across her forehead. *I knew it would be a big one. I feel like I'm walking through a shower.*

London laughed loudly as she hopped over a wide swath of mud. They tried their best to shake out their clothes and hair as they reached the truck.

"Did I just walk through a waterfall or a thunderstorm?" London asked breathlessly.

Natalie laughed and waved her hand. "Forget it," she replied. "It's a lost cause. Hop in. I'll clean out the truck tomorrow."

A moment later, she backed the Ford F150 through a track of mud and headed for the house. As their giggles died down, only the steady sound of raindrops beating against the windows and the soft squeak of the wipers could be heard.

You love her too. Realization hit Natalie like a sudden shock from the storm's electric buzz. It felt as though there was an invisible live wire between them and it rocked Natalie's awareness. Everything seemed to click and fall into place as she roughly pulled the truck up to the house. She could feel London's strange glance and she knew she was wondering what exactly was going on in her head.

Socked with the implications of her realization and filled with the same urgency that she had to get through to London, Natalie jumped out of the truck. She had to find out if she had truly meant what she'd muttered through sleep and satisfaction.

London hastily followed and they stood in the pouring rain for an uncertain moment. A bolt of lightning streaked horizontally across the horizon.

"Natalie, tell me what's going on," London pleaded. "Talk to me. You look like you have the world going through your head and something is...*different.* I can sense a change..."

"London, it's you," Natalie blurted out. She took a deep breath. "I *love* you. I'm completely head over heels in love with you. I don't want you to go back to Chicago. I don't want you to go anywhere."

London's mouth dropped open. She took a tentative step closer to her and it took all of Natalie's willpower not to close the small gap between them. She could almost see the electricity crackling between them as an ear-splitting boom of thunder shook the ground.

"I...I feel the same way, Natalie," London replied breathlessly. "I feel for you what I didn't even *know* I was capable of feeling. I've just...I've been through a *lot*, Natalie. I'm scared."

Natalie bit her lip. "Can't you feel it between us, London?" She asked, not breaking their gaze. "Why is it so scary to say it back, when you're facing me and looking into my eyes, if you feel it? You're not the only one who's scared. I've had my heart broken too. But you *know* deep in your heart that I wouldn't hurt you."

London stared at her for a long, unwavering moment. She ran her fingertips across her face and along her jaw, as though she was trying to memorize her face. "I fell for you, Natalie," she murmured. "There's no going back from there. Don't you realize what that means for me?"

Another rumble of thunder rattled the house's old vinyl siding as the rain continued to soak through their clothes. "I know you try to keep everybody away," Natalie replied. "Because in your experience, everyone eventually leaves. Trust me, London, I *know* how you feel. You stick to what's safe because you've been burned badly in the past."

A sudden buzzing noise sounded and they both glanced in the direction of the source. London's phone lit with the name "Holly" flashing across the small screen. She hit the Decline button sheepishly and opened her mouth to speak.

Natalie took a deep breath. *She needs to be out of her comfort zone* she realized. *Completely. I have to get under her skin and show her how to live in the moment, without overthinking everything. I want her to tell me how she feels. I want to hear her say she loves me too.*

"When was the last time you did something impulsive, London? Really?" Natalie asked, cutting her off before she could fill the silence. London searched her eyes.

The pool she thought satisfactorily. *Bingo*.

"Come on," she said. "Let's go to the pool."

London glanced at the backyard uncertainly. "Natalie, it's pouring."

She turned and met her eyes. "Do you trust me?"

"Yes, but..." London started.

"Then come with me," she continued. She took a few steps into the backyard and gestured for London to follow.

The pool water rippled against the whistling wind. Small waves floated from the deep end of the small rectangular pool to the water that lapped against wide, built-in stairs at the other side.

Now or never, Natalie she thought. She straightened her spine and walked to the edge of the deep end. *If you can't get through to her now, you never will.*

"Are you crazy?" London called. She had paused hesitantly just inside the backyard. "Don't even think about it. Come inside."

Natalie shook her head. "When was the last time that you lived for the exact moment you're in?" She called back. "And didn't get lost in anything else?"

"This is silly..." London started as she crossed her arms.

"I'm serious," Natalie replied. "Tell me."

London sighed. "Fine. Line-dancing earlier," she replied. "And probably when I forced myself to step onto that plane to Texas. You know, when every logical part of my brain was telling me that this was a bad idea and I had the strange sense that my life was about to change whether I was ready or not. Isn't that enough?"

"And was it a bad idea?" Natalie pressed. "Taking that chance and coming to Texas?"

London wrinkled her nose. "No," she replied. "I can't imagine *not* making that decision now. I don't want to think about being in Chicago, miserable and frustrated, if I hadn't taken that risk." She paused and met Natalie's eyes across the rippling water of the pool. "This has been the *best* experience in the world. You've changed me."

"Then come here and kiss me," Natalie responded simply. The sideways rain had already soaked through her hair. It dripped from her eyelashes as she blinked against the wet wind. Her white t-shirt clung to her skin and droplets of rain rolled down her face and arms.

She watched as London hesitated for a split second and then strode confidently from the other side of the yard. Natalie felt charged with emotion she couldn't articulate as London's piercing gaze locked onto hers. As London reached out for her, Natalie took a deep breath and closed her eyes.

Take the plunge she told herself. *It's worth it.* She took one step forward and jumped into six feet of warm water.

London froze, her bravado melted away, as Natalie's head broke through the surface of the churning water. She laughed in delight and shook her hair out.

"Have you lost your mind?" London shouted. A jagged bolt of lightning cut through the sky and illuminated the backyard in bright white light for a split second. "You're…" she paused as a loud clap of thunder drowned out her voice. "You're wearing all of your clothes!"

Natalie shrugged as she treaded water. "They're just clothes," she replied. "They can be washed and dried. Now come and kiss me."

London looked at Natalie for a long moment. Her t-shirt revealed every detail of her body. She could see the distinct outline of her breasts through her bra and tiny rivulets of water dripped down her neck. London imagined herself kissing the water droplets from her neck and running her hands along the smooth skin beneath her t-shirt. Another heavy rumble of thunder rattled the house and shook London from her lascivious thoughts.

What am I waiting for? She asked herself. Natalie's wide smile erased any lingering fear. Without a word, London teetered at the edge of the pool and jumped into the deep end. Her hands sought Natalie's body beneath the water and found her right away.

I can't let another second go by without kissing her. I love her was the last thought in London's mind before she closed her eyes and met her waiting lips. Natalie's arms wound around her waist and gently pulled her closer. She tangled her fingers in Natalie's wet hair as their kiss deepened. Two bolts of lightning split the sky as London felt the warm tip of Natalie's tongue against her own. She could see the thin flashes of light behind her closed eyes and relished the feeling of Natalie's warm, wet skin pressed against her body.

This is living for the moment I'm in London realized. *This is what she was trying to show me.* Every synapse in her brain fired sensations to nerves throughout her body. She had never felt more alive.

"I love you," London whispered against her mouth. "I love you, Natalie."

London had always wished that she knew how to stop time. From sitting with her mother for hours at the hospital, knowing deep in her soul that those minutes wouldn't be enough, to the rush of hope and possibility she'd feel years ago watching the sun rise over Chicago, there were instances in which she had desperately wanted to freeze time. An electric thrill ran through London as Natalie inhaled and rested her forehead against her cheek.

This is it she realized in amazement. *Time finally stopped.*

"I love you too," Natalie murmured. London shivered at her soft breath against her earlobe. Rain poured around them and hit the pool water with thousands of tiny splashes. "Congratulations. You're living in the moment. There's no going back now."

CHAPTER 21

London could barely come up for air as they frantically kissed their way into the house. Their hands tore at each other's shirts and belts. She was torn between an overwhelming desire to attach her lips to Natalie's and her natural instinct to breathe.

Breathing? She wondered. *Or sex?* She felt a moan escape the corner of her mouth as Natalie crushed her lips against her mouth and pressed her body against her own. *Definitely sex.* She grinned against Natalie's mouth as she took a step back and felt her shoulders hit the bedroom door.

They paused their kisses for only a moment as they ducked into the room. London gently slid Natalie's t-shirt halfway up to reveal a toned, tanned stomach. She paused at the foot of the bed and nudged the other woman onto the mattress. London knelt between her thighs and drank in the form in front of her. Her gaze trailed up Natalie's body until she finally met her eyes. Natalie stared back her silently and with a gentle intensity.

"I love you," Natalie whispered. She weaved her fingers between London's and squeezed her hand.

London rose slowly, sliding over her body, and carefully laid her back onto the bed. She wasn't sure why she was taking her time with Natalie or what was causing her to touch her so tenderly, but London knew she wanted the moment to last forever.

"I love you too," she replied before closing the small gap between their lips. She slid the rest of Natalie's t-shirt over her head and stilled as her hands slipped beneath her wet shirt.

"I want to feel you against me," Natalie murmured. Her hands explored London's upper body and finally found her nipples. Her fingertips lingered there as they teased them to attention. London sat up, straddling her, and let her pull her shirt and bra off.

London relished the sensations that Natalie was causing to course throughout her body, but she wanted to bring her over the edge first. Natalie's back hit the pile of wrinkled blankets as London kissed her way down her body and eased off her jeans. She took her time nibbling at the sensitive areas inside Natalie's hipbones and along her ribcage before slipping her fingers around her underwear.

London's mouth dropped open at the wetness that slid through her fingertips. "You're so beautiful," she murmured. She glanced up at Natalie and smiled.

"Make love to me," she whispered. "Please."

With Natalie watching her, London gently licked the tip of her index finger. "You taste *so* good," she continued in a low voice.

Natalie groaned and London bent down to kiss her slick folds. She barely registered Natalie's right hand wound in her hair or her left hand still intertwined with her own. Natalie's moans of pleasure as she continued to kiss, explore and tease her most intimate areas filled London's consciousness. The sounds grew in urgency and intensity as she ran the length of her tongue across her again and again.

Natalie froze for a long moment and then London felt her shudder and contract against her mouth. Her gasping moans turned to pants as London laid next to her and smiled. She wrapped an arm around Natalie and pushed a lock of semi-wet hair out of her half-closed eyes.

"Don't get too comfortable," Natalie warned between breaths.

London paused for a moment and then kissed the tip of her ear as Natalie cuddled into her. "Whatever you say," she replied amusedly.

In a millisecond, Natalie had flipped herself on top of London and pushed her shoulders against the pillow. "Was that a challenge, Miss Foster?" She asked with a teasing grin.

"I..." London started. She didn't have time to finish before Natalie crushed her lips against her own. As soon as she felt the tip of Natalie's tongue exploring her mouth, all thoughts of rest vanished. London was acutely aware of the growing warmth between her legs and finally let desire take over as she wrapped her arms loosely around Natalie's neck.

If this is making love London thought contentedly. *Then this is what I want to do with Natalie forever.*

Natalie opened her eyes slowly and blinked as the earliest hints of dawn gently illuminated the bedroom in glowing shades of pink and yellow. London had slept soundly against her side as the stormy night sky gave way to drizzling rain and then the rising morning sun. The television hummed at a low volume as images from an infomercial flickered by. She and London were completely intertwined and Natalie felt more content than she could remember.

She stared, unfocused, at a point on the ceiling and idly played with the ends of London's hair. *She's waking up* she realized as the other woman shifted. Natalie gazed at her for a long moment and then leaned over to brush her lips across her forehead.

London stirred and blinked after a moment. "Did we really stay up until 3 A.M. last night doing, um…?"

Natalie suppressed her smile. "We definitely did."

London rolled over and her face flushed. "No wonder I feel as though I slept like a baby!" She laughed. "Did you sleep well?"

"Honestly, I think I watched you sleep more than I slept myself," Natalie replied with a slow, shy smile.

London's mouth dropped open. "Oh my God, now I'm *really* embarrassed," she exclaimed. "Who knows what kind of faces I was making in that deep, deep sleep you put me in?" She grinned and leaned forward to peck Natalie's lips.

"You were adorable," Natalie confirmed with a laugh. "And you were way knocked out."

London stretched and settled back against the pillow. "Do we really have to go back to Fort Worth today?"

Natalie squeezed her hand and dropped another kiss onto her forehead. "We can take our time," she replied. "I'll make some breakfast before we hit the road."

London nodded. "I don't know how I can possibly be hungry with all the food I've eaten this weekend," she responded. "But breakfast sounds amazing. Do you mind if I take a quick shower?"

"Not at all," Natalie replied. She located her wrinkled t-shirt at the foot of the bed and pulled it over her head. *I don't remember falling asleep sans shirt last night* she thought with a sly grin. *I guess we were* both *exhausted.*

She padded into the kitchen and stood on her tip-toes to grab a pan from the cabinet. She half-listened as the bathroom door down the hall opened and then the spray of the shower hit the smooth tiles.

Natalie turned and took a carton of eggs from the refrigerator just as the familiar ringtone of London's phone sounded from somewhere in the bedroom. She glanced up and paused. She could hear the occasional splash from the shower as the call was finally routed into London's voicemail.

Natalie shook her head after a moment and turned to crack the remaining eggs into the wide iron frying pan. *I'm really going to have to remind London to call her friend Holly back* she thought to herself. *I'll bet anything that was her again. It must be important if she keeps trying to reach her, especially on a Sunday morning.*

She wrinkled her nose as the ringing sounded again. Somehow, it seemed more urgent this time than it did a few moments ago. Natalie listened as the shower squeaked off and the plastic curtain was pulled back. She turned back to the food with a small smile as she caught London quickly pad into the bedroom.

How ironic she thought dryly. *The first time I ever laid eyes on her, she was in a bath towel. And here she is in a bath towel again, only this time she's at my aunt's house after a crazy, amazing weekend. And a night of even more crazy, amazing lovemaking.*

All was pin-quiet in the house for the next few minutes as Natalie quickly chopped half of a green pepper. She turned to the frying pan and poured a quarter cup of milk over the eggs as they scrambled. As she reached back for the diced pepper, a strange sound broke her concentration. It was a mix between a strangled moan and a heartbreaking sob and it immediately turned Natalie's stomach with fear.

Without a second thought, she dropped the cutting board onto the counter with a loud clatter. Tiny chunks of green pepper rolled over the linoleum and spilled onto the floor, but Natalie was already halfway to the bedroom.

She threw open the door to find London hunched on the edge of the mattress in only her towel. Her phone was at her side and her hands were clenched over her eyes. She didn't look up as Natalie approached her slowly.

As she tried to process what was going on, she could see London's back quivering silently with muted sobs. Her shoulders shook uncontrollably and Natalie felt her stomach drop again.

Oh no she thought. Fear of what could have caused this gripped her. *Something happened and it's bad. Really bad.*

Natalie immediately sat next to London and wrapped her arm around her shoulders. "What happened?" She asked, her voice low. "Talk to me, London. What's going on, baby?"

London didn't answer, but finally turned to her. She fell into Natalie's arms as her shaking sobs continued. London buried her face in her shoulder as Natalie quietly held her and rubbed small circles on her back. An icy sense of dread clenched Natalie's stomach.

I have no idea what's going on she thought helplessly. *I don't have the slightest clue what's making London, my tough, cool, collected London, cry this way. All I know is that something bad happened and I need to fix it.*

"London," Natalie whispered after a moment. She pressed her lips to her temple and let her kiss linger there for a long moment. "What's going on?"

After another minute or two, she sniffled and appeared to momentarily collect herself. London sat up and finally met her concerned gaze. Natalie felt her heart practically crack at the sight of her swollen, red-rimmed eyes. She held London's hands in both of her own and squeezed them reassuringly.

"It's Tiffany," London finally spoke. Her shaking voice was raspy with tears. She swallowed hard. "I got a call from Baylor All Saints Hospital in Fort

Worth. Tiffany…" she paused and tried to steady herself. "We…We have to go. Tiffany was brought to the hospital unconscious. No one can get a hold of our father. She…She overdosed."

Natalie felt her heart plummet to the floor. "Oh my God," she whispered in shock. She wrapped her arm tighter around London. "Is she going to be all right?"

London shook her head slowly and stared at the mattress. "They don't know," she replied. "They've stabilized her, but she hasn't woken up yet. They're doing as much as they can, but they won't know the extent of any internal damage or…" she paused and sniffled. "If there's any brain damage until they run more tests or she wakes up."

Natalie felt as though the wind had been knocked clear out of her lungs. "Oh my God," she repeated. "I can't…I can't believe this."

I have to be strong for her she thought in determination. *We're not going to get any answers in Haskell.*

Natalie stood and held her hands out to London. "Come on," she urged her with a nod. "We have to go."

London blinked, as if seeing her for the first time since the phone call. "You're right," she finally replied. "We need to go now. You're right."

Natalie pulled London up. "I'll get our things together," she told her. "Keep trying to reach your dad. Maybe he didn't answer because he didn't recognize the hospital's phone number. Let's just focus on getting to the hospital, okay?"

As she headed for the bedroom door, she felt a slight tug on her hand. She turned halfway and threw London a puzzled smile. "What's wrong?"

London took a deep breath. "Thank you," she murmured. "I…I never don't know what do but right now? I really don't know what I'd do without you, Natalie."

She leaned forward and kissed a tear from London's cheek. "It's okay," she replied. "I feel for you what I didn't even *know* I was capable of feeling," she continued, repeating what London had told her last night.

London's face lightened. It wasn't a full smile, but it was the first hint of ease that Natalie had seen since the phone call. "Come on," she said gently.

"The sooner we can get to Baylor, then the sooner we can see Tiffany and get some answers."

In what felt to London like record time, Natalie gently eased the truck into the wide circular driveway of the emergency wing at the hospital. A large parking lot, dotted with thin trees planted at its corners, sprawled behind them.

I knew she had a problem London thought dismally. *I should have said something earlier. I shouldn't have questioned myself so much when I wondered if I'd make her mad or if I even had the right to say something. Of course I had the right to say something. She's my little sister and her life is far more important than any family history. She could have died. I should have* made *her listen, even if she yelled, screamed and told me she hated me. As long as she got help.*

"I'll park," Natalie spoke gently. Her soft tone filling the cab of the truck was a welcome sound in place of the blood that pounded in London's ears. "You go," she continued. "See Tiffany. I'll find you in there."

London nodded and opened her mouth to speak. The sound of her ringtone blared through the truck. She glanced at the phone in her lap and sighed. "It's my dad," she stated matter-of-factly. "Finally."

Natalie bit her lip. "You'd better take that," she replied. "I'll find you, okay? I promise."

London leaned over the middle console to plant a gentle kiss on Natalie's cheek. "Okay," she agreed. "Thank you for…for everything. Thank you."

With that, she hopped out of the truck and quickly hit a button to redial her father. She plugged her ear with her index finger and took a few nervous steps toward the large revolving door of the emergency center.

Be prepared for anything she warned herself silently. *You need to be strong and brave. Just like you were for Mom. Just like you've learned to be over the last several years.*

London took a deep breath as her father's phone went to voicemail. *If there was ever a time to fake confidence and pretend like you have it all together when you're freaking out on the inside, it's now* she thought. She tried to steel herself for whatever would come next. *Come on, London. You always know what to do…Except right now.*

She braced herself and strode into the busy emergency center. For reasons she couldn't put her finger on, something Natalie had told her during one of their first interactions popped into her head.

"*She's still your family. Sister, half-sister, it makes no difference. She's your blood. Family takes care of family, despite the differences.*"

London paused as she scanned the large room. She blinked at the frenetic rush of energy that suddenly surrounded her. She knew it was just a matter of time until her father called back.

All I want is to get to Tiffany she thought in determination. *Everything else between us seems trivial, childish even, in comparison to right now.*

She watched white-coated doctors strode down the labyrinth-like hallways. She turned and approached the circular front desk, where nurses in brightly-colored scrubs bustled around rows of clipboards.

I think I finally get it she realized. *Family takes care of family, despite the differences.*

CHAPTER 22

Natalie stood in the doorway of Tiffany's hospital room, unsure if London even realized she was there. She watched silently as she leaned forward from the chair she had pulled next to the sterile hospital bed. London tipped her face to Tiffany and gently kissed her cheek.

At least she looks comfortable Natalie thought as she gazed at London's sister. She appeared to be asleep and was lying on her back. Her shoulders and head were propped up by several pillows. Natalie swallowed hard. *Even if she does look unwell.*

Tiffany's once creamy skin looked ghostly pale. Dark shadows lined her jaw and gave her closed eyes a sunken, sick appearance. Her lips were dry and chapped, with flecks of dead skin peeling from their corners.

Natalie stole a quick glance at London. *If Tiffany's appearance is jarring to me, then it must have been devastating for her.*

"It's going to be okay, Tiff," London whispered. She reached over and squeezed one of her sister's hands. "I promise I'm not going to leave you. I'll do whatever it takes to help you get better. I'll go to therapy with you every day. I'll drive you to rehab and hold your hand while you check in. I'll take you to all of your doctor appointments. I'll…I'll…" London's voice broke and she paused. "I can't lose you too. I don't care about the past anymore. I want you to get better and I…I can be a *real* sister to you."

Natalie felt her heart breaking for London as she spoke. She was about to gently clear her throat to let her know she was in the room when a soft male voice behind her sighed.

"Oh, Tiffany," he spoke. His tone was tinged with despair. "What did you do?"

Both Natalie and London turned to find a young man, about Tiffany's age, standing uncertainly in the doorway. He balled up a Texas Rangers baseball cap in his hands and stared at her sadly.

London quickly wiped at her eyes. "Shit, I'm sorry," she mumbled. "I didn't realize you were here, Natalie."

Natalie met her eyes and smiled. "It's okay," she told her. "You need your time with her."

"What happened?" The young man spoke again. He looked between them. "I…I just saw her a week ago."

"I'm sorry, I don't believe we've met…" London started expectantly.

"Wayne Paulson," he offered quickly. "I'm a friend of Tiffany's. I…I don't understand…" he trailed off.

Natalie watched as a small smile flickered across London's features. "Wayne, of course," she replied. "I've heard about you."

He glanced at her. "I don' know if that's a good thing or a bad thing."

"It's a good thing," London replied. "She said you two have been friends for a long time."

Wayne nodded and looked back at the hospital bed. "I care about her a lot," he admitted. "I've spent some time with her since she returned from overseas, but she…she's a hard person to understand sometimes. We'll hang out and then she'll act like she doesn't know me. I'm sorry. I know you don't want to hear all of that. I've always cared about her, but she's always wanted to forge her own path." He shrugged. "I'll never stop, though."

London gazed at Tiffany for a long moment. "She's a free spirit," she agreed. She reached over and held her palm tightly. "It's not you, Wayne. What can I say? That's my sister."

Natalie's ears perked up at this. *That's the first time I've ever heard London refer to Tiffany as her sister. Not her half-sister, not a stranger…Just her sister.*

"How did this happen?" Wayne asked.

London took a deep breath. "From what the doctor told me, she overdosed on a combination of alcohol and Adderall. The components of Adderall, which wasn't prescribed to her, exacerbated the effects of the alcohol she drank. There was a lot of the drug in her system, but it wasn't enough to do any serious damage to her organs or her brain. She did have severe alcohol poisoning though. And because alcohol is a depressant and Adderall is a stimulant, they have opposite effects on the body and mix up all its signals. Since she took both in excess at the same time, it caused two seizures."

Wayne closed his eyes. "We always argue about the Adderall," he admitted. "I should have known it would hurt her eventually. I think, deep down, she knew it too."

Natalie felt a certain uneasiness in the pit of her stomach. *Guilt?* She wondered. *Because I knew early on that I should have told London about my run-in with Tiffany? Maybe if I'd brought it to her attention, despite Tiffany pleading otherwise, she would have realized the severity of her addiction. Before…this.*

"How did she get to the hospital?" Wayne asked.

"The doctor thinks she had the first seizure while driving," London replied slowly. "Thank God it didn't cause an accident and no one was injured. She was able to pull to the side of the road. Luckily, there was a state trooper headed in the opposite direction. He witnessed her cut across three lanes of traffic and said it looked like she was driving under the influence. He pulled around but by the time he reached her, she was already unconscious from the second seizure."

"Oh my God," Wayne muttered. He kicked the toe of his worn leather boat shoe against the shining linoleum floor. "I don't even want to think about what could have happened if that trooper hadn't been there."

London glanced at Natalie and bit her lip. "Neither do I," she replied. "The officer radioed for an ambulance and they brought her here. The paramedics were able to stabilize her on the way. Her car was towed to some lot in Grand Prairie and our father is on the way. He had flown to Midland for some last-minute weekend budget meetings. And that's all I know right now."

"So she'll be okay?" Wayne clarified hopefully. "The doctor thinks so?"

London nodded gingerly. "They've done a lot of scans and tests to look for internal or permanent damage," she paused. "The results aren't all back yet, but so far it's looking okay. She may be moving a little slower than normal for a few weeks, but no permanent problems."

"She's going to be in some trouble though," Wayne said, vocalizing what Natalie knew they were both thinking. "D.U.I.?"

London nodded again. "Yeah," she murmured. "And some kind of misdemeanor for being in possession of a prescription drug that wasn't hers. My father wants her in an inpatient rehab as soon as she's able to go. Hopefully the court will see that she's getting help."

"I can have my dad make some calls," Wayne offered. "Granted, his special is cosmetic surgery but he has a lot of connections to other doctors and rehabilitation centers." He paused and smiled down at Tiffany. "But she would hate that, wouldn't she? Instead, I'll visit her every day."

London stood from the chair. "You can hold her hand, you know," she said as she gestured to the bed. "Talk to her. Let her know you're here."

Wayne looked terrified for a moment. He traded his Rangers cap between his hands nervously and then finally nodded. London met Natalie's eyes and glanced toward the hallway.

They strolled arm-in-arm down the long, brightly-lit corridor. There was so much white that it practically blinded Natalie. *Sparkling white walls, shiny white floors, spotless white ceilings…*she thought miserably. *No wonder people feel uncomfortable in hospitals.*

They reached a wooden bench near a side exit door and sat. *I need to tell her* Natalie thought. *This heavy unease weighing on me is because I'm keeping something important from London. I have to tell her that I gave Tiffany that book, that she was intoxicated and she begged me not to tell anyone, that I didn't know what to do. I can't keep this from her.*

"London…" Natalie started nervously.

Without a word, London turned and wrapped her arms tightly around her. "I'm sorry," she spoke quickly after a moment. "I know you didn't exactly sign up for this. I'm sure you have to get back to the bakery and…"

Natalie kissed the tip of her ear. "London, it's okay," she murmured. "It's okay to break down. You *have* to, in order to build yourself back up. And, for the record, you're not getting rid of me that easily. It's you and me, right? Celia and Jane will certainly understand."

London shot her a small smile. "Are you sure?"

Natalie threw her a sidelong glance. "Yes," she replied, as if the answer was obvious. "You're my girlfriend."

London's smile widened at the confirmation. "Maybe…" she sighed. "Maybe you were right. You know, when you said that things happen for a reason and that the Universe purposely guides you places, even if you don't understand it at the time? I think I'm beginning to get it now."

"You *think*?" Natalie teased with a gentle wink.

London rolled her eyes good-naturedly but laughed. "I *know*. Definitely."

"I should give you some time once your dad gets here," Natalie spoke. She hated the idea of leaving, but knew that London would need to figure things out with her father. "I'll be back first thing tomorrow. Celia or Jane can open the bakery and then I'll relieve them later in the day."

London shook her head. "You don't have to do that," she protested. "I don't want you driving all over the place. You need to rest too."

Natalie squeezed her hand. "Of course I'll be back," she replied. "Maybe I can even get you out for a while too. We can go to breakfast or lunch, yeah? We can talk." *And I can tell you what I knew about Tiffany before it's too late.*

London finally relented with a nod. "That does sound good," she admitted. "My dad also mentioned that Tiffany's mom is on her way. And I wouldn't wish Diane Foster on anyone without serious preparation."

Natalie laughed. "Is she really that awful?"

London sighed. "Maybe she's mellowed out with age. But I somehow doubt it. She's stopping by the house to collect some of Tiffany's things so she'll be comfortable while she's here."

Natalie slowly stood and gently pulled London up with her. "Text me when you can. Or better yet, call me too."

The growing pit of unease deep in her gut was becoming too much to bear. *I swear if I can get this secret between us out, then I'll never keep anything from London again* she silently promised to any higher power that was listening. *The longer I keep this from her, the worse it's going to feel.*

London enveloped Natalie into a hug. "I'll be here for a while yet, but I'll be in touch periodically. After all, now I'm in love with you so I can't just let hours go by without hearing your voice."

Natalie leaned against London and felt an all-too-familiar rush of warm tenderness. She squeezed her eyes shut and breathed in her scent. *I'll miss sleeping next to her tonight. I hope she's still so open with me after I tell her. Because, either way, I can't stand to let something grow between us.*

CHAPTER 23

London wasn't sure how much time had passed since Natalie left. Wayne had politely bid her good-bye, with promises to visit again tomorrow. She gently massaged some fruit-scented lotion into Tiffany's warm palms. London tried to imagine the blood pulsing just below the surface, carrying nutrients, medicine and healing energy through her sister's body.

"Tiffany!" Diane Foster's unmistakable voice wailed like a siren. "Oh, my Tiffany!"

London immediately straightened in her chair and dropped Tiffany's hands. *Her voice is like nails on a chalkboard* she thought miserably. She took a deep breath. *Try to play nice. Her only daughter is lying in a hospital bed from an overdose. Surely there must be some kind of temporary, compassionate middle ground we can find.*

Diane blew into the room like a blonde, Chanel No. 5-scented whirlwind. She immediately rushed to Tiffany's side without a glance at London. She clasped her hands around Tiffany's as London stood awkwardly to the side.

"Oh, Tiffany!" Diane wailed. She did a double-take at the bedside table and sneered at a clear vase of flowers perched on the corner. "*What* is that? Is that supposed to be a bouquet?" Diane finally turned and looked London up and down for a long, slow moment. "Those flowers are terrible. Where did they come from, the clearance bin at Kroger?"

London realized after a moment that Diane actually expected her to answer. She shrugged. "The police officer that found Tiffany brought them up. Probably from the hospital shop. It was a nice gesture. He was worried."

Diane took a deep breath and shook her head. "A *nice gesture* would have been spending more than five dollars on a bouquet of flowers. Those are cheap. And what kind of room is this? It gives me the creeps. It's dark and depressing. I feel like I'm in a closet." She paused and shot London a disapproving look. "Not that *I* would know anything about that," she sniffed. "Though you certainly would. Where is her doctor? I'd like to have a word with him to discuss moving my Tiffany to a larger, more suitable room immediately."

Your Tiffany could barely stand having lunch with you because you're so intolerable! London wanted to scream. *I know her better in just a few weeks than you do in her lifetime!*

Instead, she closed her eyes slowly. "Right now, I think we should just focus on Tiffany remaining stable and making sure she'll be okay for the long run. She's been asleep since I've been here, but they have her on some heavy medication too. We still need to find out exactly how long they plan to keep her admitted."

"I wish you wouldn't speak to me that way," Diane replied shortly. London's eyes widened and she opened her mouth to protest. Diane held up a hand to silence her. "*I* am her parent and I will make any and all decisions regarding her care."

Vincent Foster cleared his throat pointedly behind London. She nearly jumped out of her skin at the sound. *I wonder how long he's been standing there* she thought.

"*We* are her parents and *we* will make Tiffany's healthcare decisions," Vince clarified. He strode into the room and lingered at the foot of the bed. His authoritative tone seemed confident enough to momentarily quiet Diane.

He gently laid his hand over the blanket. "Hi sweetheart," he murmured to Tiffany. "You're going to be okay, I promise." He turned to London and enveloped her into a hug. "And how are you holding up?"

London slowly returned the hug. "I'm fine," she replied automatically and then paused. She shook her head. "I'm not fine. I'm worried about Tiffany. She's going to be in a lot of trouble when she gets out of here."

"I know," Vince replied. He stroked his chin thoughtfully. "I've already spoken to the attorney on retainer at the company. He'll do the best he can, but Tiffany will have to face the consequences at some point. Hopefully when she has a clear mind. Right now she's sick and the biggest priority is getting her into treatment so she can get better."

London glanced over her father's shoulder at Diane, who was busying herself by unpacking the suitcase she had brought for Tiffany. She neatly stacked a few books and framed photos on the bedside table.

"I asked my personal assistant to look into the best treatment centers in the country," Diane interjected loudly.

"You have a personal assistant?" London interrupted dubiously. She glanced at her father and then back at Diane. "For *what*?"

Diane sighed. "To clarify, I was speaking to Vincent," she said as she cleared her throat. "As I was saying, Dorothy e-mailed me a list of the top ten treatment centers in the country. There's a fantastic facility in Utah that all the celebrities go to. Tiffany will be very comfortable there. She can have a private room and there's a world-class horse arena on-site as well as an indoor ropes course, a state-of-the-art recording studio and some of the best chefs in the region."

Vince wrinkled his nose. "Is she going on a vacation retreat or are we getting our daughter help for her drug and alcohol addition?" His tight voice shook and London knew he was struggling to control its volume. "I don't give a damn what celebrities go where! I care about my daughter and Tiffany is *sick*. She doesn't need a recording studio or a five-star chef. What she needs is an experienced doctor, a good therapist and help to learn how to stay sober! And I have every intention of being there for her each step of the way."

Diane smiled patronizingly. "Of course, Vincent," she replied. "Goodness, you're becoming cranky in your old age. All I'm saying is that this is a quiet place, away from Texas, for her to receive whatever help she needs."

Vince's mouth dropped open. "I should have known. You don't want her to get help around here because you don't want people to know that your daughter is in rehab."

Diane bristled. "Well, I wouldn't put it *quite* so bluntly," she replied with a sniff. "But let's be real, Vincent. Dallas is the biggest small town in Texas and you *know* how people can talk. They love a good scandal and a dirty story, especially when it involves those of our stature."

London rolled her eyes. "Oh, here we go," she muttered.

Diane shot her a look. "It will be less stress on all of us if we keep this quiet and send her to Utah."

Vince stared at her for a moment and shook his head. "I don't believe you," he replied incredulously. "Our daughter could have *died* and the only person you can think of is yourself. Let me reiterate to you, Diane, that I don't give a *damn* what anybody has to say. Let them talk if it helps to fill their empty lives. My only concern is getting Tiffany help so she can live a healthy, *long* life."

London bit the inside of her cheek and tried to remain quiet, but her anger at her former stepmother bubbled over. "I'm so glad Tiffany is knocked out on meds right now so she can't hear you, Diane," she spoke bitterly. "Though you should really hear yourself. You sound…"

"Watch it, little girl," Diane snapped. "You may think you're all grown up now, but you're *nothing*. You…"

London closed her eyes as she tried to tune out Diane's voice. She braced herself for her barrage of insults.

"Diane, shut your mouth," Vince cut in sharply. "London is my daughter and I couldn't be more proud of the woman she's become." He wrapped an arm around London's shoulders as her eyes flew open in surprise.

Did Dad actually just defend me? To Diane, of all people? She wondered in amazement as Vince led her into the hallway.

"Come on, sweetheart," he continued. "You need some rest. I'll deal with everything else." He shot a look back into the room.

"I don't know what you ever saw in that woman," London fumed. Her voice was barely above a whisper. "She's horrible. She's always been awful."

Vince smiled faintly and rubbed her shoulder. "We got the very best part of her," he replied. "We got Tiffany."

London sagged against the wall. She was suddenly exhausted. "I'm tired, Dad," she decided with a sigh. "Will you be all right?"

"Of course," he replied with a nod. He fished in the pocket of his khaki Dockers and pulled out a set of keys. "Here, take the Tesla. Your rental is still at the house. I'm planning to be here all night."

"Are you sure?" London asked. "I can come back and pick you up."

Vince smiled . "Get some sleep," he told her. "I'm sorry I missed Natalie earlier. Perhaps once things settle down, the three of us can go to dinner."

London nodded tiredly and returned her father's smile. "I'd like that," she replied. "She rushed me here as soon as I got the call and then stayed for hours. I think you'd like her a lot."

"If she's been making you as happy as you've been, then I think I'll like her a lot too," he agreed. "Rest up. I'll see you tomorrow."

London plucked the keys from his hand. "Good night, Dad," she said as she stepped onto her tiptoes to kiss his cheek.

She was positively exhausted as she dragged herself down the long corridor. Her eyelids felt heavy and her feet ached with every step. Finally, she pushed open the exit door and felt a rush of dry, hot air hit her face.

"After today, that big guest bed at Dad's house has never sounded so good," she muttered to herself.

London blinked sleepily in the bright morning light. A high-pitched ringing sound was coming from somewhere to her left, but the sunlight streaming between the wide Venetian blinds had temporarily disoriented her.

She flopped onto her stomach and pushed her messy black hair out of her face with one hand. She located the loud, offending object and grabbed her phone from the bedside table. She blinked in shock at the time reflected back at her and quickly pressed the phone to her ear.

Oh my God, it's 10:30. How did I sleep that late? She wondered. *The entire morning is halfway gone.*

"Hey, you," she greeted Natalie. Her voice was still low and gritty with sleep.

"Baby!" Natalie replied easily, her smile evident through the phone. "I tried to call you twice earlier. I was getting worried."

"I'm sorry," London apologized. She swung her bare feet over the edge of the bed and glared at the bright cracks in the blinds. "I really knocked out last night. I didn't even hear my phone."

"You sound like you were sleeping well," Natalie agreed. "Are you all right?"

London held a hand over her eyes. "Damn light," she muttered. "There's sunlight everywhere. This room is, like, *bathed* in heavenly rays and pure Vitamin D."

Natalie burst out laughing and the sound immediately perked London up. "Oh, you *poor* thing, you!" Natalie replied through her giggles. "I'm guessing there's not as much sunlight in Chicago."

"Not *all* the time," London replied defensively. She tried to remain stubbornly cranky, but realized it was impossible while listening to Natalie's voice and laughter. Her face broke into a grin. "So I get to see you today, right?"

"Of course," Natalie replied. "I know I probably sound like one of *those* women, but I miss you already. Why deny it?"

London smiled again as a warm feeling spread through her chest. "I miss you too." She glanced at the bedside clock and raised an eyebrow. "So I guess breakfast is out. My fault. Lunch?"

"I'm at the bakery now," Natalie replied. "Jane is under the weather today and headed to the doctor. According to Celia, she gets strep throat right around this time every summer and now that I think about it, she does. It must be some kind of weird seasonal thing. Anyway, we've been slammed here. How about a late lunch? That way, I can help Celia through Mission's lunch rush and then sneak out for the rest of the afternoon."

"Perfect," London replied. "That will give me some time to head to the hospital and check on Tiffany."

"I'll come by Baylor then and kidnap you for a few hours," Natalie went on. "Around 2, 2:30?"

"You can kidnap me anytime," London confirmed with a laugh. "But yes, I'll plan to see you then."

"Okay," Natalie replied and then paused for a moment. "I…I love you."

"Love you too, beautiful," London responded automatically. *I can't believe how easy it is to say those three words to her now* she thought. *And the craziest part is that I mean them, from the bottom of my heart.*

As they ended their call, London scanned the bedroom and paused as her gaze settled on her iPad. She realized with a sinking feeling that she hadn't spoken to Holly in days.

I really need to talk with her she thought in determination. *After everything that's happened, I can't just up and leave for Chicago.* She blew out her breath. *I don't know what that means for the promotion, or even for my career. But Natalie and Tiffany mean more.*

London's heart rate quickened as her mind's eye wandered back to Natalie. She remembered the cozy bed in Haskell and the look in her warm brown eyes as she watched her awaken.

"I'll call Holly tonight," she decided out loud. Her voice sounded powerful in the stillness of the quiet house. It flooded her with a sense of confidence, despite the nerves she felt at knowing the conversation would most likely lead to turning her back on W.H. Young. "I can't do it, can I? I can't take that promotion and I can't leave Natalie."

She smiled as her earlier words echoed in her mind. *Why deny it?*

CHAPTER 24

Natalie stepped back into the narrow kitchen of the bakery, where Celia was handing a box of pastries to a customer.

"Have a great day, y'all!" She called after them with a short wave.

"That was one of the best lunch rushes we've had in weeks," Natalie remarked with a smile.

Celia nodded. "Today has been a very good day for the bakery," she replied. "I have to admit that when you mentioned the idea of getting the food truck, I wasn't sure it would be a good investment. But you really took that idea, ran with it and knocked it out of the park. We're developing quite a following."

Natalie grinned. "It's a great way to be mobile, isn't it?" She replied. "I love that we can get our brand and our products out to people, even if they may not always come all the way 'round here. I know there's overhead with the food truck, but it's not nearly as much as the shop."

She could feel Celia watching her for a moment as she wiped down their prep counter. "It was a very smart move for the business, *sobrina*. I'm not just proud of you, I'm impressed."

Natalie glanced up and sensed there was more Celia wanted to say. "Thank you, *tia*."

After a long moment, Celia continued. "You know, *Natalia*, that you're not just my niece. You're my daughter. I may not have given birth to you, but I've raised you and I love you just like I would have if I'd carried you in my belly. You're smart and you're kind. You have a love inside you that draws everyone."

Natalie stilled, unsure what had caused Celia's sudden honesty. "I'm just me," she replied with a wave of her hand. "There's no one else I can be. And *you* taught me that, *tia*. So thank you."

Celia smiled. "I know you're ready to go," she went on. "I know you can't be expected to live with Jane and I forever. I just want you to know that, when you decide to move out of our home, you have our full support. You're still young, *sobrina*. You're only thirty years old. Surely you have other interests or professions you might want to explore. I also want you to know it's okay if you outgrow Mission Bakery, if you want to try other careers."

Natalie's mouth dropped open. "But Celia, I love Mission Bakery. Why would I want to leave? This is our family's life."

Celia patted her arm gently. "It's okay for it to be my life and Jane's life, because we have each other. Our life is already settled and Mission Bakery is just another aspect of it. You're young, *Natalia*. You need to have your own life too."

Natalie felt an unexpected pressure behind her eyes as the meaning behind Celia's words dawned on her. *She wants me to ensure there's room in my life for love - and London - too.*

"I do need to give London just as much of myself as she's given me," Natalie spoke thoughtfully. "I don't know what the future holds for either of us, but I do know that I'm going to be a part of hers and she will be part of mine. We've finally admitted to one another that we're in love."

Celia grinned. "I'm so happy to hear that," she replied. "She's a good girl. But you know that Weatherford is no place for two young girls to build a life together. You need to get out, explore and go to one of the big cities together."

Natalie crossed her arms, even though she knew her aunt was right. "You're kicking me out, *tia*?" She meant it to be a teasing jibe, but her voice came out too wobbly for her liking.

"Never, sweetheart," Celia replied seriously. "You and London could stay at the house with Jane and I, but I know you don't want that. You need your own space to start your relationship and grow."

Natalie reached over and hugged her aunt silently. "It's been tough coming to terms with knowing you're leaving soon," Celia continued. "I told Jane that I felt sort of like a mother hen, watching her baby go out into the world without the shelter that she's given them. Jane told me that's because I *am*. I've learned enough in this lifetime to know that truly loving someone is equal parts holding onto them for dear life *and* letting them be free. I like London. The love between you two reminds me a little of Jane and I, when we were young and our relationship was new. And it would be a damn shame to let something like that go, *Natalia*. You keep that love, *sobrina*."

"I will," Natalie whispered gently. She squeezed her aunt once more before taking a deep breath. "I understand."

A quick glance at the clock let her know that there was still enough time to stop by the Foster house before picking her up at the hospital. "Can I take some of these leftover sweet breads? And maybe a couple of cream cheese brownies?" Natalie asked. "I was planning to drop them off at London's father's house."

She smiled as she remembered London's original order at the bakery during their first real meeting. *Because walking in on her in a bath towel does not count as a first meeting* she reminded herself.

"Of course," Celia said with a nod. "I'm sure neither she nor her father have had any real food since her sister's emergency. Make sure you take the ones on the far end of the tray. Those are the freshest. Take some of the homemade honey wheat bread too, so they can make sandwiches."

Natalie carefully counted the baked goods into two white boxes. "Thank you," she replied. "I'm going to stop by their house this afternoon and drop this food off. Both of them are at Baylor now, but at least they'll have something homemade and fresh to eat when they get back. Then I thought I might stop at the hospital and have a quick meal with London."

"The bakery will slow down this afternoon," Celia responded. "Go. Tell London we say hello."

Natalie closed the last box with a pop and smiled at her aunt. "See you later. Love you."

With that, she rushed out the front door as the bell jangled loudly in her excited wake.

London was pleased to discover that Tiffany was awake as she quietly entered her hospital room. Her bed had been inclined to allow her to sit up. Her sister forced a weak smile in greeting.

London swallowed hard as a long moment of awkward silence stretched before them. She pulled a chair up to Tiffany's bedside and took a deep breath. "I'm so glad…" she started.

"I really messed up, didn't I?" Tiffany spoke at the same time.

They both paused and laughed. "I'm so glad you're okay," London finished softly. She reached over and squeezed Tiffany's fingers. "Everything will be okay. It's just steps up from here."

Tiffany grimaced and rolled her eyes. "A *lot* of steps up."

London tried to smile brightly and shrugged. "That's what we're here for. Dad and I. You have our full support and we're going to do whatever it takes to help you."

Tiffany slouched in the bed and stared at a point on the wall. "You know, I really thought I knew what it took to help myself," she started. Notes of frustration were evident in her voice. "I never wanted to listen to anybody else. I *definitely* didn't want to compromise my independence. Not with Dad, not with Wayne and not even with you. At the end of the day, isn't that all any of us really have?"

Oh my God, she sounds exactly like me London realized incredulously. *I guess we didn't have to be raised together to be the same. To be family.*

"I've learned a lot about independence lately, Tiff," London responded slowly. "I understand where you're coming from. But is it worth it not to let people love you? Because, honestly Tiffany, if it's genuine then they're going to love you anyway. I know I do. Sometimes it's okay to drop the defenses."

Tiffany met her eyes and smiled. "I really thought I could manage everything. I always felt like my best self either with Adderall or a few drinks in me," she paused and held up a hand as London began to protest. "I know what you're going to say, but it's true. I believed I was a better person, more sociable, energetic, ready to take on the world. Hell, even lunch with my mother was tolerable. What people don't realize is that, while you're feeling good, it starts to affect your body. It rewires your brain so you need more and more. Or at least you *think* you do."

London nodded. "You're going to be okay though," she murmured. "You could have died."

Tiffany's eyes filled with tears as she stared stubbornly at the wall. "You know, I always thought I'd die doing something amazing," she remarked bitterly. "Cliff jumping in Hawaii, traveling through volatile corners of the world, sailing across the ocean, *something*. I never thought I could actually die right here in Texas." She paused as a tear rolled from the corner of her eye. "I never thought I'd end up nearly killing *myself* by becoming my own worst enemy. How can I possibly recover from this?"

London squeezed her sister's hand again. *Think of something to say, anything* she thought desperately. She took a deep breath. *Or you could speak to her honestly and from the heart.*

"One of the craziest things I've had to accept in life so far is that it doesn't always go according to whatever plan you might think you have in mind," London started. "I never thought I'd end up in Fort Worth, Texas, but here I am. You just have to adapt. The plan that you have at one point in your life might not work so well once you begin another chapter. You have to trust that things are happening for a reason and, even if it seems really tough at the moment, you're being pushed in this direction for reasons you may not understand yet. Maybe I needed a reminder that I still have the ability to love and be loved. Maybe you needed a wake-up call to see how badly you're hurting yourself. As for how you'll recover, someone who means a great deal to me once advised me to experience things and enjoy days. And I promise you'll start to heal." London smiled and squeezed Tiffany's hand.

Tiffany regarded her for a long moment and smiled back. "Whoever gave you that advice must have been wise," she agreed wryly. "You're right, though. For the longest time, my plan was that I had no plan. I'd go wherever the world needed me. I liked the work I did, but I also loved not having any real commitments and not knowing where I'd be in six months or a year." She sighed. "I don't think I'll ever lose my free spirit, but maybe it's time to grow up a little bit too."

"No one wants you to change, Tiff," London reassured her. "We all love you for exactly who you are. Life is about learning and evolving into who we're meant to be. Personally, I'd be livid if you turned into a boring, desk-sitting, paper-pushing corporate hack."

"Like you?" Tiffany teased.

London laughed and was pleased to see a gleam back in her sister's eyes. "Trust me, it's not all it's cracked up to be," she replied. "I'm only beginning to realize what I've been missing out on."

"I could've told you *that*," Tiffany cracked. She grimaced as she shifted on the bed and swung her legs over the edge. She carefully stood, batting away London's offer for help, and held onto her portable I.V. with her right hand. "I have to pee like crazy. These nurses have been flushing me with so many liquids that I swear I've been peeing, like, every hour."

"Thank you for that information," London called after her jokingly. She sat back in the hospital chair and smiled as Tiffany closed the bathroom door behind her.

Things feel right again she realized. *Sure, it'll be a process with Tiffany and I. But right now? Things are good. We're where we need to be.*

London glanced at the bedside table and idly scanned the books and gossip magazines that Diane had brought yesterday. One of the books caught her eye and she picked it out of the stack for a closer look.

The Wisdom to Know the Difference she read silently. London turned it over in her hands to read the synopsis on the back cover. *It's a sobriety book* she realized in surprise. *To overcome substance abuse. Good for Tiffany. Maybe she knew things were spiraling out of control.*

London flipped open the front cover and glanced through a few pages as the toilet flushed. "Nice book, Tiff!" She called proudly. "Have you looked through it yet? Do you think it will be helpful?"

Her voice trailed off as she noticed an inscription above the first chapter. She froze and read it over again.

Jane: May your journey bring you peace, health, light and happiness. I am proud to be your sponsor and wish you and Celia many years of love as you weave your lives together. Sincerely, Margaret Holmes

London tried to swallow, but her throat suddenly seemed very narrow and dry. She racked her brain to recall if Celia or Jane had ever been introduced to Tiffany, but she knew that their families hadn't formally met yet.

She glanced at the date next to the inscription. *June 16th, 1982* she thought. *Before Natalie was born.*

"Which book?" Tiffany's voice roused London from her confusion. She peered into her lap as she gingerly climbed back into the bed. "Oh, *that* book…" her voice trailed off. "Well, um, I haven't had a chance to read it yet, but I plan to. It's one that, um, I'm looking forward to starting while I'm here."

London's heart sank as she watched Tiffany stammer nervously. "Did you buy it?" She asked. She couldn't shake the terrible feeling that she already knew her answer.

Tiffany met her eyes and then shook her head. "I, uh, borrowed it. Someone leant it to me."

"Who?" London heard herself ask. She traced her finger along the spine of the worn paperback as the punched-in-the-gut feeling exploded somewhere deep in her belly.

"Natalie leant to me, London," Tiffany admitted with a sigh. "She stopped by the house one morning and gave it to me. You were there."

London tried to remember the particular morning, but couldn't think past the betrayal that she felt seeping into her bloodstream. "She came to the house to lend you a book on substance abuse and sobriety?" She asked, her voice shaking.

Tiffany stared at her lap. "We, uh, *bumped* into each other the night before. She was leaving and I was coming home. You have to understand, London, I was in a really bad state. She knew it and we talked for a while. Well, *after* I threw up on the driveway in front of her." She took a deep breath. "She wanted to help. *I* begged her not to say anything to you. I made her promise."

London stared at the book. The title and tagline swam before her eyes. "She didn't say *anything* to me," London replied in disbelief. "She kept that from me. During all of the times we talked to each other and talked about our lives and our families, she never once mentioned anything. When I got the call that you were in the hospital and I sobbed the entire way from Haskell to Fort Worth, it *never* occurred to her to say a word. I was *devastated*."

Tiffany swallowed hard and tried to sit up further. "London, I *begged* her not to say anything. I was so embarrassed and I was scared of what you would think. I didn't want you to know how bad it was."

"Why?" London shot back. "I'm your *sister*! How can you and my…my *partner* go behind my back and keep something from me?"

Another tear rolled down Tiffany's cheek. "You have to understand, London," she tried again. "You came to Texas with…with this *persona*, you know? You were so closed off and this perfectionist and…"

"I am *not* a perfectionist!" London interrupted hotly.

"We've never been a part of each other's lives," Tiffany went on. "All I've wanted is a sister. You know, that love and unconditional support that you can only get from your own sibling. I didn't want anything to come between us or you looking down on me right off the bat. I was scared of you *hating* me."

London crossed her arms. "That's not fair," she replied. "I never hated you. Why would I start now?"

She knew I resented her she thought weakly. *And that's why she didn't want to come to me.*

"London, you can't be mad at her," Tiffany continued. "Please, think of the world beyond this impenetrable bubble that you've created around yourself. I was scared, but I *know* Natalie loves you. Try to see it from our point of view."

"If she loved me, there never would have been a secret this big between us for so long," London replied stonily. "You know, I have to wonder. If I hadn't happened upon that book, if your mother hadn't picked it up in a stack to bring to the hospital, would she have *ever* told me? What else has she kept from me? Lying by omission is just as big of a betrayal as lying to someone's face. *Especially* when you and that person are in love."

"See, you do love her," Tiffany replied. "She's someone you'd better hold onto and you know it deep down. You two can get past it."

"It's a betrayal," London responded shortly. "You say I'm closed off? That I don't vocalize things much? That's because I've *been* betrayed, Tiffany. I've felt like my heart was cut out of my chest and I've stayed up all night crying over someone who betrayed me. I'll be damned if I ever let myself feel that way again!"

Tiffany flopped back against her pillows. "Then be mad at me," she said simply. "Natalie is good for you. I can't let you lose her over this."

London ran a hand through her hair in distress. "And the thing of it all is that I *can't* be mad at you, Tiffany," she continued helplessly. "You're an addict. It's a disease and you weren't in your right state of mind. Natalie *was*."

"You sound mad at me," Tiffany ventured. "It's okay if you are. I'm sorry. It was totally wrong of me to put your girlfriend in that position, just like it was wrong of me to put you in the position I did at the Rangers game. I realize that there's a lot of people I need to apologize to. I'll start with you and Natalie."

London felt a strange and sudden pressure behind her eyes. It blurred her vision and closed her throat as she stood.

It doesn't matter how much I tried to protect myself she thought bitterly. *I still got burned in the end. And this time, it hurts even more because it's Natalie.*

"I'm going to step out for some air," London announced. She crossed her arms decisively. "Natalie is going to be here any minute and I…I don't know if I want to see her right now. I'll be back."

With that, she strode out of the room without a second glance. Hot, angry tears were ready to spill and she hated it. *I hate that I feel like crying, I hate myself for being weak, I hate…* she shook her head as she realized she couldn't finish the thought. *What's worst is that I* don't *hate her.*

CHAPTER 25

Natalie glanced down at her phone as she pulled her truck into the driveway of London's father's home. *Strange that she hasn't texted* she mused. She had already grown used to hearing from her often, even if it was just a silly message with a kissy face. *She must be spending quality time with Tiffany. Good. Those two need time together.*

She squinted through the bright afternoon sunlight at the wide porch as she eased her truck into Park. A woman she had never seen before slowly paced up and down the porch. Her thumbs jumped across the wide screen of her phone.

The woman was tall and impossibly glamorous, with large, shining jewels that glinted on her fingers and across her slender neck. Her black hair was wrapped in an effortless chignon and her tailored business suit was sharp and professional. *She's not from around here* Natalie thought. *She looks a lot like London did when she first arrived.*

Natalie glanced at the sleek black Lexus S.U.V. perched gently against the curb. The plate number told her it was a rental. *I suppose she could be one of London's friends or acquaintances, but she never mentioned anything about any visits* she thought in confusion.

"Hi, can I help you?" She called as she walked uncertainly to the porch. The woman's head shot up.

"I hope so," she responded crisply, enunciating each word.

Okay, she's definitely *not from around here* Natalie thought with an inward laugh.

"I'm looking for London," the woman continued. "London Foster. I may be at the wrong house, but I swear this is the address she e-mailed to me. Is this where she's staying?"

Natalie chewed her bottom lip as she wondered how much information to give away. "I'm sorry, and you are…?"

The woman met Natalie's eyes and recognition seemed to light her face. "Oh, you must be Natalie!" She exclaimed. "Of course. I recognize you from the photos."

"What photos?" She replied immediately.

"London's Instagram account," she went on. "I tried to tell her that everyone at W.H. Young was following it now, but I don't think she really believed me. The clip of you line-dancing at the county fair was *fantastic*."

Natalie's mouth dropped open as realization dawned on her. "You must be…Holly?" She was still trying to recover from the shock of this strange woman seeming to know *her*.

The woman grinned. "The one and only," she confirmed. "To think, London didn't even want an Instagram account. I only made her sign up for one so we could keep in touch during her trip. Anyway, I told her I had a client meeting in Dallas tomorrow. I flew down a day early to spend some time with her."

"That's nice of you," Natalie replied lamely. *Why do I feel like there's something big I'm missing here?*

"I have to admit, it's not *all* with honorable intentions," Holly replied. "I hate to steal London from her time off, but this client meeting tomorrow is quite important. It's essential that I brief her on them ahead of time and introduce her."

Natalie wrinkled her nose. "Her sister is in the hospital," she replied. *It's not your business to discuss* she thought as she drew on the politeness she'd been raised to adhere to. *Give Holly the basics and let London decide how much to tell her.* "She's over at Baylor All-Saints. It was an unexpected situation, so she's been sort of…unavailable. I'm sure she just forgot you were coming in."

"Oh, no," Holly gasped. She covered her mouth with her hand and looked genuinely concerned. "That's terrible. No wonder she hasn't been answering my calls. I'll have to figure out an alternative to tomorrow's client meeting. Surely there will be another once she returns that she can accompany me to."

Natalie nodded and then blinked in confusion. *She talks too fast* she thought. *I can barely keep up.* "Oh, okay," she replied slowly. *This makes no sense.* "Why?"

It was Holly's turn to appear confused. "Well, so we can start easing her into her new role once she's back in Chicago," she replied, as though the answer was very obvious. "London was given an incredible promotion. In fact, that's why she's in Texas. We agreed that, if she took some time off, we'd transition her into the role once she returned. Honestly, I couldn't be more proud of her. She's really on the fast track to a great career with the company."

Natalie tried to process this, but she felt as though she had been kicked in the stomach. "When…When she returns?"

Holly appeared to clueless to Natalie's strife as she laughed. "I spoke to her last week and she wasn't sure on the exact date of her return, but I know she was planning to leave relatively soon. I'll have to check in with her and find out how her sister is and if she'll be back once she's released. Or sooner."

The rest of the world seemed to go on mute as a tornado of emotions swept through Natalie. She could see Holly's mouth moving as she continued her rapid-fire speech and she could feel a light breeze tickling her forearms, but all she could understand was the sudden ache that pierced her chest.

"I should get going," Natalie cut in quickly. "I'm sorry, I have to run." She placed the bakery boxes gently onto the welcome mat and nodded once at Holly. "Nice to meet you, ma'am."

She could feel Holly's stare on her back as she forced her feet back to the truck. "Ma'am?" Holly's voice echoed behind her. "I'm not *that* old!"

It's Southern hospitality Natalie answered silently. *You don't get it and London didn't get it either.* Doubt began to cloud Natalie's mind as she wondered what else London didn't get. *I've been too enamored with her, too busy letting myself fall in love with her, to see if she's sincere* she thought.

Natalie turned the key in her truck with a shaking hand. *This whole time I thought she was scared. I thought she needed someone to show her love and kindness. How sweet it all could be. How do I know she really meant anything she's said?*

Am I that stupid? Natalie wondered as she jerked the truck out of the driveway. *To not see that I'm not part of her long-term plan? That she just wanted a Texas fling?*

"But she said she loves me," Natalie whispered angrily. She hit her palm against the steering wheel in frustration. "Would she really say that if she didn't mean it?"

She glared at the red light ahead of her. The sinking feeling in her stomach kept her circling back to a single thought. *If I was really any part of her future plans, she would have said something about the promotion or her job situation. She must think I'm really dumb.*

The light changed to green and Natalie hit the gas. "Well, if London Foster thinks I'm just some silly Southern girl that she can use at her convenience, then she has another thing coming."

London could hear Natalie's footsteps on the white linoleum even before she spotted her walking down the long hallway. She sat in a chair just outside of Tiffany's room and took a deep breath. She glanced up and was momentarily shaken by the stormy look in Natalie's eyes as she approached. There was no trace of the easy smile that London had fallen so hard for.

London stood as she racked her brain and tried to figure out why Natalie was so angry. She stopped short about a foot from her, but didn't reach out for a hug or kiss. London's heart sank as she realized how used to Natalie's sweet affection she already was.

They regarded each other warily for a moment. London thought again of the inscription in the book on Tiffany's bedside table and felt her insides twist with anger and betrayal all over again. Natalie glared at her silently.

"When were you planning to tell me that you gave my sister Jane's book?" London spoke tightly. "Or even just the simple fact that you *knew* how addicted she was?"

For a moment, the anger in Natalie's dark eyes was replaced by shock. Her mouth dropped open. "London, I was planning to tell you…"

"When?" London cut in angrily. "Because it's too late; she already overdosed. You had every opportunity to say something to me. *Any* of the times that we spent together would have been fine. Even on the way to the hospital, it didn't occur to you to mention *anything*?"

"I didn't know what to do!" Natalie exclaimed defensively. "I was never expecting to encounter Tiffany the way I did that night. I didn't know if it was my place to say anything. Believe me, I wish I had. Looking back, I realize I should have said something to you right away."

London stared at her for a long moment. "You betrayed my trust," she replied simply. "How can I trust you if you don't know to tell me things like that? Tiffany is my sister…"

"She begged me not to say anything," Natalie tried again, cutting her off. "I know that not saying anything was a mistake, but you have to understand the hard position I was in."

"I'm your *partner*," London replied coldly. "I can't trust someone who keeps things from me. Like I told Tiffany earlier, lying by omission is just as bad as lying outright."

Natalie's face inexplicably hardened and she took a step back. "You know, London, you're right," she replied after a moment. "Lying by omission *is* just as much of a betrayal as outright lying. Speaking of, when were you planning to inform me that you'd accepted a promotion at your company and were planning to return to Chicago soon?"

London's mouth dropped open, but she couldn't find any words to refute Natalie's accusation.

Natalie watched her for a moment. She shook her head. "Exactly," she went on angrily. "You can't even deny it. Were you planning to just up and leave in a few days? A week? You obviously weren't planning to tell me *anything*."

"For the record, I had already made the decision in my heart and in my mind to decline the promotion," London replied weakly. She hadn't expected the sudden turning of tables. "I just hadn't had a chance to tell Holly."

"You had *every* chance to speak to Holly!" Natalie exclaimed. "She called at least two times just while we were in Haskell. You were avoiding it because you weren't sure. Do you think I'm stupid, London? Do you think you're so much smarter and more *evolved* than me that you could leave Texas without so much as a conversation? You forget that I've been through that once already."

London took a deep breath. *We betrayed each other* she thought. *I should have realized all along that we would end up hurting each other, just like every other couple and every other love story that starts out with so much promise. Natalie will be better off without me.*

"Here's a piece of advice," Natalie finished coldly. "If you're fixin' to have that conversation with Holly, you ought to do it sooner than later. Because she's here. I ran into her at your father's house."

London closed her eyes. "Shit, the client meeting in Dallas," she muttered. "I completely forgot, with everything that's been going on." She shook her head. "You know, not saying anything about Tiffany was keeping something really important from me, Natalie. I…I don't know anything anymore."

After a moment of tense silence, London finally met Natalie's eyes. She looked as though she had been slapped and the expression on her face wrenched London's gut. *There's so much ice between us* London thought. *I hate this.*

Natalie finally nodded slowly. "I guess that's what I get for falling for another outsider."

The word hit London in slow motion. She blinked and felt as though she had been sacked in the stomach with a ton of bricks. Her eyes filled with tears at the word's sting. Natalie's gaze pierced through her.

That's what the problem is she realized grimly. *I'm an outsider. I have been since the day I was born. I was never supposed to be a Foster. Diane despised me, my father never wanted me and I was never meant for anyone. Even Natalie finally realizes I don't fit in.*

"You know," London started. Her voice was thick with tears. "I have never fit in *anywhere* in my entire life. I've always been the outsider who never quite blended. Thank you for that reminder. I'm sorry that you ever met me."

Natalie's mouth dropped open and she began to protest, but London was still reeling from the sting. She turned stiffly as the pangs in her heart nearly knocked her off-balance. She walked out of the side exit door without a second glance. The rest of the world was blocked out by the pounding in her ears and the simmering heat just beneath her skin. Somewhere, in the distance, she could hear Natalie calling after her, the whirring of intricate hospital machines and even the frosty air conditioning blowing through the vents, but there was only one thought on her mind.

It's time to leave she decided firmly.

London pulled into the driveway of her father's home. In the stillness of the vehicle, she sat back against the cool leather seats and took a deep breath. She stared at the oversized garage, the shaded porch and the lush brick walkway lined with imported tropical plants.

This has never been my home she thought bitterly. *My home was a beautiful brownstone in Chicago, where Mom rented out the basement unit and I went to sleep at night listening to the sounds of the city. This was never me.*

London pulled her phone from her pocket and dialed Holly. Her friend picked up on the first ring.

"There you are! I've been worried sick. How are you? How is your sister?" Holly's questions tumbled out, one on top of the other.

"She's doing okay," London replied slowly. "She's awake. Conscious and making progress. So far, there have been no long-term problems discovered. It could have been much worse, so I'm…I'm grateful for that."

"Good," Holly replied. "I'm glad to hear that. Goodness London, I've been so worried about you! It's not like you to ignore calls or texts for long periods of time. You're one of my best friends, you know? And then I heard about your sister and I was so worried…"

London felt about two inches tall as Holly continued. *What kind of friend am I?* She wondered. *What sort of person avoids someone that loves them because they're too scared to tell them how they really feel? God, I* am *an awful person.*

"I'm sorry," she interrupted quickly. "I really am."

There was a short pause. "Christ, London. Don't be sorry," Holly finally replied. "Just don't be a stranger on me, okay?"

London nodded, even though she knew Holly couldn't see her. "Of course. You got it."

Holly sighed in relief. "Look, I know there's no way you'll make the client meeting tomorrow. I've already briefed the C.E.O. as to what's going on. I'm flying out of Love Field tomorrow evening, so give me a call in a couple of days. I'll go over the meeting with you then. We'll talk more when I'm back in Chicago."

"Great," London replied as she lamely tried to muster up an ounce of enthusiasm. "Looking forward to it."

There was another short pause as London listened to Holly take a deep breath. "All right. We'll talk soon. Take care." Her voice was tinged with a strange tone akin to disappointment as she said good-bye.

London rested her forehead against the steering wheel and closed her eyes. "Well, that's two for two," she muttered. "I really have a knack for pissing people off lately."

She thought of Natalie and a sudden rush of hurt and sadness swelled through her chest. *I put that gutted look in her eyes* London thought. She felt as though a bucket of ice water had been dumped over her head. *I hurt her and then she hurt me. Who wants to stay when all they are is an outsider, anyway?*

CHAPTER 26

London stopped short halfway through the living room as she spied her father shoving half a ham sandwich into his mouth. He sat at the breakfast bar and glanced up with a smile before nodding and waving the other sandwich half at her in greeting.

"Found a special delivery from Mission Bakery on the porch when I got home," he called to her. "That was awfully thoughtful of Natalie to drop some things off. I hope you don't mind, but I dug into that honey bread. It's fantastic. With Amelia in Greece for another two weeks, I've been missing some of that home cooked taste. Care for a sandwich?"

London eyed the half-loaf of honey bread but ignored her empty stomach. "No, thanks," she replied stiffly. "I'm thinking about leaving, actually."

Vince shrugged and took another bite of his sandwich. "If you say so. Can't guarantee there will be any left when you get back though. Where to, London?"

She took a deep breath. "No, I mean I think it might be time to head back to Chicago," she clarified. "I can't stay here forever, Dad." She paused and blew out her breath in frustration. Vince froze, his sandwich halfway to his mouth. "You and I both know that was never the plan, Dad. Now that we know Tiffany will be all right and, you know, I have this big promotion at work waiting for me…"

Vince blinked. "Seems awfully sudden, London," he replied. "If it's time for you to go back, then it's time. But I thought you'd give us a little more warning. Not just me, but what about Tiffany? What about Natalie? I don't think you should just up and leave."

"Up and leave?" London repeated incredulously. She felt a surge of indignation at the guilt creeping through her veins. "Dad, Fort Worth *isn't* my home. This was only ever supposed to be a temporary trip. Of course I can up and leave, so I can return to the life that was put on hold in Chicago to be here. My *real* life." The bitterness tasted like acid in her mouth.

Even as she spoke, London knew that the life she'd never meant to start in Fort Worth was the life she loved more. *But what choice do I have?* She thought angrily. *I'm tired of everyone else making my life decisions for me.*

She felt her father studying her closely. He slowly shook his head. "You know that's a lie, London," he responded. He gestured to the stool next to him. "Sit. Please. You're an adult and, ultimately, you're going to do whatever you want, but there's a few things I'd like you to know first."

London stared at the stool for a moment before grudgingly plopping onto it. *We waited how many years to have a regular conversation?* She thought. *The least I can do is hear him out before I make my arrangements to head back to Chicago.*

"Like what?" She asked as she twirled to face him.

Vince was quiet for a moment. He looked lost in the faraway expression in his eyes as he gazed at a far corner of the kitchen. He blinked and smiled. "Do you know how you got your name, London?"

London was floored. She was torn. Part of her wanted to stand up, roll her eyes and continue her mission of getting the hell out of Fort Worth. The other half realized that she felt closer to her father in the last few weeks than she had in her entire life. *I'm different now* she realized. *I'm not the jaded woman I was before. I was too angry and resentful to listen to anything he tried to say. Now I want to hear him.*

"What…What does that have to do with anything?" She finally sputtered.

"Fleetwood Mac, live at Wembley in 1983. God, your mom loved that band," Vince spoke. His voice was filled with passion and his eyes were still locked onto that same faraway spot. "We were both studying for a year overseas in London and we met in the exchange program. Your mom was from Eastern Illinois University and I was from Southern Methodist. What a pair we made. What a beautiful city."

"You and Mom met in London?" She asked hesitantly. Curiosity was getting the best of her.

Vince nodded. "We did," he confirmed. "Boy, my parents were livid that I'd decided to, in their words, throw away a year of college on studying abroad in the U.K. I had never been outside of Texas and I knew what was expected of me once I graduated. But it was something that I wanted to do for myself and no one else; not the Foster family, not Foster Oil & Gas, *nothing*. Despite their disapproval, I was an adult so I signed up for that year away. I was a twenty-one year old kid who desperately needed to open his horizons and *experience* life. And I sure did experience it while I was there. God, London was so different from anything I'd known."

London stayed quiet as she soaked up her father's story. *They were a couple of kids* she thought morosely. *Then the pressures of society got them. At least that's how Mom always tried explaining it to me.*

"Anyway, it's hard to articulate," Vince went on. "You know when something feels like a big risk, but you have this unshakable confidence deep in your gut that it's right? Almost like, God I don't know, things beyond your sight and control are just *aligning*? You know I don't think like that. Facts, figures, statistics and data are what drives me. *Real*, tangible things. But it was the only time in my life that I've felt something like that, so I've always wondered about it."

"Yes," London replied softly. "I've felt that." *That's exactly how I felt when I was coming to Texas.*

"Well, I went to London," Vince replied. "I met your mom during my first month overseas and, God, there was no hope for me. I fell for her the second I laid eyes on her. She was beautiful all right, but when I started to look closer and see the things that nobody else did? I was a goner. And you know what, London? When your mom chose me too, that was the only time in my life that I've felt *truly* lucky. Not blessed because of the financial stability of our family or grateful for material comforts, but genuinely *lucky*."

London swallowed. "I don't understand," she replied stubbornly. "If things were so magical between you two, how did they go so awry? Why wasn't your love enough to work things through?"

"Your mother was the love of my life," Vince replied seriously. "There's no doubt in my mind about that. Things became complicated. We were young. Too young not to cave from family pressure and expectations from the outside world. The 1983 Fleetwood Mac concert at Wembley Stadium in London is when you were conceived."

London's mouth dropped open. "Oh my *God*, Dad. Seriously?"

Vince held up a hand and smiled. "Go with me for a second, sweetheart," he continued. "Your mom was so excited to see them and I surprised her with tickets. We had been going together for about six months and I wanted her to have the best seats possible. The tickets were so damned expensive, even during those times. The whole concert I knew I ought to be watching the show that I'd paid a ridiculous sum of money to be up close and personal at, but I couldn't take my eyes off your mom if I'd tried. That's how I'll always remember her, London. Young, free and dancing to the music with her eyes closed and a huge smile on her face. A sweet Midwestern gal in a crowd of thousands across the ocean. She was something else."

London blinked back tears as she thought of her mother. *I never knew who she was before I was born* she thought. *I guess no one ever really realizes that their parents were once young and filled with youthful exuberance too.*

At that moment, she wished harder than she ever had before that her mom was still alive. "She really was," she agreed quietly.

"We loved each other so much that we couldn't even wait to get back to either of the flats that we shared with schoolmates," Vince continued. "Luckily, we parked far from the entrance. I'll spare you the details but we were so in love. We drove around London for hours afterward, just aimlessly cruising and talking. And you were the result of that love, sweetheart."

"The ironic thing is," London started with a small smile. "I love Fleetwood Mac. I always have. Mom never stopped listening to them. Somehow, it all makes sense in a strange way. Did you know Mom was going to name me London?"

Vince sighed and rubbed his chin. A shadow flickered through his eyes. "When you were born, I was already back in Texas and your mom was in

Illinois," he answered uncomfortably. "We weren't, ah, we weren't much for speaking to each other then. But when I learned that you had been named London, I was overcome with this immense feeling of pride. I knew I would have given you the same name."

A long moment stretched between them. "That's right," London finally replied. "I forgot that Mom had told me you weren't present at my birth."

Vince gently took London's hand and held it. "If you can believe it, I thought I was doing the right thing by staying away," he said quietly. "Even at twenty-one years old, I hated myself for caving to my family's pressure to abandon you and your mother. I hated myself for not having the guts to stand up to them and live life on my own terms, even if wasn't necessarily according to plan. And because I hated myself, I believed that you were far better off having *no* father than a spineless, scared boy who had no idea how to care for a baby."

London stared at their joined hands. "That's not true," she replied. "You're my *dad*. I would have loved you just the same."

"The one thing I knew I *could* do was to provide for you both financially," Vince went on. "So that's what I did. And now I realize, looking at you all grown up, that I missed out on everything, including the love of my life. But seeing you now, I recognize so many similarities between us. I know that's ironic, considering how little time we've spent together."

London's head snapped up. "What similarities?"

"You hide yourself from people because you think they're better off not knowing the real you," he replied with a sigh. "You try to protect the ones you love, but in the end you just push them away. Which is exactly what's going to happen if you leave here without Natalie. You'll lose her forever, London. Trust me on that and take it from someone who learned the long, hard way."

The kitchen suddenly seemed very cramped and hot. "I don't want to lose her forever, Dad," she admitted. "But now she sees the ugliest things about me, like the fact that I'm an outsider no matter where I go. I don't fit in anywhere. Who wants someone like that?"

Vince frowned. "Who decides who fits in anywhere?" He asked. "You're a good person with a big heart, and you need to stop convincing yourself otherwise. Good people are welcomed anywhere in the world."

London shook her head. "I heard Diane talking about that evening," she replied.

"Yesterday?" Vince asked, perplexed. "What did she say?"

"No, the night before your wedding," London blurted out. "I heard her telling you that I was an outsider and that I wasn't meant to be there. It's why I wasn't a part of your wedding; I didn't belong. I was *six*."

Vince's mouth dropped open and he wrapped London into a hug. "I'm sorry you heard that conversation," he replied after a moment. "There was a change in you during the Costa Rica trip after that night. I never understood what it was. Instead, I let you grow further and further from me. I'm sorry I never stood up for you, London."

She took a deep breath. *Oddly enough, the apology feels nice* she thought. *If not a little belated. But I'll take late over never any day.*

"If there's one redeeming piece of advice that I can give you, it's to not make the same mistake with Natalie that I made with your mother," Vince spoke gently. "If she's your love, then don't let that go so easily. Anything else can be worked out. Don't curse yourself by pushing her away."

"I need to go for a drive," London finally replied. "Think things through, clear my head and get some highway under those brand-new tires."

Vince breathed deeply through his nose. "All right," he responded with a nod. "Just be safe, okay? Take a little time to think everything through. Before I forget," he paused and took a folded photograph from his breast pocket. "I wanted to give this to you."

London took the photograph and immediately recognized her parents. *Younger, slimmer and more Bohemian versions, but it's certainly them* she thought with a wry smile. She outlined her mother's profile with the tip of her index finger. The young version of her mother leaned into the young version of her father and laid her hand proudly against his chest. His arms were wound loosely around her waist and they both wore huge, million-dollar smiles on their youthful, wrinkle-free faces. *All those hopes and dreams in their heads* she thought wistfully. *Who could have predicted anything?*

Vince shoved his hands into his pocket awkwardly. "It's one of the only photos I have of the two of us," he went on. "Back in those days, you know, we didn't have cell phones with the cameras and taking selfies or whatever they're called every other hour. I kept that photo way up in the closet in a box of personal things that Diane didn't even know I had. I think you should keep it, London. After all, that's where we were when this was taken."

London couldn't bring herself to speak as she stood slowly from the stool. Instead, she embraced her father tightly and then held the photo to her. "Thank you, Dad," she replied. "This picture means everything to me." She paused and then shrugged shyly. "It sounds silly, but it means I was real. I'm going to take that drive. I have a lot of…thinking to do."

"I understand," Vince nodded. "I hope you take everything into careful consideration. I don't want you to repeat the same cycle as your old man. If Natalie is the one, put that stubborn Foster pride aside and work it out."

"Okay, Dad," London replied. She grabbed her wallet and keys from the breakfast bar and turned toward the foyer. Her quick stride was far more confident than she felt.

"Where are you going, anyway?" Vince asked as he furrowed his brow.

London half-smiled and shrugged one shoulder. "I'll let you know when I get there."

With that, she shut the door resolutely behind her and strode down the driveway. She took a deep breath as she eased herself back into the rental car and tapped her thumb against the steering wheel in thought.

Could I leave? She wondered. *It wouldn't be difficult. I could send for the rest of my things, return the car to an Enterprise in Chicago. I'd check in with Tiff regularly on the phone to make sure she's doing okay. Then I could slip back into my life like nothing ever happened. Everyone would be better off.*

She paused as her father's advice rang in her head. *But I'd be different* she realized ruefully. *I already am. Dad said he couldn't take his eyes off Mom if he'd tried. Well, I wouldn't be able to forget Natalie if I tried.*

London started the Audi and smiled absent-mindedly at the low purr of the engine as she cranked the stereo's volume. With a deep breath, she backed the car out of the driveway with only her wallet and cell phone and not the slightest clue where she was going.

CHAPTER 27

"So that's that," Natalie concluded miserably. She took another pull of the half-bottle of beer in her hand and watched silently as Isabella ran wide circles around the backyard. Her excited shrieks were punctuated by high-pitched yips as Niko chased her back and forth. Paula had been listening to Natalie lament in the private yard that she shared with Celia and Jane for what seemed like hours. The sun was quickly setting into the horizon and Natalie was nursing her third beer. She grimaced inwardly as she noticed how warm the beer had become.

"*That's that?*" Paula repeated dubiously. She leaned back in the lawn chair and shaded her eyes as she glanced at Isabella and Niko. "I don't believe it. You and London can't be through already. Even Isabella could see that you two were made for each other. All she could talk about on the way home from Haskell was how happy you seemed."

Natalie sighed. *Why does it feel like there's a knife slowly sinking deeper into my chest?* She wondered. *I forget about the sting for a while, but then someone says something like that. And then I feel it all over again.*

"I knew I shouldn't have fallen so quickly," she replied. She tapped the beer bottle against her knee in thought. "Look at me, I don't even *drink*. I knew I shouldn't have fallen in love with another outsider. But what I felt was so real that I just…didn't think twice."

She glanced at Paula and did a double-take when she noticed her friend giving her a slanted side eye. "What?"

"Maybe if you stopped referring to her as an outsider, like she's some kind of martian creature, then you could try to put yourself in her shoes. I'd be upset too if someone I loved called me that," Paula tried to gently explain.

Natalie took another sip of the smooth lager and turned the bottle over in her hands. Rays of setting sun glinted off the thick, dark green glass. "I tried to apologize," she started defensively. "It slipped out. I didn't know it would upset her so much. You should have seen her face after I said that. It was, like…" Natalie paused and snapped her fingers. "Instant. All of the sudden, the woman *I* fell in love with was gone. Her face just went blank. Like the London *I* knew disappeared."

Paula sighed as Niko bounded up to them. He nudged Natalie's hard, forcing her to scratch behind his ears, and licked her palm appreciatively.

"*Na, na, na,* Nikooo!" Isabella called in a singsong voice from a corner of the yard. Instantly, his ears perked up and he shot across patches of dry grass for another chase.

"Her wall went back up," Paula finally replied. "Can you blame her? You said she was pretty tightly wound; it's no wonder that a comment like that would make her close up again. If you give her some time to get over it, I think she'll be okay."

Natalie scoffed. "Give her time? She *walked out* on me, Paula," she replied. The hurt filled her heart all over again. "Maybe I don't *want* to chase after someone whose first instinct after every argument or bad day is to run. She's probably halfway…" she paused and waited for the tremor in her voice to disappear. "You know, probably halfway back to Chicago by now."

Paula grabbed Natalie's hand across the lawn chairs. "She won't do it," she replied confidently. "I saw the way she looked at you, just like I saw the way you looked at her. Promotion or not, she won't go back."

"I know I made a huge mistake by not being forthcoming with her about Tiffany," Natalie continued with a heavy sigh. "I know I broke her trust, but she wasn't completely honest with me either. Do you think it's too late?" She cocked her head and looked at Paula imploringly.

Paula has been through everything and back with Rudy she thought. *If anyone can give me good advice, it's her. They've been through so many hardships and trials, and they always come out stronger on the other side...Even if it's rough-going in the meantime. They give me faith. That's the type of relationship I want.*

Her friend gazed at a point somewhere at the horizon. "No, I don't think it's too late," she answered after a moment. "You know, Natalie. We've been friends for years and we keep it real with each other. I was honest with you when I told you I didn't like that girl from L.A. much, right?"

Natalie rolled her eyes but managed a small smile. "You were very honest about that."

Paula nodded and pursed her lips. "I wouldn't tell you that it's not too late if I didn't believe it," she continued. "I wouldn't get your hopes up like that. You can't fake the way she looks at you."

Natalie's eyes fell to her lap. "I love the way she looks at me," she admitted. "Except that moment at the hospital. The look on her face after I called her an outsider..." she sighed. "It made my blood run cold. I was terrified that, in that moment, I'd lost her and there was nothing I could do to take it back."

Paula reached over and patted her arm. "Hey, don't dwell on that one moment," she reassured her. "Think about all the good things. Those far outweigh that single moment, right?"

Natalie nodded silently as she drained the last of her beer.

"Then she's not going anywhere," Paula finished simply. "You both are too hard-headed to be the first to budge, but once you get past all that stubbornness? Watch out, world." She sat back and smiled satisfactorily. "Because you two will be an unbeatable force and neither of you will ever give up on the other."

For the first time since leaving the hospital, Natalie began to feel a tiny glimmer of hope. *Paula tells it like it is* she thought confidently. *She's usually spot on with things. Maybe she's right. Maybe if London and I talk,* really *talk, then we can put this behind us. I'll give her some time, but I'm not ready to let her go just yet.*

Isabella sprinted to them and ducked behind Natalie's lawn chair with a giggle. Niko loped around the backs of the chairs before covering her face with kisses and slobber.

"You ready to head home soon, *monita*?" Paula twisted in her chair and playfully tugged a lock of Isabella's dark hair.

Isabella groaned but nodded. "Okay, Mom."

"Say good-bye to Natalie then," Paula instructed. Natalie smiled inwardly at her friend's Strict Mom voice. "I'm going to get Niko secured in the car."

Paula stood and gathered the wriggling puppy in her arms. She paused and fixed Natalie with a knowing look. "And you stay positive, okay? I'll check in with you tomorrow."

Natalie started to nod and then thought for a moment. "Wait, tomorrow is the Fourth of July," she replied. "I'm going to see the fireworks at Boomtown out in Addison with Celia and Jane. You know, our annual tradition."

"That's right, I forgot," Paula said. "I'll stop by the bakery to drop off those boxes of *Gansitos* that my parents brought back from their last visit to Mexico."

Natalie perked up at this. "They wouldn't happen to be the special edition red velvet *Gansitos*, would they?"

Paula grinned. "Of course they are," she confirmed. "I know how badly you've been trying to recreate those cakes at Mission. I'll see you later."

Natalie waved as Paula trudged around the house with Niko in her arms. She was momentarily surprised as Isabella stood in a flash and wrapped her arms tightly around her middle.

"Bye, Bella," she said with a laugh as she returned the hug.

Isabella stood on her tiptoes and cupped her hand around her mouth. "Don't worry, Natalie," she whispered. "London will be right back. Remember, she's your Princess Charming like in the Disney movies. She probably just has to go slay some dragons first. She's a *tough* princess."

Natalie took a deep breath and mustered a smile. "You're so right," she told her. "She'll be back soon."

She listened as Paula sounded the car horn. Isabella grinned and bounded for the front of the house. *Maybe she's onto something* she mused. *I know, deep down, that London and I could have our very own happily-ever-after.*

"But how do you explain to a kid that sometimes the scariest dragons to slay are the ones inside ourselves?" Natalie murmured. She closed her eyes. "I know you want to work it out with me too, London."

London rubbed at her eyes tiredly. The highway stretched before her. What had begun as a busy, five-lane interstate that criss-crossed through Dallas was now reduced to two long, straight lanes into darkness. She had circled once or twice around the tall, intersecting tollways that surrounded the Dallas-Fort Worth area and then picked up Interstate 35 somewhere around the airport.

How long have I been driving? She wondered. The high afternoon sun had given way to a brilliant sunset and now it was twilight. The big sky was a deep navy blue as the Audi sped over well-traveled highway.

London shifted uncomfortably in the seat and looked around. The two flat lanes of interstate were surrounded by neat squares of farm land as far as the eye could see. *So weird that there are hardly any trees here* she thought absent-mindedly. She sped past a filling station with a small diner attached. A large sign that London was sure was older than her advertised that it had the best fried pies in Texas.

"What the hell is a fried pie?" She mused aloud. For a moment, she debated if it was worth making a pit stop. *It does say the best fried pies in all of Texas* she thought. As curious as she was, the general sense of discontent that had followed her from her father's house stopped her from veering toward the exit.

I haven't been hungry all day. Let's be honest, I've had zero appetite since… She sighed and tried not to remember the stricken look across Natalie's face.

London forced a smile and slowed the sleek Audi long enough to quickly snap a photo of the ramshackle fried pie sign with her phone. Her smile faded as her thumb automatically hit an icon to upload the photo to Instagram. *All those photos, all those adventures* she thought wistfully. *Isn't it funny that we never realize these amazing moments are actually adventures until after the fact?*

Disappointment crept into her veins and London knew it was aimed solely at herself this time. *Why is my first defense mechanism to shut down and push her away? The first sign of trouble, and I told her I didn't know anything anymore. Why did I say that?*

London remembered the ice in Natalie's voice as she made her comment about falling for an outsider. *Did I deserve that?* She mused. *No, probably not.*

But Natalie didn't deserve my backing away and questioning everything I felt about us either.

She sighed heavily as night fell around her. The insulated blanket of darkness only seemed to make the questions that swirled inside grow louder and more pronounced. "I miss her," she muttered to herself. "We're both stubborn and we both push people away. Natalie and I are equally to blame for this."

London continued to wallow in her endless circle of thoughts for another moment. They quickly came screeching to a halt at the moment she passed a tall sign on the shoulder of the interstate. Her mouth dropped open and her heart rate kicked up a notch as it dawned on her just how far she had blindly driven.

"Welcome to Oklahoma," she read slowly. "I am definitely *not* in Kansas. Or Chicago. Or, hell, even *Texas* anymore."

CHAPTER 28

London had only a short minute of realization after the shock of having driven all the way into Oklahoma subsided. In a split second, she was suddenly surrounded by bright, dancing lights as she drove beneath a flashing sign so large that it almost gave the nearby area the appearance of daytime.

"Winstar World Casino," London read as she squinted at the wide sign. Its colors flashed wildly along the otherwise dark, deserted interstate. She slowed and was momentarily stunned into silence by the sudden energy of the casino. Its sprawling size ate up miles along the highway.

As she sized up the massive casino, London suddenly felt drained. *Maybe it's all the driving that I didn't even realize I did* she thought wryly. *Or maybe it's because I have so many things to think about and I feel no closer to clarity than before.*

"It has to be at least two hours back to Fort Worth," she murmured. Without a second thought, she jerked the Audi into an exit lane and pulled off the interstate. She paused on the side of the desolate single-lane road that led to the casino. "There's no way I can drive all that way again. I'm exhausted."

London gazed again at the huge resort as its bright lights created flashing patterns along the dashboard. "I could get some shut-eye and head back to Fort Worth first thing in the morning," she cajoled herself. She took a deep breath. "Or I could get some sleep and continue heading north back to Chicago tomorrow."

Her heart pounded nervously at the prospect and she desperately wished for a moment of confidence in either decision. She felt as though she was standing on a crowded cliff, leaning over the jagged edge with her face against the wind, and staring into a long free fall to a murky abyss.

"Is this what freedom feels like?" London asked herself as she wrinkled her nose. "I could do anything right now. Go anywhere. The choice is in *my* hands this time."

London had expected to relish the feeling of total freedom, without expectations or responsibility. Instead, on a narrow, deserted frontage road somewhere in Oklahoma, the overwhelming realization that she was at one of the most important turning points so far in her life took the air right from her lungs.

"I'm completely in love with Natalie Silva," she stated in wonderment. Her voice sounded strange and loud in the silent car.

But first you need to sleep her inner voice warned her. *Before you can do anything. Besides, things always look brighter and clearer in the morning.*

"At least I can make *one* decision now," London murmured to herself. She pulled the car back onto the frontage road and made a right into the casino parking lot. "And that is that I will positively drive myself crazy if I don't force myself to get some sleep."

London couldn't quite put her finger on why, but she felt strangely lucky as she walked across the large parking lot and beneath a massive globe lit in light blue. She took a deep breath and pushed open the doors of the front entrance. Her senses were immediately assaulted with computerized music from rows upon rows of machines. Loud pings from the slot machines, excited shouts and the stench of stale cigarette smoke surrounded her.

The lobby was brightly lit and a row of uniformed casino staff stood eagerly waiting to help guests. After a moment, London turned her back to the frenetic casino floor and its blinking neon to request a room for the night.

Her eyes felt like sandbags as she stepped up to a smooth oak desk. *I can't wait to slip between the sheets and let my head hit those pillows* she thought in anticipation as she gave her mind and body over to exhaustion. *Tomorrow is going to be a big day. I know in my heart that whatever happens will be the right thing.*

London blinked at the bright mid-morning sunlight that streamed through a large picture window overlooking Winstar's swimming pool. She groaned and tried to flop onto her stomach, but realized the sheets were twisted and mangled around her limbs.

I must have really knocked out last night she thought. *And I must have been tossing and turning too.* She sighed and let her eyes adjust to the light.

"Effing sun," she muttered without animosity. She smiled despite herself. *My love and hate relationship with the sun is quickly tipping to love* she realized. *I'm actually growing accustomed to the constant bright light.*

A slow glance at the bedside alarm clock made her do a double-take as she rubbed the sleep from her eyes. "Oh my God, it's eleven," she said in disbelief. "I really was as exhausted as I felt."

She settled back against the pillows and unplugged her phone from its charger. Her eyes widened as she reviewed the five missed calls reflected on its screen. *Two from Dad* she thought. *He probably wants to check in and make sure I'm okay, since I didn't come home last night.* Guilt tugged at her stomach. *Three from Tiffany* she read silently as she bit her lip. *And a voicemail.*

London couldn't help but feel slightly hurt that there wasn't also a call or text from Natalie. *But why would there be?* She wondered grimly. *I made it clear that I didn't want to hear from her. I walked out of the hospital without a second glance. She probably thinks I'm halfway back to Chicago by now.*

The irony that she did, in fact, make it all the way to Oklahoma was not lost on London. She quickly listened to her sister's voicemail. Her heart twisted at the sadness in her tone.

"Hey, London," Tiffany started uncertainly. "Umm, Dad stopped by the hospital last night. He mentioned that you might be heading back to Chicago pretty soon. I, uh, I know you're mad. You have every right to be. So I understand if I don't at least deserve a good-bye, but just know that I don't want to lose you. I don't want to lose what we've been able to gain during your time here. I love you and I hope everything is okay. The doctor said I should be out of here by the end of the week or early next week. That's cool, right? I've been talking to Dad about some kind of rehab. I mean, I feel good but I want to feel *strong*. Strong like you, London. We'll see what happens, but we can talk more when I hear from you. I hope everything's okay and that you're finding what you're looking for. Love you. Later, sister."

A lump formed in London's throat as she set her phone in her lap and stared up at the off-white popcorn ceiling. *Strong like me?* She thought in confusion as she contemplated Tiffany's message. *How can she say that? I'm not strong at all. I compartmentalize and run away from everything, rather than deal with it head on. I bolted at the first sign of conflict from the one person that has understood and helped me to understand myself. That's not strength. That's…That's immaturity. Stubbornness. That's being hard-headed and non-compromising. That's not who I want to be.*

London picked up her phone and idly tapped the Instagram icon. She chewed the inside of her cheek thoughtfully as she scrolled through each square filtered photo from the beginning of her account to present. Each tiny picture held a memory that replayed over in her head as soon as she glanced at it.

These pictures aren't just small memories or documentation of an extended trip she realized as she watched the short video of Natalie line-dancing. *These photos are of my journey as it unfolded before me. All of these represent one of the small steps that's led me here.* She paused over a candid shot of Natalie. The exhilarated smile that lit her face caused London's heart to beat in double-time. *God, she's the most beautiful woman I've ever met.*

London studied the first picture they had taken together by the duck pond. Natalie relaxed comfortably in her arms. The sun glinted off her hair and highlighted deep golden streaks across swaths of dark brown. They both wore easy smiles and, although they hadn't yet shared their first kiss, their body language read perfectly content with one another.

She recalled a specific part of her sister's voicemail as she scrolled through dozens of photos. "This *was* what I was looking for," she murmured. "Not just Natalie, but *everything*. I'd found it and I didn't even realize it."

London returned to her and Natalie's first photo as her eyes fell on her jeans. In her late-night exhaustion, she had stripped her pants off and dumped them onto a small corner desk. The contents of her front pocket had spilled halfway across the smooth wood and the photo of her parents faced her.

London looked at their photo for a long moment and then glanced back at the photo of her and Natalie still displayed on her phone. She swallowed and looked back at her parents' photograph before glancing again at her own picture.

She's the one London thought with sureness that she felt deep in her veins. She was more positive of this than anything she'd realized before. *Natalie is the one and I am totally, hopelessly in love with her.* London blinked as realization washed over her in waves. *I'm going to be making the exact same mistake with Natalie that Dad made with Mom if I go back to Chicago and force myself to place her in the past.*

In that moment, London knew that returning to Chicago without Natalie was no longer an option. *Was it ever, really?* She wondered.

She took a deep breath and thought of her high-rise apartment, her comfortable job and the familiar sights and sounds of the city she had been raised in. *It's bittersweet* she decided. *I'll miss it.*

But London also thought of the crushing sadness, the dreams that had slowly been pushed into a corner until they turned to dust, the jade that had seeped deep into her heart and the underlying anger that had come very close to searing her soul. She recalled the cloak of anonymity that only a big city allows, which she had been all too eager to use as a buffer to keep everyone away. *But I won't miss it too* she thought with a wry smile.

London's gaze fell on the small bathroom across the room. She pushed back the blankets and swung her bare legs over the edge of the bed. "First things first," she murmured to herself. "Shower. And then there's one more person that I need to speak to." She glanced down at her phone as a momentary shot of melancholy coursed through her at the thought of Holly.

I know she'll be happy for me London reasoned as she padded into the bathroom. *But she's the only true friend I've had. I know, out of all things Chicago, I'll miss her the most.*

As she stepped under the warm shower, her mind returned to Natalie and a decision was made.

It's time to grow up and stop hiding.

CHAPTER 29

The high afternoon sun beat down in heat waves as Natalie hauled sacks of sugar into Mission Bakery's food truck. It was parked at the back of the bakery in a tiny slice of shade, but it was still impossibly hot. She stopped for a moment and rested her hand on her hip before swiping at her brow with the back of her palm. The familiar honk of a car horn caused her to turn expectantly.

Natalie forced a smile at the sight of Celia and Jane in their tiny Hyundai Accent. Celia waved a hand excitedly out of the open driver's side window. *Why was I expecting anyone else?* She thought dejectedly. Disappointment filled her heart, but she didn't want her aunts to think she wasn't happy to see them.

"What are you waiting for?" Celia called as she pulled the vehicle alongside the truck. "If we want to have any hope of finding a place at Kaboomtown, we'd better head toward Dallas now."

Natalie wrinkled her nose. "I thought we were taking the food truck?"

Celia paused and then shook her head. "Nah," she replied laconically. "I know we tossed around the idea, but I thought it'd be good to take a night off. Hang out just the three of us, no work allowed."

Natalie blinked in surprise and turned to Jane. "Who is she and what happened to my *tia*?"

Jane laughed and gestured for Natalie to hop in the car. "Oh, come on," she coaxed. "Take a night from that busy social life and that new girlfriend of yours and hang out with your favorite aunts."

Natalie's heart stopped and she was sure that her face went white. Celia quickly leaned over the middle console and whispered something to Jane. Natalie swallowed hard as Jane's face instantly lost all its color.

"Oh, I'm so sorry," she continued hurriedly. "I know there was a, uh, *tiff* but I had assumed it was all worked out now. I'm sorry, sweetheart. Now you *have* to come with us and get your mind off things."

Natalie shoved her hands into her pockets and kicked the toe of her sneaker through the brown dirt. "Yeah, that sounds good," she admitted. "I've never missed Kaboomtown's fireworks. Don't want to start now."

Fourth of July is my favorite holiday she reminded herself silently. *No use in letting your favorite holiday get ruined because of everything. Try to make the best of it. That's why you have your family.*

Jane smiled broadly. "That's our girl," she replied. "Why don't you hop in and talk to Celia, and I'll get the truck locked up? We'll be on our way in just a few minutes."

As London sped straight down I-35 with the windows down and the warm breeze ruffling through her hair, she began to appreciate the possibilities that the open road offered. Without thinking, she stuck her hand out the window and let the rushing wind guide it up and down along the weather strip. She grinned as she passed the "Welcome to Texas" sign that was planted staunchly along the shoulder of the interstate.

An abrupt *ding* from the dashboard caught London's attention. She squinted as the neon orange gas alert flashed twice.

So much for the open road she thought ruefully. *I didn't even think about how low on gas I would be this morning.*

London knew she was still in close vicinity of the casino as she pulled off the highway at the nearest exit. The gas station advertised slot machines among its offerings of soda, beer, snacks and ice. She pulled alongside an empty pump and quickly snapped a photo of the sign to upload to Instagram.

Who can resist? She thought with a grin. She pocked her phone with a sigh as she filled up the shining Audi. As the pump shook and clicked with each release of gasoline, London briefly wondered if the station had been there since the beginning of time.

She sidestepped a tumbleweed that bounced across the parking lot as she jogged into the station. An elderly cashier who looked bored out of his mind sat on a stool in front of the old cash register. He barely acknowledged London's presence.

"Um, thirty on pump two," she spoke hesitantly. She slid a twenty and a ten across the dusty counter.

The elderly man grunted, picked up her bills and pressed a few buttons on the cash register. "Thank you."

London smiled. "You're welcome," she replied. She turned awkwardly and then turned back. Three sleek slot machines were lit up along the back of the old gas station and stuffed between the slushy machine and a tall rack selling B.B. gun ammo.

Again, who can resist? She thought. *Why not waste a dollar?*

She nodded once at the slot machines. "I'm just going to…Yeah," she trailed off lamely. She had a feeling that the cashier thought she was as big of an idiot as she felt. *Screw it.* "I'm going to try one of those machines. I'm feeling lucky."

London was almost positive the old man rolled his eyes at her, but he nodded and waved at the machines. "All right, then."

Man of few words London thought with a grin. *That's okay. I am feeling lucky. What the hell?*

She realized how silly she looked as she slid four quarters into the shiny chrome coin slot. *Oh London, what on Earth are you doing?* She wondered. *You have more important things to attend to today. Namely, finding Natalie and getting her to talk to you before it's too late.*

London pulled the lever with a slight shake of her head and then turned in embarrassment. She nodded at the cashier and pushed the door open.

"*Wait!*" A gravelly voice croaked. London turned in confusion. The old man had hopped off his stool, a feat that she would have deemed impossible just a few moments before, and was stabbing his knarled index finger at the slot machine. "You won! Holy smokes, you won!"

London stared in disbelief as the machine flashed and loud music filled the tiny gas station. "I...I *won*? I don't think I've ever won anything in my life."

A wide smile stretched across the spotted, leathery skin of the old man's face. "Dang it, girl, I've worked here for sixty-somethin' years and I ain't never seen *one* person win so much as the lint from the bottom of their pocket! You won $1,000!"

"I...I...Oh my *God*," London replied. She wrinkled her nose as the strange realization set in. "I can't believe it."

"Oh, you better believe it," the old man continued with a partially toothless smile. "Look, that machine is called 'Home Sweet Home'. You must be in the right place then."

London stared at the machine as her heart pounded. *I barely read the name of the machine* she thought. *I just stuck my quarters in and pulled the lever. What are the odds?*

"I...I guess I must be," she agreed, after her voice had caught up to her gaping mouth.

"Well, I gotta' have you fill you out some paperwork," the old man said with a sigh. "State rules and whatnot. I'll have to find it, but I think it's packed away in the store room. Probably covered with dust. I'm tellin' you, we ain't never had a winner in over half a century. Bet you feel *real* lucky now!"

All London could do was nod and stare in wonderment at the machine as its bright colors danced before her.

"I got to call the owner of the filling station too, but, well, the owner was my wife and she passed away some fifteen years ago," the old man went on. "So I'll cash you out, but don't you move. I'm going to look for that paperwork."

London nodded and placed both hands on the counter as the old man stumbled into a back room. She took a deep breath and leaned onto her elbows. *Granted, $1,000 isn't much* she told herself. *It's not like I won half a million or something. But what are the odds? Those crazy, faraway odds?*

Images of Natalie, of herself, of her father and sister and of the rolling Texas sky flashed through her mind. "I'm exactly where I need to be," she murmured with a knowing smile.

"What's that you're saying?" The old man called as he returned from the store room. He held a packet of paper in his arms. "The old ears ain't as good as they used to be when I was your age. What are you gonna' do with that grand, anyway?"

London shook her head slowly as she took the paperwork and a ballpoint pen from his shaking hands. *I already knew I was staying in Texas* she thought. *But what was the plan after that?*

"Getting a place in Texas," she decided out loud. The words tumbled from her lips before she could stop them. "I'll use it to pay off my current lease and get an apartment here somewhere. I have a lot of exploring to do."

The old man nodded and grinned. "Ain't that the stuff of life," he remarked. "Good for you, ma'am. Good for you."

London waited quietly as the old man punched a few keys on the register. It popped open with a jangle and he began carefully counting out twenty dollar bills. A thought occurred to her as she absent-mindedly watched his wrinkled fingers smooth each bill before adding it to the stack.

"You know what," she spoke again before she could think twice. "How about a lucky split? Give me half. You keep five hundred."

The old man froze. His eyes widened behind his thick bifocal glasses. "You…You don't have to do that, you know," he started. London swore she heard a tremble in his voice. "That's your money. You won, fair and square. You were right, you *are* lucky."

London looked down at the stack of bills on the counter and then back at him. *The stuff of life* she thought as she recalled his words with a slight smile. *It's not always money.*

"I want to," she clarified. "I think that's fair, don't you? A bonus to the gas station that had the lucky machine?"

The old man appeared to consider this and then nodded slowly. "If you're sure. I mean, I could do a lot with that bonus, ma'am. But…"

London held up a hand. "I'm glad you agree," she cut in with a grin. "So five hundred for you and five hundred for me then."

He nodded again and smiled back. "Well, I don't know what to say except for thank you. That's mighty generous."

London glanced out the doors at her car and then back down at the counter. *Today* is *a lucky day* she realized. *More importantly, it's a* good *day. I just hope Natalie is willing to talk.*

"Okay, I have to know where you're at and what hole in Texas you've crawled into," Holly's voice cracked loudly through the phone.

It was nearly evening as London cruised through Denton and passed the large University of North Texas buildings. She had been deciding how to approach her next conversation with her friend, but Holly had beaten her to the punch and called first.

"Oh, you saw the photos?" London asked, amused.

"*Hello*, I've been following your Instagram since you left!" Holly replied. "I just got off the plane at O'Hare and I swear they must be getting our luggage from the seventh circle of hell or something, because I've been standing at the baggage claim for almost an hour…"

"Holly, *breathe*," London cut in with a giggle.

"Right," Holly replied. "Sorry. Anyway, I saw those new photos. I have to know where in the world you must be. Where can you find slot machines in gas stations and fried pies? What *is* a fried pie, anyway?"

London laughed. "I honestly don't know," she replied. "I only stopped for the sign. I *did* spend the night at a massive casino in the middle of nowhere. And then I won five hundred dollars on a slot machine named Home Sweet Home when I stopped for gas."

"You spent the night *where*? Wait, you won five hundred…Did you take a quickie trip to *Nevada* or something?" Holly asked.

London laughed again. "Not even," she admitted. "Evidently, this is what happens when you travel outside of the big Texas cities. Um, speaking of which…" she coughed once. Her heart pounded and her palms became clammy as her mind raced with how to broach the subject.

"What's up?" Holly asked expectantly.

"I can't…" London paused and took a deep breath. She hated that her trembling voice sounded so tiny through the crackling line. "I'm sorry, Hol, but I can't take the promotion. I know you've been grooming me for it and I know you're really excited about what it has meant for my career." She paused and listened to the silence fill her ear before forging ahead. "I'd been excited about it too, honestly I was. But I…I need to decline the promotion and formally give you my notice for my position at W.H. Young. Please don't be mad at me."

There she thought as she inhaled deeply. *It's out. No going back now.*

"It's Natalie, isn't it?" Holly replied after a moment. London was cautiously relieved to hear no anger in her friend's voice. Instead, she found only curiosity and understanding. "You're in love with her?"

London swallowed. "Yes," she replied. "I am. I can't…I can't go back to Chicago and leave everyone. Tiffany still needs me and my dad…God, he'll never outright admit it but I think he does too. He's going to be retiring soon. I can't leave Natalie without giving what we have a real chance. She's so different from anyone I've ever met, Holly. She makes me think about things in different ways. When I'm with her, it's like we're the only people that exist."

"Then I think you should go for it," Holly replied easily.

London blinked. "Wait, what?" She asked. She was thrown off by her friend's confident reply. "You think I should…?"

"Go for it, London," Holly replied in mock exasperation. "You love her. What else is there? You'll regret it forever if you come back to Chicago and let her get away. You forget that I *know* you. You think you're so good at hiding your feelings and keeping yourself locked away from everyone, but you're not *that* good. I can tell from hundreds of miles away that you're in love with her. *This* is what you've been missing, London."

"I don't even recognize the person I was when I left Chicago," London admitted. "It's strange, I never thought I could change that quickly. Or ever. I thought about leaving yesterday. Two months ago, it wouldn't have fazed me to up and leave and continue to keep everyone at arm's length. But I'm…I'm not that person anymore."

Holly sighed. "You were *never* that person, London," she replied. "The hardest thing for me has been to watch a close friend stumble and fall.

Watching her believe she was unworthy, a bad person, someone who should keep others away. You've *always* been deserving of someone like Natalie. You just needed time to get rid of all that shit you've used to insulate yourself and rediscover the real you. And it sounds like you finally have."

"You don't think I'll be making a mistake by giving up this promotion and sacrificing my career at W.H. Young to take a chance on love?" London asked. She chewed her thumbnail nervously.

"You don't think you are, do you?" Holly countered. "I can tell from your voice. In those photos of you two. In that genuine smile that I haven't seen in I don't know how long."

"No, you're right," London replied. "I don't think I'm making a mistake at all."

"Then you don't need me to tell you that you're not," Holly concluded. "I could never be mad at you, London. I'm glad you're finally living your life and letting yourself love."

"Me too," London agreed. She took a deep breath. "I can't even describe it, it's such a different feeling. Like some big weight off my shoulders and my heart, but so much more. Natalie has helped me face myself in so many ways. It's almost scary."

"It *is* scary," Holly replied. "It's love."

"And it's time to grow up," London said as she ran her fingers through her wind-blown hair. "Time to stop using the same tired defenses and shutting people out. Time to tell her what she really means to me."

"Good," Holly said decisively. "That's exactly what you need to do. Natalie is worth it. She wouldn't have stolen your heart if she wasn't. Don't think about it so much, London. Just tell her exactly how you feel and what's in your heart. Let it out without it getting caught in your mind. It's the *only* right way to let her know how much you love her."

"I think you're right," she replied with a sigh.

"Wait, can you repeat that?" Holly cut in with a laugh. "I think the line must be breaking up. Can you say that once more so I can record it this time?"

London burst into laughter. "Oh, stop it!"

"Oh shit, the airport crew must have just returned from hell. The baggage claim is making the most awful cranking noise, which I'm assuming means it's going to start moving soon. Maybe I'll actually get my bags before I'm fifty. Got to go, girl."

"Holly?" London tried.

"Oh, I'll send an e-mail to the Mr. Hanson when I get home," Holly continued hurriedly. "I may need you to write a formal resignation letter for me, but you can just e-mail that over tomorrow."

"Holly!" London practically shouted.

"What?" She asked.

"Thank you," London replied. "For everything. But, most of all, for being the absolute *best* friend I could have ever been blessed with."

"Hell, you're going to make me cry," Holly cracked. She sniffed. "You don't have to thank me, London. Remember what I told you? People love you, you just had to learn how to let us. We'll talk soon, okay?"

London grinned as she hung up with her friend. *It's done* she thought. She blew out her breath in a sigh of relief that she hadn't even realized she'd been holding. *Natalie and I both deserve this. A real chance.*

Her stomach twisted anxiously as she entered Dallas County. She knew there wasn't much further and there was only one place she could think to go. She drummed her fingers against the steering wheel and picked up her phone again.

"Siri, take me to Natalie's house," she spoke loudly. "Before I run out of road with these nerves."

CHAPTER 30

London's heart was beating so fast that she was sure its pounding was audible throughout the car. She slowly pulled down Natalie's street and bit her lip.

"You have arrived at your destination. Your destination is on the left," the robotic female voice of her phone's built-in G.P.S. informed her.

She eased to a stop against the curb and blinked at the small house. *No choice but to ring that doorbell* she told herself. *You didn't drive all this way to park outside like a creep.*

London slowly opened the door and stood on shaking legs. *One step at a time* she reminded herself gently. She thought of all the small steps she had taken, the photographic reminders displayed on her Instagram account, to become who she was now. She remembered each step as she took another and her slow but steady walk up the driveway felt as though it was taking hours.

London had nearly reached the wide porch when she heard a car pull into the driveway behind her. She jerked around and watched as Paula parked. Isabella swung open the back door and raced up the walkway. She immediately threw her skinny arms around London.

"London!" She screeched. "I knew it! I knew you'd come back. I tried to tell Natalie that you were slaying the dragons, but I think she already knew. I'm so happy to see you!"

London glanced nervously at the front door and then back at Isabella. She hugged the little girl tightly.

"Of course I'm back," she replied with a smile. "I'm happy to see you too."

Paula cleared her throat pointedly. "Isabella, sweetheart, can you bring the Gansitos inside and leave them on the kitchen counter? Remember we promised Natalie we would drop them off today?"

Isabella nodded and grabbed a few boxes of what London could glean were pastries. She plucked a key from Paula's open palm and skipped up the rest of the walkway.

"Look, I know you probably don't want to see me…" London started shyly.

Paula's hard stare morphed into a friendly smile. "Of course we want to see you," she replied. "You're family now. It's about time you made an appearance."

London blushed. A rush of warmth and familiarity coursed through her as Paula's words sank in. *So that's how it feels* she thought satisfactorily. *To have family.*

"I…I'm sorry," she stammered, unsure of what to say.

"Don't be sorry," Paula replied quickly. "Natalie is like the sister I never had. I know that she can be stubborn. I know that she sometimes lets words spill that she doesn't mean when she's upset. She misses you. More than I've ever seen her miss anyone."

"Where is she?" London asked. She glanced uncertainly at the nondescript home.

"Kaboomtown," Paula replied.

London realized her face must have betrayed her confusion as Paula blinked and then continued. "In Addison. It's the biggest annual fireworks show in the Dallas-Fort Worth area. Natalie loves it. She goes every year with her aunts."

"That's where she is?" London asked. "Okay. Then that's where I have to go. Thank you." She started quickly down the driveway, but then turned halfway and cocked her head. "Um, do you know where Addison is?"

Paula rolled her eyes with a heavy sigh but grinned. "Come on. We'll take your car."

Isabella loped out of the house and handed the key back to her mother. "Where are we going?"

"Kaboomtown," Paula answered as she met London's eyes knowingly. "To see Natalie, Celia, Jane and the fireworks."

Isabella pumped her fist in the air excitedly. "*Yes!*" She shouted. "Let's go!"

Exactly one hour later, London groaned as she slowly circled the parking lot. "You didn't tell me Kaboomtown was *this* big," she complained. "There must be a hundred thousand people here already."

Paula nodded seriously from the passenger's seat. "Probably," she replied matter-of-factly. "Everything is bigger in Texas."

"I'm never going to find them in this crowd," London replied, hating the whine in her voice. "We'll be walking around forever and we won't find them."

"Are you stressed?" Isabella piped up imploringly from the backseat.

"Isabella!" Paula started warningly. "Let London and I find a parking spot." She turned back to London. "I should have remembered when I tried to call her that she usually leaves her phone in the car for the fireworks. She's like a little kid with them; she loves them. Always has."

London sat back against the driver's seat and sighed. "I'm sorry," she apologized. "I'm just worried that I won't find her in time."

Paula perked up as they crept past the main entrance again. "London, how much do you trust me?"

London shot her a sidelong glance. "Why?"

"How about you get out here and start looking for Natalie?" Paula asked. "I'll find a parking space and then Isabella and I can catch up with you."

London chewed the inside of her cheek as she thought it over. She wasn't keen on someone else driving the rental, but she knew her options were limited. "Okay," she finally agreed. "Fine. Nighttime is chasing us and I'll *really* never find her in the dark. If that's what I have to do to have a shot at finding Natalie, then I'll leave the car with you."

Paula grinned and shooed her out the door. "Don't worry, London," she called out the window as she scooted over the middle console. "I'll find a good spot. *You* go find your girl."

"Bye, London!" Isabella called from the backseat with a wave.

London waved back and then turned toward the entrance. *Okay* she thought as she set her shoulders back determinedly. *I can do this. One hundred thousand people, and more filtering in every minute. I can find Natalie.*

After nearly a half-hour of walking the perimeter of a big, grassy field and squinting at anyone with dark hair, London was ready to give up. She hadn't heard from Paula yet and hadn't spotted Natalie, Celia or Jane. Darkness had all but closed in and recognizing faces was growing more difficult as each second ticked by.

London leaned against the trunk of a tall, thick tree and sighed. She scanned nearby small groups that had spread out on blankets before her. A strong stench in the breeze caused her to grimace before looking around. She quickly recognized where the offending odor had originated and smiled despite herself at the neat row of blue Porta-Potties set up a few yards behind the tree.

Porta-Potties she thought. *Disgusting no matter where you go. At least some things never change.*

She turned back toward the crowd as a single firework was shot into the velvety evening sky. It exploded in a burst of white as the crowd oohed and aahed. A smattering of applause rose from the field. *Great* London thought. *The fireworks are going to start any minute. I'll never find Natalie.*

London turned back to the line of Porta-Potties and then glanced at her phone for word from Paula for what felt like the hundredth time. *Still nothing* she thought. *This was a bust, wasn't it?*

She raised her eyes from the ground and immediately went stock-still as a Porta-Pottie door swung open. Natalie gingerly stepped out of the tiny restroom. Her face read disgust as she squeezed hand sanitizer onto her palms and then quickly pocketed the small bottle. Despite the expression on her face, London thought she never looked more beautiful.

She stood, frozen, as Natalie took a few steps away and pulled her phone from her other pocket. London watched as she glanced at it, shaking her head in disappointment, and then pushing it back into her shorts.

Paula said she didn't answer her call because she leaves her phone in the car during the fireworks show London thought, perplexed. *She ignored her friend's call, but brought her phone with her? She looks...sad.* London wondered for a split second if Natalie had brought her phone this time in hopes of hearing from her, but chose not to dwell on it.

It's now or never she told herself as she straightened her spine. *This is everything I want. She is everything I want.*

"Natalie!" She called as she stepped around the thick wooden trunk.

Natalie stopped short and looked around in surprise.

"Natalie, it's me," London tried again. She took a few tentative steps closer.

Natalie craned her neck and glanced around as her eyes finally found London. She crossed her arms protectively around herself.

I miss when we used to throw ourselves into each other's arms the second we saw each other London thought as she tried to ignore the strange pressure on her chest. *We can make this right.*

"I...I..." London stammered and then closed her eyes for a moment. She recalled her earlier conversation with Holly. *Tell her exactly how you feel and what's in your heart. Let it out without it getting caught in my head. It's the only way to truly tell her how I feel.*

"Natalie, I love you," the words tumbled out of her mouth, falling clumsily on top of each other, as she met her guarded eyes. "I'm here. I'm not going anywhere. I promise you, from the bottom of my heart. I'm not going back to Chicago. I can't...I can't imagine leaving without you. I won five hundred dollars from an old man at a gas station in...in...Gainesville and I'm going to use it to buy out the little bit left on my lease and get an apartment here. Well, maybe not *here* in Addison, but somewhere around here. I..."

"London..." Natalie started and then faltered. She bit her lip.

London forged ahead again. *Time to put it all on the line.* "I love you, I really do. I know, with everything I am, that we can make this work. Where will we end up, where will life take us? Who knows? *I* don't know. For once in my life, I don't know and I'm completely at peace with that. Because,

Natalie, as long as we have each other then we'll be okay."

The first two firecrackers lit up the sky and exploded with loud booms. *Shit* London thought. *I'm making her miss her favorite part of the Fourth of July.*

Three firecrackers followed in short succession as London opened her mouth and then closed it. "You kept asking me if I believed that everything happened for a reason. Looking at you right now, I can answer that *yes*. Yes, I believe that everything happens for a reason and *yes*, I believe that I was led here. I didn't understand it in the beginning, but I do now. Maybe our paths were *always* meant to cross and maybe I had to get to that point where I could be the right person…"

London's voice grew louder as the fireworks continued popping and exploding high in the sky above. The occasional burst of color lit Natalie's face in hues of blue, red and white as London trampled on. She swallowed. "You're…You're so beautiful. I just wanted to tell you that I love you. Very much."

"London," Natalie repeated her name with more insistence this time. She stepped closer and gently laid her hand on her forearm. "London, hey…Hey," she repeated as she wrapped her into an enveloping hug.

They held each other tightly for a few long moments as the firecrackers' loud booms shook the nearby tree. Natalie pulled back slightly and ran her fingers along London's face. "London, all you had to do was say that you love me and you're not going anywhere," she said. A wide smile spread across her features. "But everything else was really nice to hear too," she finished shyly.

London looked into her eyes and felt an immense rush of relief. She didn't recognize sadness in her face anymore. It was lit with the same playful sparkle that she had come to fall in love with. "I'll say it," she replied shakily. "I'm not scared anymore. I'll keep saying it if it means you won't be sad anymore. I'm so sorry for everything."

Natalie leaned in and rested her cheek against London's shoulder. "I'm sorry too," she said with a deep breath. "I missed you."

"I missed you too," London murmured as she rested her lips against the tip of Natalie's ear. "I'm not going anywhere."

Natalie looked up as another round of firecrackers exploded in a rainbow of color overhead. "So, tell me again. You won five hundred dollars *how*? Start from the beginning and tell me all about this old man at the gas station. And why were you all the way in Gainesville?"

London laughed and followed Natalie across the field as their joined hands swung casually between them. "It's a long story," she replied warningly. "But I think it's a good one."

"You *think* so?" Natalie teased as she met her eyes.

London grinned. "I *know* so."

"By the way," Natalie whispered as she stepped closer. "You just made my dream date come true. Remember?"

They paused at the trunk of a smaller tree and gazed at each other for a long moment. *There's so many things to say* London thought. *But sometimes putting it all into a kiss is enough.*

She leaned forward and met Natalie's waiting lips. The tree shook as firecrackers thundered above. All other eyes were directed at the magnificent sparkling display overhead and allowed them a few moments of privacy. She and Natalie kissed and the world spun around them as the lingering moments transitioned from desperate to playful to content and back again. London smiled as she realized that she was home.

EPILOGUE - TEN MONTHS LATER

The door of the house swung open and the smell of fresh paint floated onto the porch. London stepped aside to let Natalie walk into the new home. She grinned at her and followed before setting a heavy armload of boxes onto the clean ceramic tile of the foyer.

London put her hands on her hips and surveyed the home in wonder as Natalie disappeared into a bedroom. They had been lucky to snap up the three bedroom, two bathroom home on the outskirts of Austin. *The Realtor said that this is one of the fastest growing cities in Texas* London marveled as she took in their new surroundings. *I can see why. The nature around us, the city's appreciation for art and development, the sense of possibility and promise. Even this home feels right.* She looked around again and smiled at their blank slate.

Natalie padded from the bedroom and shook out her arms. "Only how many more boxes to go?" She asked.

London laughed. "I don't think we should count until the truck is at least halfway empty."

Natalie shook her head ruefully and slid her arm around London's waist. "There's a lesbian U-haul joke in there somewhere."

London grabbed Natalie's hand and led her to the sliding glass doors on the other side of the living room. She peeked between the blinds and grinned at the fenced yard before them. "You know, I've never had a yard before," she said. "That high-rise Chicago apartment certainly didn't and the flat I was raised in with my mother only had a little square that we shared with whomever rented the basement unit. I think I'm going to like having a yard."

Natalie shifted behind London and wrapped her arms around her waist. She rested her chin on London's shoulder and gazed out at the empty yard that now belonged to them.

"You know what *I'm* going to like?" She replied. "No, scratch that. I'm going to *love* expanding Mission Bakery to Austin. I still can't believe how well our last couple of years went. I mean, I knew we were busy but I guess it never occurred to me."

London twirled around in Natalie's arms and met her smile with a kiss. "The second food truck is going to be huge," she agreed. "Austin is the perfect city for it."

Natalie sighed and threw a sidelong glance at the open front door. "Next time I have the bright idea that we can move everything ourselves, please stop me. Especially in the springtime heat."

London laughed. "Hey, don't worry about it," she replied. "Why don't we focus on the essentials first and then bring in the…not-so-essential?"

Natalie nodded. "That sounds good," she agreed. "I just want to make sure we have enough moved in by the time Tiffany and Wayne arrive. When do you think they'll be here tomorrow?"

"Around four," London replied. "But you know Tiffany; she says four and means six. I'm just glad she has Wayne to keep her organized and grounded."

"We still need to find a restaurant for the dinner reservations," Natalie replied. "But I guess we can do that in the morning. There's only thousands of restaurants in Austin to choose from."

London leaned on the breakfast bar and thought for a moment. "You know," she started. "I have the strangest feeling that Tiffany and Wayne are visiting to tell us that they're engaged. I mean, they've been inseparable since she finished rehab. Sobriety has done amazing things for her."

Natalie smiled across the room at her. "What is it now, ten months?"

"Give or take," London replied. She eyed the box of dishes that she had left in the foyer and groaned as she pushed herself off the long counter.

"So what are your thoughts on it?" Natalie asked.

London sensed a change in atmosphere and wondered what it was. She groaned again as she hoisted the dishes back into her arms. "On what?" She asked. "Tiff's sobriety? I think it's fantastic. She's taking it seriously and Wayne is great for her."

"No, on…you know, the other thing," Natalie hedged.

London blinked. "What other thing?"

Natalie sighed. "You know, the getting engaged part. *Marriage*. What are your thoughts on it?"

London felt as though all the air had been knocked out of her and she struggled to not drop the box. "My thoughts on Tiffany and Wayne possibly being engaged or on, you know, *us* getting married?" She suddenly felt light-headed.

Natalie walked over to her slowly and helped her place the box onto the breakfast bar. "On us getting married," she continued after a moment. "I know it's still early and snagging this house was a big step. But I'd like to eventually, you know? Maybe not *tomorrow*, but…" She took a deep breath. "Not too distant in the future either."

London wondered if she was supposed to feel scared or threatened, as though her freedom was taking its last breath. *Maybe once upon a time. But all I really feel is happy* she thought with a grin.

She whirled around and kissed Natalie again. "Of course I would," London replied breathlessly. "I would marry you in a heartbeat, Natalie."

Her wide smile was enough reply for London. They kissed in the empty kitchen for a few lingering moments. London was all too aware of Natalie's body, still slick with sweat, rubbing gently against hers as they explored each other's mouths.

London stepped back with a muffled moan. "If we don't stop right now, I'm going to march us into our bedroom without a bed and have my way with you on the floor."

Natalie met her eyes wickedly. "As responsible as I'm trying to be, that really, *really* doesn't sound like a bad idea."

London glanced over Natalie's shoulder at the open front door. "Hold that thought," she replied. She raced around her girlfriend and quickly shut the door. For good measure, she slid the deadbolt lock into place resolutely. "The last thing I need is any new colleagues at the software start-up wandering by."

"Good idea," Natalie replied with a wink. "You said the office is only about ten minutes from here?"

London nodded in confirmation. "As much as I'd like to extoll the virtues of how bad-ass working at this start-up is going to be and how much I'm going to enjoy having a meaningful role at a small, growing company, I really can't stop thinking about you and I, um, taking a moving break in the bedroom."

A split second later, Natalie was kissing her again. Hands slowly caressed each other's bodies over their clothing as the heat in the house rose. London paused for a moment and watched Natalie with unbridled passion.

"What?" Natalie whispered with a cheeky grin.

"I love you," London whispered back. She tucked a lock of Natalie's hair behind her ear gently. "We've got what it takes."

"You know so?" Natalie replied. She smiled again and held London's eyes. "Because *I* know so."

London nodded and fell into Natalie's kisses again. "I know so."

THE END

Ashley Quinn is a devout writer, avid reader and lover of all things art. A bonafide Chicago girl, Ashley relocated to Dallas, Texas in 2014 and quickly discovered that she loves Tex-Mex, craves deep-dish pizza, is terrified of Texas drivers and doesn't miss the blizzards.

With a B.A. in Marketing Communications from Columbia College Chicago and a wide range of professional Communications experience across a wide array of industries, Ashley's first love remains creative writing. She enjoys writing fiction and lesbian romance featuring relatable, developed characters and unique situations. *Texas Blues* is her second novel.

She lives in the Dallas-Fort Worth area with her partner and their two spoiled dogs. They are perpetually planning their next adventure while Ashley continues to plan future books. She can be contacted through her website at www.ThisIsAshleyQuinn.com or on Facebook at www.facebook.com/AshleyQuinnWrites.

Printed in Great Britain
by Amazon